AT PACIFIC HOSPITAL, SOME OF THE SICKEST PEOPLE WERE NOT THE PATIENTS

If you were a doctor at Pacific Hospital, you were supposed to play the medical game according to the rules, no matter how unfair some of those rules were and no matter how corrupt some of the players.

If you were a patient at Pacific Hospital, you were supposed to put your faith and your fate entirely in the hands of the all-too-human medical gods.

If you were a truly dedicated doctor or a patient who refused to lie back, you had to find your own way to be heard.

At Pacific Hospital, everything that could go wrong did—from professional in-fighting to tight money to labor walkouts to power failure. A once great metropolitan hospital had itself become a disaster area—where only the strongest and shrewdest would survive. . . .

PACIFIC HOSPITAL

Big Bestsellers from SIGNET

Pacific

Hospital

Robert H. Curtis

A SIGNET BOOK
NEW AMERICAN LIBRARY
TIMES MIRROR

SIGNET, SIGNET CLASSICS, MENTOR, PLUME AND MERIDIAN BOOKS
are published by The New American Library, Inc.,
1633 Broadway, New York, New York 10019

FIRST PRINTING, JANUARY, 1980

1 2 3 4 5 6 7 8 9

PRINTED IN THE UNITED STATES OF AMERICA

To Joan, with love

Prologue

Viewed from a distance this stormy December dawn, Pacific Hospital looked asleep. The lighted windows of the five floors above ground offered the only signs of life. However, were one to focus a high-powered lens up to its walls and then to see through to the inside, that impression would be erased by the continuous motion in progress. Concerned with the problem of sickness and its constant companion death, Pacific Hospital was beginning another day.

Only the top floor, home of hospital administration, was deserted, aside from two lighted offices. But directly beneath it, the activity of the fourth floor contrasted with the silence of the fifth. Under bright lights, those doctors and nurses not already in the operating theaters were checking the black bulletin board with its now reduced schedule of surgery. Clothed in green gowns, caps, and masks, they stepped aside occasionally to make way for orderlies pushing patient-loaded gurneys. Nearby, the pathology laboratories, though less busy than usual, were in operation. One pathologist was cutting into a lump that had just been removed from the lung of a young woman. He was preparing to rapidly freeze the biopsy tissue and then to look at a thin slice of it under a microscope. In only a few more minutes, the pathologist would focus his scope, and what he saw would determine whether or not the woman would need radical surgery. Beyond pathology were two wings of patient rooms but the beds were empty. In anticipation of possible real problems in nursing care because of events in progress, all patients had been moved to other areas.

The floor below, the third floor, was entirely devoted to patient care and housed, in addition to the usual private and semi-private rooms and the nursery, two specialized areas to

1

care for the sickest patients in the hospital. In the first, the coronary care unit, the three heart patients were in various stages of awakening. They all felt relief that they were alive, a relief mixed with fears for the future. In the intensive care unit, where acutely ill non-cardiac patients were cared for, a young woman, comatose from a barbiturate suicide attempt, stared sightlessly at the ceiling as a machine breathed vital oxygen into her lungs. Moving southward, the dialysis room, located at the end of the corridor, was not yet in use, but the rest of the floor was active. In the 3 South nursing station, nurses, technologists, orderlies, scurried like ants in and out. Occasionally, two of them would halt to avoid a collision, determine a pathway, and then continue on their individual treks. Some would remain inside the station itself, talking there or resting briefly before moving on. Up and down the adjoining corridors, hospital personnel and patients appeared with the energy characteristic of a new day. In the afternoon and evening, everyone moved more slowly.

On the second floor, a few patients lay on gurneys in the corridor of the Xray department. All were there for diagnostic films, except for one man. He was waiting to be taken to another section of the department for radiation therapy. Next door, technologists in the sprawling clinical laboratories already were at work. They were in the midst of performing the complex tests—blood counts, chemistries, bacteriologic studies—that had become, since their invention, so important for the diagnosis and treatment of illness.

The main level of Pacific Hospital resembled, in many ways, a hotel. Behind the lobby, the Admissions Office was surrounded by other business offices handling insurance, patient accounts, and discharges (or checkouts.) Along the main corridor behind the lobby, the Pharmacy, the Gift Shop, and Beauty Parlor lined up in a row. The other end of the main corridor was the site of the emergency room, and there, an older doctor with a gray crew cut was sewing up a laceration.

Finally, beneath the other five floors, the physio- and occupational-therapy departments in the basement were preparing to receive patients with acute injuries as well as getting ready the rehabilitative props of the department. The basement was also the home of myriad storerooms which housed supplies *brought each day by trucks that unloaded at the dock in the courtyard. The purchasing department was located in the basement, as was the morgue, the repair shops, the incinerator, the laundry, and the huge engineering department with its generators and boilers and hot-water heaters and pumps and pipes and eighteen men who manned the equipment. Of all of them, only one, a thin man repairing a step-down transformer, would remain on duty after six p.m., but it was too early to think of that. The hospital was almost eleven hours away from what would normally have been the relative calm of evening. Thus, from the basement floor heading skyward, almost every part of the place was in motion, and one could see that running a hospital was not unlike running a ship, or a hotel, or a city.*

PART I

Morning

Sam March cursed the rain as his trim frame bisected the electric-eye beam and the glass doors opened. Inside the lobby of Pacific Hospital he took off his raincoat and shook it angrily. He was sore at the rainstorm, he was tired of the labor negotiations, and he was furious at his wife. He wished he was drinking mai tais on some tropical beach—but what the hell, he acknowledged, who wouldn't?

March scanned the huge deserted lobby and then spotted Liz Scripps, the young director of nursing, talking with the admissions clerk. Her back was to him and his gaze shifted to her rear end, voluptuously entrapped in white pants. March was fascinated with the bounce which accompanied a foot tap each time she emphasized something to the clerk. He remembered reading that female buttocks were designed as an anthropologic ploy to lure male primates to procreate. Wasn't nature smart? he asked himself, and concurred. He felt better already.

"Hey, Liz," March said when he reached the desk.

Scripps turned and looked up at the partially balding man whose blue eyes were fixed on her.

"What's our census this morning?"

"One hundred and twenty, half-full, Sam. Five probably discharges, but we won't know for sure until the doctors come in. Make my life easier and work things out today, will you?"

March leaned over the desk and stared down with interest. "Just keep those gorgeous tits pointed straight ahead and I'll do my best."

He'll always be an intransigent chauvinist, she thought, but that didn't block the strong stirrings she felt for this married

7

man, the most attractive man she knew. "How's Karen?" she asked.

"Don't spoil my fantasies," March answered. "By the way, if there's more than a ten-bed shift, I want to know about it."

He moved out of the lobby and stepped into the elevator. He pressed Five and got out at the top floor, the home of the hospital administration. This floor was smaller than the others and oval in shape, so that it resembled a crown sitting atop the rest of the building. Here were housed the various administrative offices, the ornate board-of-directors room, and a solarium. March walked quickly down the hall. He turned a corner and gasped. The corridor was dark, but he could see the body of a man hanging from a light fixture. He raced toward the dangling figure. The rope from the ceiling encircled only a neck of bloodstained sheets. March stepped closer and examined the effigy. Shit, he thought. The damn thing almost stopped my heart. He read the sign pinned to the figure: "WHITESIDES! GIVE IN OR ELSE!" He decided against cutting the effigy down. The old bastard needs some shaking up, he thought. He walked quickly to his office. Usually he enjoyed the solitude up on the fifth floor each morning. Before Lester Whitesides arrived, before the director of volunteers arrived, before the secretaries arrived. Ordinarily the gold-lettered title on his door, *Assistant Administrator*, made him feel good. He had done it the hard way, had forged his own success story. But now he felt lousy—his hospital was in trouble.

An elevator opened and interrupted his reverie. He wondered who was arriving this early, and the heavy footsteps answered his question. Only Lester Whitesides, administrator of Pacific Hospital, made such sounds. He waited quietly until he heard an echoing yell. *Oh, My God!* The footfall resumed, augmented now by wheezing respirations.

"In here, Lester," March called out.

"Did you see what they did out there?" the fat man asked. He lowered himself with effort into a chair and mopped his forehead with his maroon-monogrammed handkerchief.

"Sure I saw it," March replied. "How the hell could I miss it? I left it there because it gives you a better image, Lester. They took fifty pounds off of you and made you look like you did when I first met you."

8

"Don't be funny with me, Sam. I'm not in the mood. And it's not that stupid union thing in the hall. I couldn't sleep last night. This hospital has been serving the community for one hundred and eight years. I've been here for forty of them. I won't allow those vultures to call a strike against us. They might not love the hospital, but they should respect it."

"Come off it, Lester," March said to his boss. "It's not a matter of respect. You know better than that. It's a matter of financial security. It's jobs and money, not respect."

"Unions will never run my hospital. That's final."

"It may be settled." March looked at Whitesides. The fleshy face was adamant, but March continued. "We're meeting with them at two P.M."

"They said it wouldn't do any good," complained Whitesides.

"For Christ's sake, Lester. That's a game and you know it. You've gone through this crap a lot longer than I have. They're not idiots. They're not going to say, 'That's great of you hospital guys to give us another chance.' They have plenty to lose and they know it. This time it's different. The rock is up against the hard place. They *know* it, Lester. Take my word for it." March slouched back in his chair. He didn't like lecturing his boss, but Whitesides had been slipping during the past several years, and the strain of the six weeks of labor negotiations had further impaired his effectiveness. What particularly irked March was that Whitesides had told him that he had no intention of retiring for at least three years. And the board of directors was unaware that he, March, was carrying the major load of hospital administration; the board apparently was satisfied with things as they were. Whitesides, like Pacific Hospital, was an institution not to be trifled with.

"What's our census this morning?" Whitesides asked.

March sighed. "One-twenty, and the staff is complying with the emergency-admission order. With luck, admissions will balance discharges. We're lean and trim and tough, Lester."

"The fourth-floor pavilions are closed, aren't they?"

March looked startled. "Yes, all of the patients on four have been moved to the third floor. Three South is a real mixed bag now, medical and surgical. I can tell that you're not getting much sleep, Lester. We toured three and four yesterday. Did you forget already?"

Whitesides shook his head in disgust. "I'm being stupid. Of course. Too much on my mind, I guess. Did Miss Scripps find out which nurses will refuse to cross the picket line?"

"She'll have answers by noon. But I don't think we've got a problem there."

March stopped talking as the sound of footsteps was heard once again in the corridor. He and Whitesides turned toward the open door as two men walked by, each carrying a dripping raincoat. One of the men was stocky and grizzled and wore a rumpled old suit. The other was an athletic young black, neatly dressed. Both men nodded as they passed, but neither spoke. The footsteps faded, and March and Whitesides could hear a door close.

"They didn't say a word about that rotten effigy," Whitesides complained.

"Why should they?" March said. "They didn't hang the damn thing up, and they're sure as hell not going to admit that someone in the rank and file did."

"What are they doing here so early anyway? We don't meet until two."

"They've gotten to like that office you gave them for a caucus room, Lester. I suppose that they're planning strategy. Who knows? Frank O'Brien and Jackson Armstrong. What a pair! I heard a rumor that they're going to meet in the laundry with the workers later this morning."

"They can't have a meeting like that. This just isn't permitted. The contract specifically forbids it."

"Lester, there's no reason to get yourself so excited about this," March said. "Look, we want to work things out, right? I'm not sure about that meeting, but let's assume that I'm correct. Does it make sense to get everybody pissed off by forbidding it? Come on, Lester"—March's tone was placating—"we don't want to blow the whole thing over something like this. What the hell do we care what they say to the laundry people or what the laundry workers say to them? It's what O'Brien says to us this afternoon that's important."

Whitesides sighed. "You're right, Sam. I'm too damned edgy. Just tell me one thing. What do you make of Armstrong?"

"We should have gotten to know him better when he worked for us. Smart, educated, young, black—in that order. Now, aren't you glad you asked me?"

"Thanks for nothing," the fat man grunted.

The phone rang. "March here," the younger man answered. He listened for a moment. Finally he talked to the caller. "Any clues? Didn't anybody see anything?" He listened again. "Okay," March finally said. "Keep working on it. I'll be right there." He slammed down the receiver. "Shit, the effigy was only the beginning. Now somebody's stopped up the public toilets near the lab with hand towels. Water is backing up and spilling on the upper floors. They're showing us how it's going to be. Cave in or else."

"It's those troublemakers in the laundry!" Whitesides shouted. "That lousy union is doing that to us."

"So what else is new?" March asked as he headed for the door.

Dr. Anne Simpson sat in the cafeteria absorbed in the morning paper. Dressed in the uniform of a house officer, a stethoscope protruded from the side pocket of her white jacket. Her brown hair, pulled tightly back, might have given some other woman a severe appearance. With Anne, the shapeless outfit and the hairstyle had a paradoxical effect. Without a trace of flamboyance, the tall young woman was sexy. She ignored the constant clatter of dishes and the staccato noises of multiple conversations. But her concentration was not strong enough to keep her from sensing the approach of the man walking toward her. She looked up, waved, and a few seconds later he was sitting opposite her. At age fifty, Dr. Leo Vanni did not look like a matinee idol, but his features were strong and he possessed a quiet virility that women adored. Of this attribute, he was completely unaware. He was of medium height, dark, and stocky. The most memorable feature of his face was his eyes, dark brown, soft, luminous. They usually projected a kindliness that warmed, but when, on rare occasion, they narrowed, it was wise to take heed of the signal; it was one of mounting anger.

"Got yourself pretty wet, Leo," she said as she leaned over and kissed him gently on the cheek.

"I wish this storm would break," he answered. "Three days

of continuous rain sufficeth." He pointed to the paper. "What's new in that rag?" he asked.

"Pacific Hospital is getting lots of attention today. The editors are worried about a strike."

"So am I," Vanni said. "I don't think it will happen, but I don't even like the possibility of this place closing down."

"But, Leo," the young woman said, "how else can those underpaid workers ever get ahead? How can they support their families?"

Leo paused for a moment, temporarily distracted by the sounds of the Cafeteria, which was animated by the clatter of rattling dishes and coffee cups. Conversations were rifling back and forth in at least ten languages and from the kitchen, breakfast-tray preparation added to the general noisiness. Empty trays with diet sheets on them traveled along a conveyor belt. They were progressively added to until they were filled, and then stacked into a cart for transport to the floor.

"That's the idea of negotiations, Anne," he finally replied. "They'll get a raise. The problem is that there is simply not enough money to meet all the demands." Vanni accepted her look of disgust with equanimity. "I think that the hospital is telling the truth. You know, sweetheart," Vanni added, "many, many years ago, when I was chief medical resident, I knew everything. Then I got older and smarter. I got so smart I married you. So now you're the chief OB resident and you know everything. Nothing wrong with your thinking that time won't take care of. You just need a few worry creases in that baby-ass complexion."

The young woman was annoyed with her husband. "Don't patronize me, Leo. I'm twenty-nine, not sixteen. I've been around your medical establishment for several years. I didn't marry a crusty anachronism like Lester Whitesides. I married you, and you could be a little generous, you know. You're making a good income."

Vanni stared at his wife's even white teeth, and his gaze moved up to encompass her lovely face. She *did* marry me, he thought. One of life's minor miracles. They had been married almost three years and he still wondered why she had chosen him. He sighed voluntarily to show that he was dealing with a hopeless idealist. "I know I'm not overpaid, that's what I know. I'm not crazy about getting up in the

12

middle of the night, and I want to get paid for it. You weren't thrilled by my last night call."

"That's true," Anne admitted. She remembered exactly what it was that the phone call had interrupted, and she reddened at the recollection. "But you know what I mean."

"Listen, more money is spent in this country on pets and cigarettes and booze than on doctors. Okay, I like practicing medicine and I'm acting out of self-interest, but so is everybody else, union officials included."

"Don't act naive with me, Leo. You're plenty cynical, so don't try to tell me all doctors are like you."

"Did I say that there weren't crooked doctors or cold doctors or stupid doctors or lazy doctors? Tell me, sweetheart, did I say that?" Vanni continued before his wife could answer. "There are plenty of doctors in all those categories, but they're not a high percentage, believe me."

"You forgot 'arrogant,' Leo. Add that category to your others. And you know that there are a lot more lousy doctors than you're willing to acknowledge, so don't sing me any sad songs about love of humanity and all that stuff."

"Who mentioned love of humanity? All I'm saying is that most doctors are in the profession because they find it exciting, but they like their patients, they *care* for their patients. Let's change the subject. Were you busy last night?"

Anne had been on duty the preceding night and had slept in her room in the house-staff residence. "Nothing much," she answered. "I missed you. That clinic patient I told you about, Sheri Johnson, telephoned. She's the one who finally managed to get pregnant at age thirty-nine. She had a few contractions, but they stopped. I told her to keep checking with me. She's overdue, and if she doesn't start up again soon, we'll have to induce."

"What's your morning schedule?"

"A D-and-C and then I'm assisting at a hysterectomy."

Vanni was staring at his wife in a way she had learned to recognize. "So everything's quiet, huh? What time is your D-and-C?" His voice was a little huskier, a little self-conscious.

"I've got thirty-five minutes."

He reached under the table and gently stroked her leg. "I don't like being a minute man except when I have to," he said. "Let's go."

They left the cafeteria hand in hand and walked quickly to the passageway on the second floor which connected the house-staff residence to the main hospital. By the time they reached her room, he was fully aroused. He silently urged her to hurry as she found the key and turned the lock. Inside the room, he kissed her and pulled her close.

"Lock the door, darling," she said.

"I already did. Two nights is too long to wait."

They undressed quickly and clasped each other with urgency. Usually she demanded tenderness, and Leo could be tender, but there was no time, and besides, her desire as well as his came now from more primitive, noncerebral areas. He was a magnificent animal, *her* magnificent animal, and she rode him with abandon, urging him on, feeling him respond. Dimly she remembered that there were times for civilized intercourse, and there were other times, like now when satisfaction came only from Leo fucking her.

Afterwards Vanni lay alongside his wife. He looked at her body now with appreciation. His lust had been quelled for the moment.

He remembered the day he had first seen Anne. There had been women, to be sure, from adolescence on. But those relationships had been no more than sexual liaisons, pleasurable but without sufficient substance to be termed love affairs, let alone to lead to marriage. Those many women found him eligible, attractive, and a confirmed bachelor. And so he remained until that day when Anne Simpson appeared on the floor, fresh from medical-school graduation. If it wasn't love at first sight on Vanni's part, at least it was something far stronger than infatuation with a lovely young woman. Perhaps the age disparity began to snap the bonds of comfort that had tied him to life as a single man. It later seemed irrational to him that none of the more contemporaneous women had moved him so, but he accepted his awakening as a gift from the gods, not to be explained.

Anne, along with another intern and two assistant residents, had been assigned to make rounds with Vanni. She had presented a case she had worked up, and then the group went to see the patient. Afterward they all discussed the case.

"What do you think, Dr. Simpson?" Vanni had asked.

"It's a pretty obvious case of an acute exacerbation of chronic pyelonephritis, Dr. Vanni."

"Likely but not obvious," Vanni responded. "We have no confirmed history. I've seen other patients with fever and unilateral flank pain and CVA tenderness that turned out to have the flu. But tell me, Dr. Simpson, what tests do you want to order to establish the diagnosis?"

"Urinalysis, BUN, creatinine, scan, and IVP," the young woman answered without hesitation.

Vanni leaned back in his chair. "Those are all very fine tests of kidney function, but only one of them is needed right now. The earlier episodes of back pain are undocumented and may be just that—back pain of a chronic nature. Do you know how much those tests you suggested will cost?"

"No, I don't know, Dr. Vanni, and I don't really care that much. My primary concern is for the patient. Anyway, this is supposed to be a teaching hospital, isn't it? At least, that's what your internship brochure states."

"This is indeed a teaching hospital, Dr. Simpson, but I must disabuse you of the idea that there is only one kind of teaching. Now, there is a philosophy adopted by some teachers in medical school that practicing physicians, local medical doctors—LMD's is the deprecating term—eschew all theory and treat their patients in a kindly but Neanderthal fashion, that salvation for the really sick is to be found only in those sanctuaries directly attached to a medical school. This is known as the town-gown syndrome, and the mutual hostility engendered serves neither the town nor the school well."

"I don't remember a single professor in medical school standing on a soapbox, Dr. Vanni."

Vanni ignored the insult. "You did hear about LMD's, I presume?"

"Yes, I did," Anne replied. Her tone suggested complete indifference and Vanni, who had a good relationship with house staff, was not used to either hostility or lack of interest. He was annoyed, but he was also intrigued.

"Well, let me tell you what this LMD would do if the case you presented were mine. Instead of ordering almost three hundred dollars' worth of laboratory work, I would take a morning specimen of urine and test it myself. If it were com-

Robert H. Curtis

pletely normal, I would know that the patient does not have
chronic kidney disease."

The young woman looked directly at Vanni. "What you
say makes complete sense."

"Thank you," Vanni said. He obviously was amused.

Over the next few weeks Vanni tried to be fair, but he
found that he was directing most of his questions to Anne.
What's happening to me is crazy, he thought, and hoped that
the one-way romance was not visible to the others. Then one
night he received a phone call.

"Dr. Vanni. This is Anne Simpson. I'd like you to take me
to dinner, or I'll take you to dinner, or we'll go dutch. I've
never eaten with an LMD before."

The phone rang, and Anne stretched out her arm. "Yes,
Mabel," she said. "He's here." She turned to her husband.
"For you, lover." She passed the phone over his chest.

As her husband listened and talked to whomever Mabel
had connected him to, Anne, in unspoken communion with
him, continued with the recollection of that initial date. If she
had sounded self-assured when she called Leo, it was purely
an act of self-control. Her heart was beating furiously, because while she sensed reciprocal interest, she was not
sufficiently convinced that she would not be politely but firmly
rebuffed. And it was not humiliation she primarily feared.
She wanted Leo very much, and aside from the fact that he
was a bachelor, she knew nothing of his personal life. Was
this man seriously involved with another woman? If so, was
the expression in his eyes when he looked at her, Anne, something different from what she wanted it to be? Before Leo,
she had heard all about the metaphor of chemistry and
scoffed at it, the chemistry of infatuation, whatever that was.
And then one fine morning, this middle-aged man conducts
ward rounds, and whammo, there it is! Chemistry—the real
thing—all kinds of Simpson atoms and molecules in frenetic
collision with Vanni substances.

"I'm not a liberated man," she had heard him reply. "The
pleasure is mine, and so is the tab."

She was new in town, so he took her to Henri's, a dimly-
lit quiet restaurant that featured French cuisine. Instead of
an explosion of excited dating talk, both were cautious. As
they sipped thir wine and ate, they asked each other ques-

16

tions that might have sounded superficial to an outsider but that were, in reality, surgical probes for important feelings. And one joyous fact she valued more than all the others uncovered during that first dinner together. He had no commitments, which meant that she had no rivals. She had to win this man, but at least she didn't have to win him away from somebody else. Womanly wiles, she thought, feeling deliciously unliberated, are going to hook you, Leo Vanni, you poor unsuspecting paisano bastard.

After dinner, he drove farther downtown and pulled up to a jazz place. After they got out of the car, he took her hand and led her inside. It was a week night and still early, and the room, though large, was empty aside from one couple. On the stage, the great Turk Murphy band, visting from San Francisco, was playing for its own enjoyment until Turk looked up and spotted Leo sitting with Anne at a side table. He motioned to the others, who then looked out to the floor. At the conclusion of the number, Turk walked to the front of the bandstand. "Leo," he commanded, "stop wasting time and get up here."

Vanni excused himself. He walked behind a curtain and appeared on the bandstand. There was handshaking all around. The clarinet player handed his instrument over to Leo and produced a saxophone for himself.

"Solace," Turk announced, and tapped his foot several times. Simultaneously the six musicians began to play. As the sounds of the Joplin classic drifted through the room, Anne took her drink and moved to a table near the front. In the middle of the song, Turk pointed to Leo. As the bass strummed and the other instruments remained silent, Leo began his solo with the most haunting sounds she had ever heard. Anne cried as he played, and through her tears she could see that it wasn't just because she was in love, because if that were the case, so were the other musicians. There they were, professional all, and she could see that they regarded as an equal the middle-aged doctor making magic sounds with a clarinet. The room slowly began to fill with customers as the sextet, now a septet, played song after song, some of them with vocals by Jimmy Stanislaus. "Storyville Blues," "Of All the Wrongs," "Doctor Jazz," "Yama Yama Man," each following the other without a pause. Finally after one solid hour

of playing, they stopped. The ovation from the now-filled room was long and genuine. "If this man would only give up wasting his time with a stethoscope . . ." Turk commented to Anne during the break, sensing that she could influence Leo to spend more time where he belonged—sitting in with a jazz band.

Later, in Vanni's apartment, they danced to romantic records, their arms wrapped around each other. As the passion of their embraces increased, so did Leo's need to find an answer to a puzzle. "I know I want to go to bed with you," he whispered to Anne, *"and I think you want to go to bed with me, but I have a question."*

"Ask away," Anne answered.

"Are you looking for a father-figure?"

"No, Leo Vanni, I'm not. I've found one."

Six months later they were married.

Now Anne lay in quiet contentment, watching her husband conclude his conversation. Finally he hung up.

"Arnie Jacobs wants me on the floor," Vanni said. "Chernock's gone sour. No surprise. Also, I have an accident case en route."

"I'm sorry about Chernock," she said.

"Me, too," Vanni replied as he dressed quickly.

"Mabel asked me why you didn't answer your page."

"Because I hadn't gotten in yet," Vanni answered. "I'll see you later."

The small house had a worn, tired look about it, but it was spotless. A stranger entering the place would have surmised that its occupants were trying very hard but were having a difficult struggle. The rugs and drapes were frayed, multiple cracks in the walls and ceilings were apparent, and the furniture was cheap and without character. The stranger's assumptions would have been correct, because Herbert and Sheri Johnson were indeed struggling to keep afloat financially. Even now, their joy and excitement over the baby, whose birth was imminent, was on occasion not complete. Every once in a while Sheri wondered whether the new arrival would put too much strain on Herbert, while her husband hoped that he still would be able to provide a few things not absolutely necessary, a few "luxuries" for the wife he adored.

"Coffee's ready, Herbert," Sheri announced, and in a little while she walked with effort from the kitchen to the breakfast room. She was still in her nightgown and bathrobe.

"I better leave for the store early today. The traffic will be very heavy downtown," Herbert said when he had finished his coffee and toast. He worked as a clerk in the men's section of Thornton's largest department store, the Emporium, one of hundreds of trading posts scattered throughout the United States so named. His salary was average because his "book" was average. Herbert had no real talent for sales. He was a nice guy, but not at all imaginative, and he had no strong opinions about the suits, sport jackets, shirts, ties, bathrobes, and the like stocked by his department. Thus he never was able to really sell anything. What he did was handle transactions for the customer who had already made up his or her mind. He had watched, without rancor, younger people in the department promoted to sales-manager positions. He understood that he simply was not equipped to assume this type of responsibility. "You'll call me the minute something happens?" he reminded Sheri.

"You know I will," she answered, "but it seems everything has stopped for the moment. Last night, for a while . . ." She suddenly looked troubled. "You think the baby is going to be all right, don't you, Herbert? I mean, I can feel kicking."

"Everything is going to be wonderful. You know what Dr. Simpson said. You're a very healthy girl, Sheri, and we're going to have a very healthy baby." At first he had wanted to take out a loan so that Sheri could go to a private obstetrician instead of remaining in the clinic. Sheri had said absolutely no, the clinic had good doctors. And indeed, they both had complete faith in Anne Simpson. Even though Sheri was two weeks overdue, Dr. Simpson had said there was nothing to worry about, that doctors weren't all that certain of the expected date of arrival of babies.

"Well, I think I'd better go." Herbert walked to the closet and put on his raincoat and hat. He called to his wife. "Let's take a look together."

Sheri knew what he meant. They were both superstitious and liked to look in the small nursery as often as they could. The viewing, they both felt, although neither had communicated the compulsion to the other, would bring luck to the baby, their baby, who within a short time would occupy the room. This nursery, in contrast to the rest of the house, sparkled. Herbert had repainted the entire room white, as well as the secondhand crib. The walls were covered by decals of animals, half of them pink and the other half blue. A mobile which played Brahms's "Lullaby" was attached to the side of the crib, and the now-silent carousel was suspended over a blanket covering the sheets. A chest of drawers painted white contained several baby outfits which Sheri had knitted. In the closet, a stroller, bassinet, and a box of Pampers awaited use.

"Darn it, I wish I would start up again," Sheri said, staring at the crib.

"We've waited so long," Herbert said. "We can wait a little longer."

Sheri was surprised by her husband's remark. He sounded more definite than he usually did. She walked him to the door and looked outside. Rain was making splashes in the puddles that had formed, and as Herbert backed their old Chevrolet out of the garage, Sheri suddenly felt very nervous. She wanted to shout out to him to be careful, but instead she bit her lip. She watched the car turn and disappear and then went to clear the breakfast dishes. In the kitchen, she stopped washing the plates for a minute because the baby had given a hard kick. She patted her distended abdomen affectionately, relieved by the activity within it. When she had returned the dishes to the kitchen cabinet, she walked to the bedroom and looked at herself in the full-length mirror. She turned first for a profile view and smiled with satisfaction. They had made a decision to wait for a while to have a baby because they really could not afford one when they were first married. But the years passed, and then the time came when Sheri was thirty-five and they could no longer afford, in a health sense, to wait. Family obligations had painfully stretched their budget, but they were determined to produce a child. For a time it seemed that not only the financial fates but the fecundity fates were against them as well. Because while Sheri twice had been able to conceive, both pregnancies had quickly been ended by miscarriages. And now at age thirty-nine, this girl—for Herbert still thought of her as his high school girlfriend—was about to give a child to the husband she loved so much. She looked at her profile again and savored the pregnant-matron reflection. After the baby was born, Herbert wanted her to stay at home for at least three months, but she knew that she would have to return to her job at the bank as soon as possible. She took a final look in the mirror. "Do you know," she informed her unborn baby, "that your mother was the prettiest cheerleader at Thornton High? And you'll be too, if you're a girl, because your father is still just as good-looking as he was." Herbert, the nondescript Emporium salesman, was more handsome to Sheri than Paul Newman. Such are the ways of love.

Sheri walked back and forth in the bedroom. Although she was very tired, she thought that doing something might start up labor. But the double bed was too seductive, and Sheri lay down to rest for ten minutes. An hour later she was awakened by the phone ringing. It was her neighbor Zelda Meyers inviting herself for coffee.

Shortly afterward Sheri opened the door for Mrs. Meyers, who shook out her umbrella and leaned it against the side of the house. Then the older woman, followed by Sheri, walked to the closet and hung up her raincoat then before she moved to the living room and settled herself in an armchair.

"How's my little mother?" Zelda asked. A widow, she had married children living in Chicago and Washington, D.C., and had "adopted" Sheri and Herbert as her own. She visited several times a week and called every afternoon to make sure that Sheri was all right.

"I don't think my baby is in any hurry, Zelda." She sighed. "I'm so big and I'm late and I don't know if the baby's even all right." Sheri began to cry. She was far more worried about being an older first-time mother than she admitted to her husband.

Zelda comforted her. "It's normal to have the jitters," she commented after relating the latest neighborhood gossip. "I did too with Willie."

"How is Willie?" Sheri asked.

"He's fine. Told me last Sunday that Carol and him want me to visit in the spring. During the vacation when the kids are out of school. They're sending me a ticket. How's that for children?" She continued before Sheri could answer. "And my Emily. My little scamp is giving me another grandchild.

Called me last night. I'll have eight grandchildren and two great-grandchildren. How's that for a woman who weighs ninety-six pounds? Well, I've stayed too long already. Don't get overtired and don't worry. Your little boy—you're carrying low, so I'm sure—he's going to be just fine. Just don't try to rush him."

Sheri laughed. "As if I could," she said.

Just before she left, Zelda turned and asked quietly how the "folks" were. It had been a while since she had inquired, and secretly she hoped that Sheri would have some sad news to relate, because Sheri's parents and Herbert's father were all patients in Sunny Glen Convalescent Hospital. Herbert's father had been senile for eight years, and Sheri's parents were invalided by circulatory problems and were severely depressed. Neither wanted to live, but they survived year after year. And the financial drain had been enormous, despite Medicare, especially in view of the Johnsons' less-than-spectacular incomes. "No change, Zelda," Sheri answered. "Daddy Johnson thinks he's on a troop-transport ship. It's always 1918 for him. And my folks keep crying. They can't get excited about my baby. Why should they?"

The question was rhetorical, and Zelda said once more not to worry and to call if Sheri needed anything.

After she left, Sheri felt a gas pain. It was different from last night, so she thought nothing of it. Then, twenty minutes later, she had a hard contraction. She got to the phone as quickly as she could maneuver and dialed the hospital and asked for Dr. Simpson. "It's an emergency," she added.

The operator told her that she thought Dr. Simpson was between cases, and connected her with Surgery. The surgical nurse who answered found Dr. Simpson and put her on the line. When Sheri told her about the hard contraction, much worse than last night, Anne told her to come to the hospital to be admitted.

Sheri then called the Emporium and asked for the men's department. Herbert answered the phone. "Come home, Herbert," she said. "Labor just started, and Dr. Simpson wants me admitted."

"St-stay there, honey," Herbert stuttered. "I'll be home right away. Be careful."

"Herbert. I'm all right. Drive slowly. Please!" After she

hung up the phone, she got dressed. Then she carried her already packed suitcase to the living room and stood by the window, watching for her husband to arrive. As she watched, she prayed silently for her baby to be all right.

Vanni walked down the 2 South corridor and entered Chernock's room. The patient was gasping like a fish out of water. He had been comatose for two days as the result of overwhelming infection, and it was understood that there were to be no heroics in this case. Suddenly Chernock clenched his teeth and stopped breathing. His face turned blue, and a trickle of blood oozed from the side of his mouth and rolled past his chin and onto his neck.

"When did it begin?" Vanni asked the intern, pointing to the dead patient.

"About five minutes ago. I was in the room when the agonal breathing started."

Vanni noted the time, felt for a pulse, listened to the silent chest, and checked the pupils, which had started to dilate. "Notify the floor, Arnie, and then come back." Vanni moistened a washcloth and wiped the blood off the dead man's face. He wondered about what he had just witnessed, about the vital force that was no longer in Chernock. The differences between life and death could be classified in a definition, but the essence of life was incomprehensible.

"What was the immediate cause of death?" he inquired of the intern when the latter returned.

"You mean besides the pneumonia?"

"Yes."

"I'm not sure," Jacobs answered, running his hand through his thick curly black hair. Vanni was his preceptor for the month, and the intern followed all of Vanni's patients in addition to those of several other doctors.

"Well?"

"Respiratory-center failure?" Jacobs ventured.

"No. Guess again."

Jacobs hesitated. "How about a heart attack?"

"Use your head, Arnie," Vanni said. "This patient has been bedridden for two months."

"Pulmonary embolism," Jacobs said, the logic registering.

"Why not? I'm sure his leg veins are full of clots, and a big one broke loose just now. The pneumonia might be entirely responsible, but I don't think so. We'll know at the post."

Vanni stopped talking for a minute as a nurse came in and attached a tag to Chernock's toe. Chernock was now officially baggage on his way first to the hospital morgue, later to a mortuary. "Call the transplant bank," Vanni said. "He left his eyes."

"I just did," Jacobs answered. "The technician will come early this afternoon. The bank said Dr. Lusk will be admitting an eye patient who's been waiting a week for a donor."

"All right," Vanni said. He left the room, and after phoning Mrs. Chernock, he climbed the stairs to Pathology. On the fourth floor, he walked quickly to one of the doors and poked his head in. He could see the back of a lanky man who was sprawled in a chair, one leg up on a cluttered desk. The man was reading a newspaper, and Vanni watched him briefly as he turned the pages, simultaneously sipping coffee from a paper cup.

"You're working at your usual furious pace, I see." Vanni addressed himself to the pathologist, Ed Fraser, who slowly swiveled in his chair until he had completed a half-circle and now was facing Vanni. He folded his paper with great deliberation, and showed by his suffering expression that he was prepared to accept interruptions like this bravely. Then he peered toward the door, squinting in concentration at the visitor, as if he were having difficulty in identifying him. Then he smiled benignly.

"Vanni, Dr. Leo Vanni. So good of you to come." He spoke in slow, doleful tones. "I would suggest our mahogany model, the one with brass handles and a white satin lining. It has the quiet dignity, and besides, it's waterproof." Fraser stopped and peered once again. "You are *the* Doctor Vanni?" he intoned. "The one who provides us with so much of our business, and I might say that we are deeply appreciative of—"

"Okay, gorgeous," Vanni said. "You can knock it off. I can't sell your act, and I'm in a hurry besides. Do you have any special plans for this morning?"

"Nothing special. Are you proposing?" Frasier wriggled his eyebrows like Groucho.

"Listen. My patient Chernock just expired. You remember,

the fellow with amyotrophic lateral sclerosis. You and I reviewed the muscle-biopsy slides last month. I think the terminal event was pulmonary embolism. Anyway, could you do me a big favor and post him this morning? His wife wants the funeral tomorrow or I wouldn't have dared to interrupt your journal reading."

"Tch, tch, tch," Fraser replied sadly. "You really did come for our mahogany model. Yeah, I'll find out where you fucked up, buddy boy. How's eleven o'clock for you?"

"Thanks," Vanni said. "That's perfect I'm going to the CPC for a while, but just have me paged."

"CPC," Fraser said. "Well, that's not *my* worry. Our *chief* pathologist runs that conference, so I'll be able to hack away at your mistake. I'll page you, buddy boy. Remember that in June, when I become chief, you won't get such prompt service.

"Knowing how long it takes you to even set up, I'll expect your call at noon," Vanni said. "I never realized," he added, "that each time I watch you at work in your abattoir, underneath that mask of stupidity and indifference the real Ed Fraser stands, a highly intelligent creature who has a heart of gold. Thanks again, sweetheart."

Skid row is the saddest place of all. It seems incredible that such areas are taken for granted, but freedom demands certain penalties for its very existence, and one of them is the inurement of society's survivors to the plight of its losers.

The downtrodden of Thornton lived most of their lives within the confines of nine square blocks, blocks whose bones were cheap hotels and pawnshops and bars, and whose corpuscles were its defeated inhabitants. On sunny days, one would find the occupants of skid row in some sort of motion, talking in small groups, or snoring on the sidewalks clasping wine bottles in brown paper bags, or brawling ineffectively. (Although occasionally someone's head collided with the pavement.) People driving through the area might notice that more than an average number of men—for this was a predominantly masculine world—limped or even had to use a crutch, and that more than the average were double amputees bound to wheelchairs, and that most of the men wearing dirty pea coats or sweaters, sneakers, and knitted caps, had a week's stubble surrounding their vacant faces. But more likely these aberrations would not be observed at all as driver and passengers traversed the small autonomous metropolis of losers. Certainly today, with the continuing downpour, there was nothing special to see, for whatever life existed was not on the streets.

Inside the Palace, a decrepit four-floor walk-up hotel for transients, a gaunt man gazed out of his window. From his top-floor room he looked for a moment toward the large gray post office which commanded the horizon of his view. Absent from its steps were the panhandlers who solicited strangers coming in and going out of the building, which, like the man staring at it, now appeared desolate and isolated. Finally he turned away from the window and sat down in a chair next to his bed. The fact that the man, Victor Bates, looked fifteen years older than his actual age of fifty-eight was in no way unusual, because many inhabitants of the area had haunted, ancient visages. What was noteworthy, however, was the fact that Victor Bates, aside from the desk clerk, was the only one in the hotel earning a regular salary. He was, and had been for the past two years, employed by Pacific Hospital as a mangle hand in the laundry. He operated the big machine that rolled and smoothed the sheets. It was the steadiest job that he had ever held, and as he thought about it now, he smashed his hand down on the table as his features became contorted by anger. Because after today, through no fault of his, this job would no longer exist. And in a life characterized by repeated thumpings from the fates, this injustice was almost too much to bear. Maybe they'll settle, he thought suddenly, and his face brightened for an instant, but then he remembered that this was the final day for negotiations and became glum again.

For a time immediately after World War II it had appeared that his life might become steady. He had married a waitress, but three months after he became the father of a son, he returned to find his wife and baby gone and a note saying that she was going to spend her time with somebody else and not to try to find them. Bates had neither the financial nor the imaginative resources to trace his wife and child. Since then he had been a loner and a drifter, but he had always worked. However, people avoided him because of his strange personality. His inability to take criticism had cost him innumerable jobs, all of them menial, for he was equipped for no other kind. A job lasted two months on the average, but after he was fired he would always manage to find another job as a dishwasher, or a watchman, or as a sort of postman delivering advertising fliers for various neighborhood hardware stores or grocery stores. Sooner or later—almost always sooner—he would lash out at his employer over some real or imagined slight, and the next day he would be job-hunting again. He had worked in over twenty American cities, but for the past ten years he had lived in Thornton. During that period of time he had made one friend, an engineer at Pacific Hospital. Even though this friendship was on a working-hours-only basis, he valued it as he did his job. For some reason he found the noise in the laundry soothing, and he was able to do his job without getting into any arguments. He felt that his work was not appreciated by the hospital, but while he grumbled to his friend about it, he still felt that he would live out the remainder of his working life in the laundry. That is until recently. With the onset of contract negotiations for his union, Bates became more and more apprehensive. He wanted things settled soon. His life was now a secure one, and he did not want it disrupted. He lived in the best room of the Palace, and because of his two-year tenure at the hospital, he felt superior to the skid-row residents he lived among. If a strike came, he was convinced he would be terminated, and once again he would be off in search of odd jobs and no longer in communication with his friend Phil Wray.

He looked at the alarm clock on the table. Time to go. Ordinarly he felt good in the early morning of a weekday when he was ready to leave for work. Not today, however. He had decided that the hospital and the union could not settle their differences without sacrificing his job. If that was the case, this would be his last day at Pacific Hospital. He clenched and unclenched his fists several times. Then he stood up and put on his coat. He slowly walked down the three flights to the lobby, where, because of the rain, more people than usual were sitting around. The desk clerk, a scrawny, pimply-faced bully, watched the older man complete his descent.

"Lousy day, huh?" the desk clerk offered.

"How much do I owe on my room?"

"You don't owe nothin', Mr. Bates." The clerk kept his eyes glued to the account book. "You're paid up until next Tuesday." He tyrannized the other residents of the hotel, but not Bates. He was frightened of Victor.

Bates turned and looked around the lobby. A woman and two men shared a worn mohair couch. The six chairs were filled with men, two of whom were sleeping. One man who had just come in slouched against a corner, completely absorbed in watching the water drip from his clothes. All the others who were awake stared at Bates. He was a curiosity to those residents of the hotel who were sober enough to observe him. He spoke to no one, ever, except for brief inquiries of the desk clerk. But it was not his behavior that attracted the rheumy-eyed questioning glances of the Palace clientele. Many of them were better educated than Bates, and one of them was a Ph.D., a former teacher. No, what puzzled all of them was why Bates chose to live among them. A workingman, a man who paid for his room and his meals and his clothes from a semimonthly paycheck, a man who touched neither wine nor whiskey—why did such a man choose to live among the doomed? They could not recognize that for all his differences from them, he *belonged* in this part of town, in this hotel, in this lobby. They were too far gone to comprehend that he was one of them.

"Wet out there," the man in the corner volunteered in a tentative attempt at friendship. Victor Bates did not answer. He turned up the collar of his coat, opened the entrance door, and walked out into the storm.

"Just like the union hall, isn't it, Frank?" asked Jackson Armstrong. He slowly waved an extended right arm across the room and pointed out toward the sea. "From these Olympian heights, the gods of Pacific Hospital gaze serenely at the Pacific Ocean—on clear days, that is. When we look out of the window at the union hall, we see one cleaner's, one grocery store, three tenement buildings, one porno movie theater, and a massage parlor. That should tell us something right there. Establishment looks down, we look across, and we rarely like what we see." Armstrong returned to his chair and sat down.

The older man, Frank O'Brien, executive secretary of Local 175 of the Hospital and Institutional Workers Union, AFL-CIO, stared at the young man who had just spoken. How did I hire myself a smart-assed college kid like this, and a colored one besides? he thought, but as usual he did not answer the unspoken question. "You're talking a lot of philosophy this morning, Jax," he said. "Did they teach you those highfalutin thoughts at the university?"

"Yes," Armstrong replied. He refused to apologize. "Exactly who are the gods of this hospital?" Armstrong continued. "After all the time I've spent in this cathedral of healing, I'm still not sure. Whitesides and March imply that it's the medical staff—the administration acts only as a sort of servant for the doctors. The doctors don't agree. They say the administration really runs this place, using the influence of the board of directors. But the board says it only acts on advice given by the administration and the doctors. If that's true, the board is just for show. But we know the courts have made hospital boards accept responsibility. They're not rubber stamps anymore."

"Every hospital is different," O'Brien replied, "but as far as we're concerned, they all run it—Whitesides, the board, the docs. Nobody will admit that they have any control when we ask for something. It's part of the game. Wait till you've been around as long as I have," the gravelly voice continued, "you'll learn to play the game. Just remember to keep it simple. It's them against us. You don't need a college degree to figure out that *we* don't get nothing given to us."

"You really think it's a game?" Armstrong asked. "Our brothers and sisters in the laundry don't think it's a game, Frank. They don't think having their jobs on the line is play."

"Don't get fancy, kid," O'Brien answered. "The army has war games, but they're not for fun. I'm sixty-two years old and I know what's serious and what isn't."

Armstrong studied the older man. "The strain is showing, Frank. You shouldn't lose your cool. I know that it's them against us, and you and I are sitting in this nice caucus room sniping at each other. I'm worried because you don't realize how desperate the—"

"I don't realize? I was at this game before you were born, and *I* don't realize!" O'Brien slammed his fist on the desk.

"You think stupid things like that hanging dummy out there are going to help us?"

"Just listen, Frank. No, you *don't* realize that this time it's different. I'm closer in age and background to the rank and file, and I know them better than you do." O'Brien put up his hand in protest, but Armstrong kept talking. "Just let me finish, Frank. You keep needling me about my degree from State. What about all the part-time jobs I had? You know how long it took me to graduate. When I worked at this hospital as a security guard, I had to schedule my classes around the job."

"I don't need a history lesson about you, Jax. I know your story."

"I worked here and I became active in the union, and the people I worked with got to know me and respect me. They *liked* it that I was going to college, because one of their own was making it and could represent them because I was one of them. Not only my black brothers and sisters, but the Chicano brothers and sisters and the Filipino brothers and sisters and all the rest who can hardly speak English. They liked it that I could speak for them. Cut the crap, Frank. You didn't hire me into your lily-white office because you thought I was so smart."

"As a matter of fact, that's exactly why I hired you."

"You hired me to take the pressure off, because you weren't one of the angry brothers or sisters of the union." O'Brien tried to interrupt, but Armstrong waved him off. "I'm your safety valve, proof in glorious color that you head a democratic union. I like the job because I believe in the movement, but don't tell me that you didn't breathe a little easier when I became business agent of the union."

"I never hired you because of your color," O'Brien protested.

"Bullshit, Frank. I'll tell you what. Why don't you try to fire me right now and see what happens."

"We're at the critical stage of the negotiations, and you just said we should work together, so what do you do? You bait me with a challenge. Hell, I like you, Jax. Don't make this into a race war."

"Have I ever?" Armstrong asked. "Have I once acted as a black man in preference to a union man?"

"No, you haven't, and that's what confused me now. Why are you picking this time to start a fight?" O'Brien's tone was softer, conciliatory.

"I'm telling you that times have changed, Frank, and you damn well better realize it. You've sat through many hospital-contract negotiations and you've never come close to a strike, right? But what were the issues? Mostly wages, and as you said, it was a game of ending up on the fat side of the compromise. But you saw our meeting when they voted. I know the old tactics of whipping up enthusiasm for a strike by the diamond-shaped seating pattern, so twenty vocal men could sound like a hundred. Did I use the diamond? Did I have to?"

"You think I'm blind?" O'Brien asked. "I know the rank and file are worked up."

"But they're not worked up about wages. It's the other issues, mainly the laundry, because they know that if the laundry is subcontracted out and closed, and the hospital can get away with that, Dietary and Janitorial are next. We're in the last day, dammit, and the hospital hasn't budged."

"I've told you that today they *will* make concessions. They're putting up a real fight, but until now there was a tomorrow. Lester Whitesides is more nervous than I have ever seen him. He doesn't want a strike." O'Brien swung around in his chair and looked out toward the ocean. The gravel had returned to his voice. "And frankly, I don't neither."

"We're moving backwards. Nobody *wants* a strike. But if we come back to the membership with anything less than major concessions on all the issues, we're going to get lynched."

"Look, Jax. We need a short break." He looked uneasily at the business agent. "Not in this dump," he explained. "At Albie's."

Armstrong nodded, and the two men left to go to the luncheonette across the street from the hospital. Once inside, they took a booth and remained silent until the waitress, a stout white-haired woman, brought two menus to the booth.

"I want the usual, Jean," O'Brien said.

"Ditto," Armstrong instructed the waitress.

After she had placed the two steaming cups on the Formica tabletop, she made another trip to the counter and extracted, with tongs, two jelly doughnuts from a dirty plastic bin. She was slow, unruffled, and inefficient.

"Busy day," O'Brien commented, pointing to the empty counter.

"It'll pick up, Frank," she said, retrieving the menus.

"Where's Albie?" Armstrong asked.

"He's got the flu. I'm it, me and Louie." She pointed to the short-order cook. "He don't look too good either, if you ask me." She retreated to her station behind the counter and began to straighten out a stack of menus. She was interrupted as the door opened and a husky young man who had just parked his small pickup truck walked to the counter and sat down.

"Coffee, mister?"

"Yeah. Just coffee. It's cold in that rain."

The waitress turned to the Silex, poured a cup, and placed it in front of the new customer. Then she ambled a few steps to her left and slid one of the sugar containers down the counter.

"Just like a western," the man remarked.

"This *is* the West, mister," she answered.

"Well, it's not the desert West of the movies. More like pneumonia gulch out there. People in the city getting sick, and over across the street, some goddamn janitors' union is trying to hold up the hospital." The man stopped, seemingly oblivious of the two men sitting in a nearby booth. He was waiting for a reaction from the waitress, but she wasn't in the mood for conversation. "Times are getting pretty bad," he continued, "when the greedy unions can get every damn thing they ask for. Nobody pays my doctor and dentist for me. Nobody is giving me every holiday that comes along, and nobody is giving me any paid vacations. I'll tell you something. If they try and picket tomorrow, I may just drive my truck along the sidewalk and turn the pickets into part of the pavement." He turned for approbation to the only other customers and saw a furious Frank O'Brien approaching. He estimated that he could take this old man coming toward him, but what if the other one joined in?

"Meet the head of that janitors' union, mister," the waitress said.

O'Brien, considerably older and shorter than the customer,

was also tougher. He reached an arm out and grasped the front of the man's jacket, pulling him to an upright position. The man dropped his coffee as he struggled for balance, one foot on the counter step, the other on the floor.

"Tell me again what you're going to do with your truck tomorrow." O'Brien pushed the man back in his seat and released his grip.

"I was only kidding," the man answered. "I'm going to be out of town."

"You better be," O'Brien said.

"Let's go, Frank." Armstrong had left the booth. He stared at the seated customer for a few seconds. "You know," he finally said, "you're one dumb bastard."

Back at their meeting room on the fifth floor of the hospital, O'Brien remarked, "I coulda flattened him, but what good would that have done?"

"No good at all," Armstrong answered. "Anyway, you half-believe what he said about this strike being a holdup."

"Don't you even want to know my reasons for not wanting to go out? Listen to this." O'Brien picked up the morning paper from the table and turned the pages quickly until he reached the one he wanted. "Here! Listen carefully. This is from the editorial section." He began to read: " 'The institutional workers traditionally have been at the low end of the pay schedule, and we recognize that they must press hard for improvements in their situation. However, they should continue to use and never abandon the negotiation process. A strike against Thornton's largest hospital would be dangerously against the public interest, and therefore will not be tolerated by the citizens of this city. While the union officials are threatening strike tomorrow, we feel certain that they can best serve the community and themselves by extending the deadline and continuing to bargain with Pacific Hospital until an agreement acceptable to both sides is hammered out.' That's the Thornton *Star*, no surprise. But that's also the community this time, and you know it, Jax. You just heard it at Albie's. This may be a union town, but striking a hospital is much tougher in its way than striking General Motors."

"Frank . . ." Armstrong's voice was deliberate. "You and I don't really care what the *Star* says, do we?" He was not asking a question. "And we really aren't overly concerned with what the citizenry tolerates or doesn't, are we? Nobody but us gives a shit what happens to our people. The way I see it, we'll be on the line tomorrow. The hospital—namely, Whitesides—is being hard-nosed. We're going to have to squeeze them, because we're not doing it with the yak-yak."

"Why don't you listen, kid? Haven't I taught you that there's an old saying in the labor business: if you don't win in two weeks, you've lost the strike. It's not just the *Star*. You've been talking to the public, Jax. You can feel the heat, and we haven't even struck yet." O'Brien was almost shouting.

"I read that crap in the *Star* when I woke up this morning. 'Traditionally at the low end of the pay scale.' Damn right. 'Should never abandon the negotiation process.' What's the union supposed to do? Talk for three years while we get clobbered? You puzzle me. Why do you look at everything from the public-opinion aspect? You're our executive secretary, Frank. For Christ's sake!"

"Stop fighting with me," the older man said. "I'm not talking against you. All I said is I hope we settle, because this strike is going to be a son of a bitch to win, whether you like it or not. When we meet in the laundry this morning, I just want our people to know what we're in for. If we go out, it won't be easy for them. You know that discipline is hard to maintain, and once a strike ends, it leaves a lot of bad feeling behind. Those who went out, against those who scabbed. That kind of thing."

Armstrong stared at O'Brien. "I know that. But I want *you* to see how our people act this morning. I want you to see for yourself that they won't settle for a handout."

O'Brien was about to answer when the door suddenly flew open. Framed in the doorway was the hospital administrator. His face contorted by anger, he held a piece of severed rope with its attached bloodstained effigy high in the air. He stood silently for a moment, then hurled the effigy into the room. "I hear you're meeting in the laundry this morning, Frank," he finally sputtered. "You better tell your people one thing. Tell them that they'll never intimidate Lester Whitesides." Then he slammed the door.

The coastal city of Thornton had prospered. Located between Monterey and Santa Cruz, its population during the past thirty years had quadrupled to a census of 160,000, heterogenous as to ancestry and income. The old-money families of the city lived in the section called Sealawns.

The largest and most graceful of Sealawns' homes belonged to Dr. and Mrs. Asa Porter. Thornton people called it "Redhouse," and a man walking his dog might describe to his wife the length of his hike by stating that he had gone two blocks past Redhouse before turning back and heading for home. Actually, the mansion was owned by Asa's wife, Beulah Thornton Porter. Her grandfather Eliot Thornton had been a financial wizard, and after he had become the town's richest citizen and founded Pacific Hospital, the city fathers of that era renamed the community after him. Redhouse was a colonial structure located atop the highest of Sealawns' three hills. Its white portico could be seen from parts of the city miles away. Two marble lions stood guard over the arched entryway, and a driveway made a meandering U between the street and the house. Surprisingly, no iron gates protected the driveway at entrance or exit, and it was presumed that the structure was imposing enough by itself to keep intruders away.

Inside the mansion, in a large den adjoining the entrance hall, Asa Porter sat talking to his wife. Seated in an armchair, he spoke as if he had been born to the manner. He was dressed impeccably in a vested brown pin-striped suit. His prominent features included a slightly bulbous nose and large ears. He was bald except for a ring of reddish hair. His voice was deep and resonant, and he was never unaware of its impact.

"It should be an interesting session today, Beulah," he said to his wife. "They always manage to throw the toughest cases at me. That's a compliment, of course."

"What session are you talking about, Asa?" she asked indifferently. She had been reading as he talked, and she looked up from her notebooks.

"I've mentioned it this week, but I expect you weren't listening." He sounded annoyed, almost petulant, but continued. "I'm in the hot seat at the monthly Clinical Pathology Conference. As you've no doubt forgotten, the discussant tries to determine—"

"I know. The discussant tries to determine the diagnosis of a patient who has died for obscure reasons and only the pathologist knows the cause of death. It will be your job to deduce from the patient's record the disease that did him in. Did I omit anything, Asa?"

Porter stared at her but said nothing.

Beulah Porter at fifty was an attractive woman, but this was the result of illusion. Scrubbed clean, her face was plain; she knew, however, the way to best use cosmetics to compensate for nature's lack of vigor, and she put this knowledge to expert use. "I'm sure you'll do brilliantly, Asa," she continued. "You always do, don't you?" He again remained silent, and she continued in an apparently new vein. "You know, I miss your father. Every time I see his portrait in the hospital lobby, I remember what affection and esteem he evoked. He wasn't what you would call a financial success, was he, Asa? Compared with, say, my father or grandfather. But he was so dedicated, and everyone in the medical community remembers him as a great teacher. You remember how he traveled to University Hospital and to the medical school three times a week, and that fifty-mile round trip must have been difficult in his later years when his arthritis was so bad. But he never complained, did he? He loved teaching and he loved people. He loved me, Asa, and I loved him." She stopped and looked directly into her husband's eyes, as if to study the effect of her next remark. "Your mother was a bitch. I don't miss her at all."

Asa returned his wife's gaze but didn't say anything for several seconds as the tension in the room increased. "Don't start up with me, Beulah. I don't know what your game is or why you're playing it, but I'm telling you to cease and desist," he said finally. "My father was a dedicated man, but you know what he was dedicated to. Medicine, not his family. I'm glad that I have not behaved toward our children and grandchildren as he did toward me. We—my mother, whom you call a bitch, and I—were ignored so my father could pursue his goal of fame. That was probably the main thing to which he dedicated himself, and you know that when *I* look at his portrait—I try not to, but I see it by accident occasionally—I have entirely different feelings from you. So I'm warning you to cease and desist."

"You've upped the stakes, Asa. A few seconds ago you were telling me; now you're warning me." She laughed. "All right, I stand warned." She waited for a reply from her husband, but he was angry and said nothing. "Lester is very concerned about the strike. He and Sam March believe that the union will settle, but—"

"Since you've become chairman, I mean chairperson, of the board of directors, your interest in Pacific Hospital has been commendable, but don't you think that perhaps it's somewhat all-consuming? I mean, little else seems to concern you. I'm sick of hearing about all your meetings over the strike situation."

"But, Asa," she answered with a faint mock surprise, "until five years ago, I was happy merely volunteering in the gift shop once a week. You seem to forget that it was with your encouragement, I could even say *urging*, that I became more active in hospital affairs. Something about helping you advance your medical career, wasn't it? Remember last year. You began to talk to me about the upcoming appointment of a new chief of medicine. You wanted the job because the other candidate, Leo Vanni, didn't deserve it."

Porter retreated. "I'm delighted by your hospital activities, and I think you can help me get the job. But I did you no disservice by suggesting that you would find more involvement rewarding. My only complaint is that lately you seem more distant, hardly interested at all in what I'm doing. Today's CPC—the pathology conference—is just an example."

"I almost forgot that it's Wednesday, the doctors' afternoon off." Beulah pointed to the rain splashing against the windows. "You're not going out to the boat and tinker around in this weather, are you?"

Porter looked carefully to see if there was any trace of mockery, anything in the remark which might have made it a double entendre. He found nothing. "I'll probably take some journals out to the boat and catch up on my reading later this afternoon. I'm going to the hospital for a few hours, then I'll get away from it all on the boat. I'll probably sleep aboard tonight. No outside work today, that's for certain."

"Amen," Beulah said. "Maybe I'll join you." She laughed

at her husband's worried expression. "Don't be concerned. I won't go near your plaything. I despise it. Anyway, I have to be at the hospital later."

Porter frowned and looked at his watch. "I must leave. The pathology conference, which seems trivial to you, is at eleven, and before that I want to see my patients and go to the library." He got his coat, entered the side door to the garage, and left for the hospital in his small English sports car. Driving through the rain, he realized that his wife had not said good-bye to him. This was getting to be a habit he didn't like. After his appointment as chief of medicine was announced, there would be no need for Beulah to spend so much time at the hospital.

"This is going to be a long, boring day," muttered Dr. Harry Albright. He was seated at a desk inside the glass-enclosed nursing station of the emergency room. The nurse to whom he was speaking remained silent, and he continued. "Look at those soaked rats out there," he said, indicating the reception area, where a few patients, accompanied by family or friends, were waiting to be seen. Dripping umbrellas and raincoats spilled water on the white vinyl floor. "What was that call about, Latimer?"

"That was Leo Vanni. City ambulance is bringing in one of his patients. Auto accident. He wants the man admitted after you check him. I guess it will be a busy day, doctor." She looked at him and smiled the smile that had become, for him, the happiest part of his work. Her calm demeanor made him feel better.

"What have we seen so far, Latimer? Two bladder infections, a kid with an upset stomach throwing up, and four minor lacerations. I shouldn't complain. That's what the hospital is paying me for, but I'll tell you, I feel like a fifty-seven-year-old boy scout."

"I know that all the patients we see aren't serious emergencies, but they all need help. You do help them, Dr. Albright."

"You know what I wanted to be when I was an intern? A heart surgeon, a famous heart surgeon. I actually did have one year of surgical training, but my wife was so goddamned greedy that she couldn't wait for the long haul. She wanted me in practice making money right away. And she was married to just the dope who did it."

"You would have been a good heart surgeon."

"I might have been, but I doubt it. I probably would have botched that up like I did the rest of my life. After she got enough money out of me, my wonderful wife divorced me. She'll never remarry, because she enjoys killing me with alimony payments." Albright sighed. He did not tell the nurse that he had lost so many patients because of his personality that he was forced to apply to the State Medical Society for a paid job placement. That's how he got this position. Neither did he tell her of his frequent thoughts of suicide. He had completely lost confidence in himself.

"Do you think that we're going to have a strike?" Marilyn Latimer asked, changing the subject.

"It won't make any difference to us one way or the other. We'll be just as busy, and my twelve-hour shift won't get any shorter. But to answer your question, no. The hospital politicians and the union politicians will work something out somehow," Albright answered wearily.

"I'm working a twelve-hour shift today too. I'm taking half of Michelle's shift," she said.

"Yes, I know. I checked the schedule."

Their conversation was interrupted by a siren, followed seconds later by the arrival of an ambulance. The attendants unloaded their patient and quickly wheeled him into one of the treatment rooms. His clothes were spattered with blood and the bandage around his head was soaked through with fresh blood.

Albright looked at the slip which the ambulance attendant had handed him. Then he crumpled the sheet of paper and threw it on the floor. In a few minutes, when he was told the patient was ready, he entered the treatment room. "Morley. Karl Morley, isn't it? What happened to you?"

The patient turned toward Albright. He was a young man, and despite his messy condition, he retained an air of hauteur. His thin but somewhat long nose gave him an aristocratic appearance. "I was in an automobile accident. I thought you might have guessed."

"Don't get sarcastic with me, Morley. I know you were in an auto accident. What I want is your version of it."

"I was on my way to my antique shop. I'm not fond of driving in this city, especially in dreadful rain like this."

"The accident, Morley. Get to the accident."

"If I had waited at home five more minutes, I would have been someplace else and not involved with a moronic driver. His pickup truck did more than batter *me*. It smashed my vintage Cadillac. He ran the stop sign, and I had to jam on my brakes. My car swerved to the right and hit a lampost. I was thrown forward and my head hit the windshield. Also, my stomach must have hit the steering wheel, because it's very sore here." Morley pointed to his abdomen.

Albright tried to be sympathetic. "Don't worry about all the blood. These things often look worse than they are."

"I'm certain of it," Morley said. "As soon as you take care of the cut on my head, I'd like to go home. I did not lose consciousness, doctor. And I know that's very important. All I have is a headache and a sore abdomen."

Albright walked to a cabinet and returned with some pills and a glass. "Here's some aspirin," he said.

"I can't take aspirin. It gives me a stomachache."

"Well, you can't have anything stronger. I'm not going to mask the signs, in case your head injury is more serious than I think it is," Albright replied. "We'll dissolve the aspirin in a glass of water and follow that with four more glasses of water. Then you won't get a gastric burn."

Morley reluctantly downed the aspirin and water as instructed. Then Albright proceeded with the examination after unwrapping the patient's bandaged head. "You're not dying," Albright said. He turned to Latimer. "Eight stitches should handle this cut. Pulse and blood pressure are normal." Albright continued the physical examination. Morley winced when Albright pressed down on the left side of his rib cage. "We'll get some chest films before you go to the floor and make sure you haven't broken any ribs. No big deal if you did. Just some tape."

"What did you say about the floor?" Morley asked. He was perturbed.

"Dr. Vanni wants you admitted for observation."

"There is absolutely no need for me to go into the hospital. I feel better now."

"I just take orders around here. You'll have to fight it out with Vanni."

Marilyn Latimer opened the suture set. Albright injected lidocaine around the gaping edges of the head wound, waited for a minute, and then quickly completed the sewing. "Okay, Morley. We'll send you to X Ray and then you can have the pleasure of sacking out for the day." He turned to Latimer before leaving the examining room. "I wouldn't mind changing places with him. I can't think of better treatment for a tired old boy scout."

Sam March sat with his feet up on the desk. He had thrown his jacket on his office hide-a-bed couch and had loosened his shirt and tie. He looked at his watch. Karen should be here by now, he thought. Her phone call had upset him. He had enough to worry about today without mystery added to his troubles, and Karen had sounded mysterious enough. She had to talk to him, she had said, and she didn't want to discuss it on the phone. He would wait five more minutes, and then the hell with her. There had been happier times, he thought, weeks and months without the kind of anger he felt now. He reflected on how much had changed in his marriage. A year ago it would have been impossible for him to have anticipated his present mood.

Born in a lumber town in Oregon, he was the youngest of three boys. His older brothers and his father still worked in that town, but his feelings during his stint in the navy precluded his return home. He had been very young when he was in the service and had first seen Thornton. His ship had been anchored in Thornton Bay for a week, but that single week was sufficient; he had fallen in love with the place. And he had had time to explore it with a shipmate from Thornton, who showed him around. Both boys were members of the black gang, the engineering crew, and the sight of white buildings lining beautiful beaches was particularly appealing, since they had spent much of their working time below deck. Liberty had been generous—only a skeleton crew manned the anchored ship—and each morning as the tender carried him toward the Thornton shore, his decision to make the coastal city his home was reinforced. His friend's father, an attorney, had taken a liking to Sam and offered to help find him a job someday. That had been his ace in the hole. but it had not been needed. When he got out of the service, he made the rounds of Thornton employment agencies as well as investigating every promising newspaper advertisement for help needed. Partly because of his engineering experience, and partly because of his enthusiasm, the personnel director at Pacific Hospital had hired him to work in the divison of Buildings and Grounds. He felt at home with blueprints, he was imaginative, and he was a hard worker. He began to climb the administrative ladder, and three years ago, just after his marriage, he was appointed assistant administrator. If he had a single failing, it was his irrepressible honesty. It was an honesty that he was unable to temper with lip service, so he was never political. The art of diplomacy completely eluded him, and he said and did whatever his inner code dictated to him. Another man with these qualities would have been fired somewhere along the line, but since Sam was so completely open, his intemperate talk and actions were tolerated as the idiosyncratic qualities of an excellent administrator. Despite his bluntness, and sometimes because of it, everybody liked him. "That's Sam," his associates had concluded. Most of them secretly identified with this man who daily seemed to risk his job because he was unable to dissemble. That quality was giving him particular trouble in his home life, because he never really comprehended that other people, especially his wife, were capable of significant dishonesty.

He had met Karen for the first time four years ago. He walked into the medical-staff office one morning to meet with the hospital chief of staff. In the outer room, somebody new, blond and strikingly pretty, was sorting some cards. She looked up at him, smiled, and without a hint of self-consciousness introduced herself. She told him that she was glad to be at the hospital because since she had been born in it and had her appendix taken out in it, the place was comfortably familiar to her. "It's better, though, to be working here," she said, "than being cut up." She laughed easily as she made a few more comments about Pacific, but Sam was not paying attention; he was too busy wondering what her appendectomy scar looked like. He did hear her say that she was an only child and that she had gone to secretarial school after graduation from high school. When he went to pick her up at her apartment before their first date, he should have been forewarned. She showed him her senior yearbook. "Karen is ambitious," the caption under her photograph read. "She will get whatever she wants." What Karen really seemed to want, March thought ruefully a few weeks ago, was simple: MORE. More money, more social standing, more of everything that Sam both could and could not provide. But those early days of courtship had been idyllic, and after that Sam thought he had hit the marriage jackpot. When Karen had smiled during their first meeting, he knew that this girl would become something in his life but he had no idea that that something would be Mrs. Sam March; he was not, as he had convinced himself so many times, ready to settle down. But Karen was ready, and the yearbook had prophesied well. Exactly when had it all begun to go sour? March wondered.

The sound of her pleasantly husky voice brought him into the present.

"Hello, Sam." She stood at the door for an instant, and as he looked up he had almost the same feeling that had hit him when he first saw her four years ago. This girl is a knockout!

"Come in, Karen, close the door. I want to know what in the hell is so important that it couldn't wait until tonight."

Karen closed the door quietly and took off her gloves, rainhat, and raincoat. She placed them neatly on the couch and moved slowly to a chair. She was not in any hurry.

"Well?" asked March.

"I thought we should have a little talk about us, Sam. Don't you think it's about time?" March stared at her but said nothing. "Your behavior this morning, for example. Don't you think we should talk about that?"

"Your riddles are getting annoying, Karen. What behavior this morning? You mean at three A.M. when I tried to have some carnal knowledge of my wife and you said no go? Is that the behavior you're bitching about? Or was it at five-forty-five this morning when I got dressed as you slept, made my own coffee, and drove to the hospital? Don't tell me, I know. You wanted me to wake you up and tell you I was leaving. You were concerned that I didn't wear a muffler."

"There's no need for sarcasm, Sam. You know what I'm talking about. The car. Remember we can only afford one

43

car. And remember that this week was my shopping week. I haven't bought anything for six months and the year-end sales are going on now. You knew that. The shopping centers I use are all miles apart. You stay in one place—at this hospital every day—and still you've taken the car every day this week. You promised I could have it."

"Are you serious? You planned to go shopping in that?" March pointed outside. "It's been this way for three days and you want to go shopping?"

"Yes, I do. These sales don't last forever. And the good things go early."

"You're one lovely broad, Karen. You've had the car two days a week since we've been married. We're getting another car as soon as these negotiations are over, and you cry like a fucking baby because this week I've had to get to the hospital early."

"Save your vile language for Pacific Hospital. They appreciate it."

"You ought to know, Karen," March replied. "You worked here until I got my raise last year. You threw a fourteen-thousand-dollar-a-year job in the medical-staff office out the window because you wanted 'more out of life.' Is volunteering for every museum, symphony, you-name-it committee getting more out of life?" March looked evenly at his wife. "Or could it be just social climbing? Is your not being 'ready' yet for children getting more out of life?"

Karen stood up and began pacing up and down the length of the office. She was dressed in a black ultrasuede pantsuit and white satin blouse. Her figure was lithe and youthful and her shoulder-length blond hair bounced as she walked. March was aware that most men were strongly attracted to Karen and envied his marital prerogatives. *Little do they know,* he thought.

"Look, Sam. I'm not going to trade recriminations with you. I came here for two reasons." Karen had stopped pacing and stood facing her husband. "First, I came to pick up the car keys. I'm going shopping whether you like it or not. You can call me tonight when you're ready for me to pick you up. Second and more important, I'm telling you as honestly as I can that our marriage is in trouble and we might as well face it. I can put up with your language—I knew about that when

I married you—but I didn't know about your disposition. Ever since these negotiations began, you've been impossible. And you have made no attempt to straighten things out."

"Things are straightened out now, Karen. Every night. I'm trying for a little relief. And the rest of what you said is a pile of shit. You closed your legs tight months ago, long before the negotiations started. Christ, you've been acting like some goddamn vestal virgin. We got trouble, baby—no doubt about that—but don't play me for a sucker. You've got fifty percent of the action."

"I repeat, Sam, I'm not here to argue with you. It's just that things have been getting steadily worse and somebody better have the courage to mention that ugly word, 'divorce.' Since you've shown no inclination to face the facts, I'll have to force the issue. You must be some kind of an animal—you and your precious champ over there." She pointed to a framed picture on the wall. "Marriage is some prizefight to you. You don't care if you take punishment as long as you can get a punch in regularly. Sexual or any other kind of abuse."

"Abuse? What the hell are you talking about?" March stood up and walked over to her. "Have I raped you? Have I hit you? Are you saying that we should consider divorce because I have normal sexual instincts I want gratified? Is that what you're saying?"

Karen backed up. "Why don't you gratify them with Liz Scripps? She's always had a yen for you."

"Maybe I'll just damn well do that. But you haven't answered me. What kind of abuse?"

"You don't know how to give affection, Sam, and I need it so badly. I can't make love to you without tenderness. You just don't know how to show me your feelings. It's not all your fault. I don't think I'm the right woman for you."

March turned his back on his wife. He spoke softly, half to himself. "You never said anything ever. Not once in the three years we've been married did you say anything. No complaints at all until a few months ago. Then you bitch about tenderness and provoke fights and begin to turn to ice, and still you don't say anything. Until just now." He turned around and faced his wife again. "And now you say we should consider—that was your word, wasn't it?—divorce.

And you say that *I'm* the one who doesn't have any feeling?" He reached in his pocket and tossed the car keys to Karen. She caught the key chain with its plastic boxing gloves attached and nonchalantly put it in her purse. Then she walked to the couch and put on her coat and hat.

"We'll talk about this later, Sam. I only meant to mention it, not to have a long discussion now. Please, just think about what I've said." March stared at her without answering, and finally she shrugged and left the office.

He stood motionless for a moment. Then he walked over to the wall and stared at the picture Karen had mentioned. Karen knew only that it was a photograph of him posing with the light-heavyweight champion of the world under the big guns of a battleship. Both men were wearing boxing trunks. For some reason, March had never told his wife the story behind the picture. Now his mind went back in time. The photo had been taken just before an exhibition bout fifteen years earlier when he was in the navy. The bout was three rounds, and in the second round the champ had decided to amuse the assembled officers and men at March's expense. He began to pepper the young machinist's mate with stiff jabs that hurt and put March's head into motion like a horizontal yo-yo. Everybody but March was laughing. His face was red from the leather staccato and his nose was bleeding, but in the final round he made up for it all. With two minutes gone, he slipped one of the jabs and threw a fast hard right hook. He literally decked the champ, who was confused and shaky when he got up. The champ then clowned for the rest of the round as if it had all been intentional, but he danced away and didn't throw any more jabs.

March turned from the wall and sat down at his desk.

The young woman in Room 301 was crying softly as she remembered the trip. If I had only told Dr. Vanni! she thought. He wouldn't have let me go. Why didn't I tell him? Why didn't I tell myself? Why was I so stupid? She looked at the man sitting uncomfortably at the foot of her bed. Alex, sitting there reading a magazine—he was the reason she had not told her doctor that she was going to the snow country. And yet, he was not to blame. Susan Royal was thirty-four years old, and it was she who challenged the fates and lost.

For at least that much, she acknowledged, she was responsible. Somehow, she thought that if she kept reviewing what had transpired, she could mentally force its reversal. Ludicrous. She always ended up in Room 301.

"How much longer, Alex?" she asked.

The man glanced at his watch. "At least a half-hour till they come for you, Susan." It seemed as if he wanted to say something else, but he didn't, and fell silent once more.

Susan had been so excited that morning three weeks ago. She had packed the night before, assuring Alex that she would be ready at seven the following morning. She would split the expenses of a week in Squaw Valley, a glorious week with a man whose interest in her had begun to wane a bit when she earlier had rejected the idea of a snow-country vacation. That had been unfair to him, since he loved skiing, and so she had second and third thoughts, finally assenting to the trip. Once that decision had been made, she felt as if a burden had been lifted. Alex was happier with her, and she vowed that she would be careful, that she would take care of her diabetes even more meticulously than she did at home. An impossible task, but a vow nonetheless. She had never skiied before, but she would learn. This was another vow. She tried not to think of herself as an invalid, and if she could get away with an active sport like skiing, she would be able to share much more of Alex's world. She had rented skis and boots and bought an outfit that stretched her budget. But, she reasoned, the ski clothes represented an investment toward a future with a man she hoped to marry.

They had left promptly at seven. Alex had picked her up at her apartment, loaded her suitcase, placed her skis alongside of his on the rack, and they were off. From Thornton, north on the Coast Highway to Half Moon Bay, where Alex had headed inland and picked up Interstate 280 to reach the Bay Bridge and the beginning of Interstate 80.

The State of California resembles an elongated football stadium. The Coast Range is its western grandstand and the Sierra Nevada range its eastern grandstand. The playing field is a large central valley extending from Redding in the north down to Calexico at the Mexican border. Transecting this central valley on the northern thirty-five-yard line is Interstate 80, a superhighway that begins in San Francisco and ends at the George Washington Bridge entrance to New York (or at least that is the viewpoint held by Westerners). The highway heads in a northeast direction until it reaches Winnemuca, Nevada, and then it takes a horizontal course over the rest of the United States. Traversing that segment of Interstate 80 that would take them to Squaw Valley, the car picked up speed. Alex had checked with the CHP, and all roads were passable, although chains were required. The snow from a storm two days earlier had been mostly cleared.

Alex rarely talked when he drove, but Susan did not object to his silence. Passing Vacaville, Dixon, Davis, and Sacramento, she felt an increasing elation as they headed toward a destination she had never before reached. Actually, she had never been farther from Thornton than two hundred miles, and having exceeded that distance now, she wondered how in the jet age she could have taken her renunciation of travel, the neuroses of her deceased parents, for granted. Life on the outside, she thought, is great fun. They passed Auburn, heading in the general direction of Lake Tahoe. She resolved to do this sort of thing more often, maybe fly to Florida or Hawaii. They had chains put on by a young man who looked half-frozen, stamping his feet several times after he had fastened the chains. "He really earns his living," Susan said as they got under way again.

"We're probably supporting him on welfare and food stamps," Alex answered. "He pockets plenty, and I doubt if he reports a cent of it." A precisely judicious mind, not a compassionate heart, was Alex's forte. The snowbanks were higher now as they passed Emigrant Gap. Why not Europe? Alex had been there twice. Of course, next time Europe with him. They passed Cisco Grove and continued the climb toward Donner summit. Soon they were there, 7,240 feet above sea level, over a mile and a half in the sky. Alex listened to the radio and Susan gawked at the scenery. Shortly before Truckee, they took Highway 89 and traveled south, reaching the inn by two P.M. After the registering and unpacking, Alex left for the slopes, telling Susan that he would be back by cocktail time. Also, he would register her for ski school for the following morning.

As soon as Alex was out of the room, Susan did her unpacking. She carefully retrieved the paraphernalia of her disease from the side pocket of her valise, the case containing her testing equipment, her syringes, and her insulin bottles. Once she and Alex had begun sleeping together, she had thought that the routine of managing her diabetes could be performed without fuss regardless of whether he was present or not. But when he first saw the syringe, he had paled and had told her that he did not like sickness and that whatever duties she had in connection with her "health" should not be done in his presence. She put the case under her clothes in the bureau; she would test and inject later, secretly, after Alex was asleep.

She was so euphoric about the drive up and the week which was to follow, that she quickly dismissed the episodes of anguish which had characterized her life. Everybody has problems, she understood. Susan Royal had lived with diabetes for so long. The disease had been discovered when she was ten years old, and blood tests, urine examinations, and insulin shots had become part of her daily routine. She adjusted to the requirements of taking care of herself better than her parents did. They were terrified every time Susan got a cold. Susan's sister, twelve years older than she, was married and out of the house during Susan's adolescence, so she could not help the younger girl in her fight to lead a normal life, a fight which she gradually lost. Inwardly she refused to think of herself as sick, but nevertheless Susan withdrew from friendships and social life in general so she could reassure her mother, in particular, by just being in the house. When Susan was seventeen, her life was devastated by a cruel, incomprehensible tragedy. Her parents were killed in an automobile accident only a mile from their home. Her sister, in Thornton for the funeral, tried to persuade Susan to return to Milwaukee to live, but she refused. The girls had been left some money, certainly enough for a college education, but Susan elected to stay in Thornton and to go to work after graduation from high school. She began with a typing-pool job with an insurance company, and because of her diligence, she had been promoted to a minor executive position with the company, Western Mutual. Eight years ago, the doctor who had taken care of her since birth died. For her the pain was very great, and mitigated only because Leo Vanni, who became her doctor, was compassionate and changed practically nothing in the way her diabetes was handled. Five years ago she had noticed that her left calf occasionally pained her when she walked, because of reduced circulation to the leg. Dr. Vanni warned her about extreme cold. Therefore, she had told him nothing about this trip. She could confess later, but she could not accept any interdiction which might ruin things with Alex. She had dated very little during her life, had lost her virginity at age thirty to a drunken executive during a company convention. That meaningless night of painful accession was the closest she had come to romance until she met Alex. She was excited by the attentions of this youthful, handsome man who had come to work as an adjuster in the company. They had begun to go out on dates five months ago, and not long afterward had begun sleeping together. The affair, for Susan, represented her first real hope that she might have found someone with whom she could share her life. Alex was not a man to make commitments, and so Susan was especially encouraged when she was asked to take the trip. In no way could she have refused.

The first evening of the vacation had been its high point. After a brisk walk through the snow, they sat on a couch near a blazing fire. Alex was exuberant from his afternoon of skiing. As he drank his martinis—Susan could not drink—he looked only at Susan.

In bed that evening he murmured that it was wonderful having her with him and that who knows, someday they might both want a more permanent arrangement. Susan snuggled happily against him. She had no way of divining that this was the closest Alex ever would come to a proposal. The following morning at ski school, Susan fell several times just trying to stand in line on a slight slope as the instructor was explaining fundamentals. Snow spilled into her socks as she untied and tightened her loose ski boots. That afternoon a rope lift pulled Alex and Susan to the top of a beginners' slope. Her ski lesson had paid off, because she made it to the bottom with only one fall. Alex told her to keep practicing, and he went off by himself to try Little KT before taking the gondola to higher altitudes. Susan's leg began to hurt by midafternoon, and she did not ski the following morning, claiming that she had twisted her ankle. Alex could tolerate a twisted ankle but not ill health. Susan stuck it out for two more days as her leg got progressively worse. Finally she told Alex she had to see a doctor. When the physician at Squaw Valley saw the leg, he said she required immediate hospitalization and should be rushed to Thornton by ambulance. Her left leg was frostbitten and infected, and the doctor phoned Leo Vanni to tell him the situation. Alex drove to Thornton behind the ambulance. He was annoyed that his vacation was spoiled but relieved that the ambulance attendants now had the responsibility of caring for a sick Susan.

Two days ago Leo Vanni had sat by her bedside as she screamed. He had just told her that the leg had to come off. Vanni kept talking to her and finally forced her to realize that nothing short of cutting off her leg could save her life. She would become the youngest diabetic amputee Leo Vanni had ever treated.

Now, in her drowsy state, fears surfaced. What did the new artificial limbs really look like? Were they natural or would she appear deformed to people on the streets? Would people turn away self-consciously as she limped down the pavement, or would they stare at her, pity or curiosity on their faces? Would she ever again be able to wear a short skirt?

The door opened and the intern Arnie Jacobs came into the room. He asked Alex to step outside for a moment. "Last-minute exam, Susan," he said. "Sorry."

"I know," she answered. "Dr. Vanni was here earlier. I've already been prepped and they gave me my pre-op shots. I'm beginning to feel dopey, and I know that when I wake up . . ." She stopped talking.

"When you wake up it's going to be very tough for a while. But you're going to be fine, Susan." Jacobs felt emotional and he hoped it didn't show. He looked at her. Even though she was six years older than he, she looked younger. It was as if the diabetes paradoxically had taken years from her face while it aged her arteries. Her cheeks were flushed from medications and the crying, and her black wavy hair was in disarray. Her nose was small and straight, and altogether, her determined chin included, Jacobs had fallen for her a little. He knew that aside from a married sister in the Midwest she was alone. Susan had told him yesterday that after the amputation she would surely lose Alex. Since Jacobs could not be certain that this was an unwarranted fear, he had said nothing. A lot of Susan, he felt, resided in a dream world, and her apprehension about Alex represented at least a stab at reality. Jacobs hoped that she was beginning to chart her life more sensibly.

Jacobs thought for a moment about diabetes. It was almost two diseases. There was the insulin thing—not enough of the stuff being made by the pancreas, so that the blood sugar got high without treatment. That part could be controlled by diet and shots of animal insulin. But there was no effective prevention for the second part of the disease, the circulatory complications of diabetes. No matter how well the blood sugar was controlled, blood-vessel damage might proceed on its inexorable course, and the result could be blindness or kidney disease or stroke or other calamities. Blood vessels were everywhere in the body. Fortunately, most diabetics did not develop these kinds of complications. Susan was not one of the lucky ones.

Jacobs gently patted Susan's cheek, and then he lifted the cover off the frame that was protecting her legs.

"Arnie," she mumbled, "it was horr . . . it was horrible knowing there wasn't a damn thing I could do to stop what was happ . . . happening to me."

Her words were beginning to slur, and Jacobs proceeded quickly with the examination. He inspected the infected, gangrenous left leg. He noted the blackened toes and he noted the level of the left calf where the infection had finally been contained by large doses of antibiotics. He quickly felt the cold foot and confirmed the absence of pulse under the knee. He knew it was an intrusion—a necessary intrusion, but an intrusion nonetheless—to examine this dying appendage, this leg that in less than an hour would no longer be part of Susan Royal. When he had completed his observations, he replaced the sheet.

"Arnie," she whispered hoarsely. "Do you know what they're doing now in surgery? They're boiling the scalpels."

Just behind the emergency room on the main floor, the PBX office sat like a compact box. The chief operator, Mabel Catlin, reigned like a queen over her court of telephone operators. All of them had worked at Pacific a long time, but none could match either the service record—forty-two years—or the sharp tongue of their boss. The PBX room was really Mabel's home, because she loved the place. As a result, she spent more time there than she needed to, often working extra shifts.

When not talking into her headset, Mabel kept up a continuous conversation with the other girls, relating the latest gossip. Lester Whitesides had once told her that she was the historian of Pacific Hospital, and this pleased her. Mabel, a bleached blond, knew all the hospital dirt because she waved for silence anytime a conversation that she deemed juicy was taking place. Once, a girlfriend of one of the residents called the hospital to talk with him. At one point in the conversation the resident told her to stop discussing personal matters because "the operators listen in." Both the young doctor and his girl were startled by an indignant "We do not," rendered by Mabel in her unmistakable shrill staccato.

Now, lights were flashing on all of the boards as agile fingers plugged and unplugged connections. "Pacific Hospital, just a moment please." "I'm trying my best to connect you, sir." "Yes, she's a patient in Room 246, just a moment and I'll ring the room." "No, sir, I know Dr. Chase isn't available, he's scrubbed in surgery . . . yes, sir, I'm sure, I just spoke to surgery, why don't you try in about forty-five minutes." The four operators were working at full speed, when suddenly Mabel waved for silence.

"Girls," she pronounced, "some guy just called me for the third time asking if we do those sex-change operations at Pacific. I told him no the first two times, but you know what I just told him?"

"What, Mabel?" the operator at the far left asked dutifully.

"I told him that if he bothered me again, he could come in here and I'd do the operation for him free of charge." She cackled for a moment and then admonished the other girls to get back to work.

"It's a rainy day. Weird things will happen," she advised her assistants as she returned her attention to the switchboard.

"That's exactly the kind of thing I was talking about," O'Brien said. "A reporter collared me fifteen minute ago. I said we knew nothing about it and we don't condone it." He and Armstrong were sitting in the lobby discussing the effigy incident and the minor sabotage to the toilets. "Dumb things like that play exactly into the hospital's hand. That's what the public will be reading about tonight and seeing on TV."

"The whole thing was stupid," Armstrong agreed. "Does anybody know who did it?"

"No. Who's here that early? What time you got now?"

Armstrong glanced at his watch. "We have a few minutes yet."

"Here. Look at this." O'Brien took a sheet of paper out of his briefcase and handed it to Armstrong.

"Looks fine to me," Armstrong said, and handed the list of proposed picket captains back to O'Brien. "Besides the laundry workers, the rank-and-file committee will be there too."

"You already told me that twice. Do you think I'm deaf?"

"Every time I tell you something, you accuse me of thinking you're blind or deaf or stupid. I'm just telling you again, for emphasis, that our people are looking over our shoulders. They're not convinced that you're with them, Frank. At least not one hundred percent."

"Am I supposed to be a leader in this union or a rubber stamp? Are you saying I'm not one hundred percent for the interest of our people?"

"I'm not doubting your motivation, Frank. It's just that during these weeks of negotiation, I'm not convinced that we see eye to eye so far as strategy. Specifically, I'm not convinced that today's marathon session won't seem more productive to you than to me, and I think that you would be more willing to settle short of a strike than I would."

O'Brien grunted. "You're always three jumps ahead of where you should be. One thing at a time. Let's go downstairs."

Even before they reached the laundry, angry voices could be heard arguing. Armstrong, looking grim, flashed a see-I-told-you-so look at O'Brien. The latter's tough old face remained expressionless.

As the union leaders entered the laundry, the noise quieted down. Men and women stood around in groups of twos and threes. Occasionally a loner could be seen leaning against a wall or a piece of equipment. O'Brien and Armstrong made their way to the back of the laundry. It was quieter there, and they could see all of the rank-and-file union members, about thirty of whom were present.

"Can you all hear me?" O'Brien began.

A chorus of nos answered him.

"Turn off all those machines," he ordered. In a minute or so the room was quiet. "Come closer. Let's close ranks." O'Brien waited until the assemblage had consolidated. "I hear that those of you who work in this laundry wanted this meeting so you could learn the progress of our negotiations."

"What progress?" somebody shouted, and there was some jeering laughter. There was also some noise as some workers translated to others what was being said.

"I see signs that we are making some progress. Management has already conceded that a wage increase is justified, but we think that we can do better for you than what they're suggesting." There was stony silence except for the translation, and O'Brien continued. "I know what your interest is, and I haven't forgotten it for one minute since these contract talks began. You want this laundry to keep operating! You want your jobs, right?"

Now there were loud cheers and whistling and stomping. "A wage increase is no good if there's no job to go with it," shouted O'Brien, and he was again answered with cheers. "Now, we are meeting with Whitesides and March this afternoon, and tonight again if necessary. I think we'll break 'em. I think we'll make 'em realize that this hospital is a big family." O'Brien's voice rose to a rough crescendo. "You good people. You hardworking, underpaid people of this hardworking laundry, we're not going to let anybody push you out of the hospital family."

As the cheering started, Armstrong frowned and looked at O'Brien, but the latter was waving and smiling in acknowledgement of the cheering. Subtle, Armstrong thought, very subtle. Once more he was forced to reappraise O'Brien. The old warrior had a million tricks. Armstrong applauded mechanically.

"What about the strike?" a woman sorter asked before O'Brien could continue. "Suppose the hospital don't give in, then what?"

O'Brien waited for the noise to subside. "Your rank-and-file committee"—he pointed to the group of four men and two women standing nearby—"authorized Jax and me to call a strike if the talks break down. The Central Labor Council has given its okay. And I think I'll have some good news. The Teamsters haven't made up their mind, but they think we're fighting for something important here at Pacific. I talked to someone at Teamster headquarters yesterday afternoon, and they may decide to make us a test case. If they join us and honor our picket line, you know how much that will help us."

The combination of words "picket line" and "Teamsters" galvanized the crowd, and the cheering was louder than ever. Armstrong frowned again. Yesterday morning O'Brien had told him that he didn't think the Teamsters would go along, and he hadn't related the telephone conversation to Armstrong.

Finally the noise died down, and O'Brien was ready to continue when a voice shouted out, "You ain't going to win a strike! My job here is finished. You're talking bullshit, O'Brien, and maybe you can con these foreigners, but don't try to bullshit me!"

While the other workers were mumbling to each other about the outburst, O'Brien turned to Armstrong and whispered, "Who is this guy?"

"He's a mangle hand. His name is Victor Bates."

"Mr. Bates," O'Brien said. "I don't know who you've been talking to, but somebody has been handing you a line of crap. It's my business—Jax's and my business—to make this union stronger, and I'll tell you one thing, Bates, defeatist talk like that doesn't help the union one goddamn bit. Now's the time we better all stick together."

"Sure. You union guys stick together and the hospital bosses stick together and you all get fat salaries, but who cares about us? Nobody, that's who! So the laundry closes and we lose our jobs. They'll retrain the young ones, but I'm fifty-eight. Are you going to be out of a job, O'Brien?"

Armstrong studied Bates. The man looked desperate and angry. He was thin, on the verge of emaciation, and his hair was a scraggly gray. He was a familiar figure at the hospital because he spent so much of his off-duty time there. Prior to now, he had been the quietest man who worked in the laundry.

"Bates he is right!" one of the Chicano workers, a press operator, shouted out. "Listen, Mr. O'Brien. You listen to this *New Labor Hospital Paper*." He walked over to Bates and handed him a mimeographed sheet. "Here, Bates. You read this!"

Bates took out a pair of glasses and began to read. "What are Pacific Hospital union officials doing for us? Look at their past record! They settle for small increases and minor changes in working conditions. Do they really challenge the hospital? The answer is NO! THEY NEVER FIGHT! They bargain. WHY? UNION LEADERS LIKE O'BRIEN HAVE A PERSONAL COMMITMENT TO THE BOSSES AND THEIR CAPITALIST SYSTEM. NO WONDER! Our dues pay them good salaries, and they get under-the-table payoffs too. THEY ARE SPIES OF THE BOSSES.' "

Bates finished reading, and now there was a cacophony of boos, yells, and cheers. Arguments broke out all over the laundry, and everybody was speaking at once. O'Brien looked confused and angry, but Armstrong looked furious. He walked out into the crowd and stopped in the middle of the room. "Is there anyone in this room who doesn't know me?" he asked. The response was silence. "I'm glad, brothers and sisters. I'm powerful glad." He paused and looked around "Have I ever once lied to you? Have I? When I worked here and was on the rank-and-file committee, since I've been business agent of the union, anytime? Well, have I?" He looked around slowly this time, trying to fix each worker in his gaze.

The men and women began shaking their heads in the negative. A few shouted out "No," and one black man yelled in a falsetto voice: "Jax, you is my main man!" Everybody including Armstrong began to laugh.

"Okay. Cool it!" Armstrong was quickly serious again. "I don't know where you got that paper from, Manuel," he said, addressing the Chicano, "but that's exactly the kind of garbage that can beat us, just that kind of garbage that helps the hospital, not us. Brothers and sisters, we stick together or we sink. What do you think 'union' means?" He looked around the room, searching each face out. "Well, what does 'union' mean?"

"Together!" shouted out a black woman, a hand ironer.

"Right on, sister! Together. Now, I've known about Frank O'Brien for a long time. When he was fighting for workers' rights in the painters' union, he was hit by a car and beaten up by scab strikebreakers. The lives of his family were threatened. Does that sound like the kind of man who's working for the bosses? Do you see Frank O'Brien rich and driving a big car? You're damn right you don't."

As Armstrong talked, O'Brien shifted uneasily from one foot to the other. He was on the one hand grateful for the defense but on the other disturbed about both the need for it and the fact that it was Armstrong who was controlling the meeting. Ten years ago, he would have cracked some heads, if necessary, to defend himself.

"All right," Armstrong continued. "I want you to promise me one thing. If you see any more copies of that kind of scab sheet, tear them up. I ain't never heard of the New Labor party, but I can tell you they ain't out for us."

Armstrong found his lapses of grammar occasionally useful in reminding the workers that he was still one of them and always would be. "Our union is too strong and too good to be hurt by shit like that!"

Suddenly one of the workers pushed Manuel Valdez and then grabbed the paper from Bates. The man tore it up, throwing the pieces in the air. There were some cheers, but when quiet was restored, Bates said bitterly, "You didn't hurt Manuel and me none. We don't believe O'Brien and we don't believe Whitesides. Me, I don't believe nothing and I don't believe nobody. I have no future. This job is my life." Slamming his hands against a dryer, he stomped out of the meeting in a rage, followed by Valdez.

"I'm sorry Victor said those things," said Armstrong quietly. "I don't know why he and Manuel have given up before we've even started to fight, but I know one thing for damn sure—the rest of us have faith! All of us here know that if we strike, we're not going to have a picnic. We're in for a hard fight and we'll have to make sacrifices. But we're not going to be pushed around any longer! We knock our brains out for this hospital, and this hospital is not grateful. This hospital doesn't give a shit for this laundry or for you good brothers and sisters. That's all right. If that's the way they

58

want it, fine. We don't want their love!" Armstrong's voice had grown louder. "We just want one thing from this hospital—OUR RIGHTS! And you can be sure of it, we're going to get our rights. Are you with me?"

There were a few yeas.

"Louder, much louder! ARE YOU WITH ME?"

Now Armstrong received the vocal response he wanted. "Okay, then," he told the group as he began to roll up his sleeves. "If we decide to go out tomorrow, here's what we're going to do. Before I start, I want to hear it once more loud and clear. ARE YOU WITH ME?"

The 3 South station was especially active this morning. The patients from the fourth floor had been moved to the lower floors, mostly the third, so that patient care could be concentrated and more efficient. But uncertainty of the status of Pacific Hospital had created tensions not usually manifest this early in the day. Near the elevator the kitchen personnel had left a cart still stacked with breakfast trays. The cart's location managed to inconvenience almost everyone walking down the corridor, but nobody thought to move it or even to complain to the diet kitchen.

Inside the station itself, the confusion and noise were augmented by a loud argument between the ward clerk and a frustrated laboratory technologist who had been trying to track down a patient. "It wouldn't have hurt you to let me know the patient went to XRay," the technologist complained. "I don't like lugging these tubes around for the fun of it."

At the chart rack, Arnie Jacobs paid no attention to the hubbub as he extracted the chart he was looking for, thumbed through the lab data, and dropped the chart back into place. But he was aware that the argument at the desk had stopped abruptly. He looked up and saw Liz Scripps. "What are you doing here?" he asked. "The boss nurse on lowly Three South. We're honored."

"Just checking some procedures on the station in case of the strike. Sam March isn't taking any chances. He has a contingency plan so that supervisory personnel can run this place if necessary."

"The LVN's will go out tomorrow if there's a strike, so

you'll be able to practice some nursing skills probably rusty by now," Jacobs teased. "You know, making the patient without mussing the bed, and all that stuff a nursing executive has long forgotten."

"Ah, yes. The good old days. But you're wrong. *I* won't be making beds tomorrow, no matter what. The Women's Auxiliary, that gracious army of pink-uniformed volunteers, will man the trenches, attack the bedpans and all of that sort of stuff."

"Susan Royal went to surgery a little while ago," Jacobs said, changing the subject. "Below-the-knee amputation. Hard to believe. She's the wrong sex. Diabetes hits one woman in twenty-five—twice the incidence of men."

"I'm sorry about Susan," Scripps said. "She's a nice woman. But we're not the wrong sex. We live longer than you macho marvels."

Just then the beeper of Jacobs' pager sounded. "Dr. Porter wants you in the library," the small box squawked. Jacobs frowned. All of his encounters with Porter were unpleasant. Porter's hostility was tempered, never overt, but he resented house officers. There was tension between Vanni and Porter, but aside from a few attending physicians, it was mostly the house staff who saw Porter for what he was—glib with facts gleaned from textbooks but lacking clinical judgment.

Standing outside the library door, Jacobs could see Porter sitting at a long table, books and papers piled in front of him. Porter was wearing a brown suit, and from the rear, the semicircular tonsure of red hair made him look like an absorbed monk.

"Yes, Dr. Porter, you wanted to see me." Jacobs spoke in a polite, flat tone. He deliberately remained by the door so that Porter was forced to turn around.

"Oh, yes, Dr. Jacobs. Come over here if you will."

The intern moved across the library and sat opposite Porter. The latter continued reading and making notes for what seemed like a long time. Finally he looked up.

"I'm preparing for the CPC. You've seen the mimeographed summary of the case, Dr. Jacobs." It was an assumption rather than a question. For a minute Jacobs wondered if Porter was trying to pump him for information. "We're dealing with a very complex case, and I have just a half-hour left to hone in on it."

Jacobs glanced at his watch. It was 10:30 A.M. He wondered why Porter was wasting time talking to him. Then he realized that the books and notes were all a sham. Porter had been given the patient's record ten days ago and he had had plenty of time to study it. By now he must have been completely familiar with the case, all except for the path findings that would reveal the answer. Jacobs was certain that Porter knew every word he would say one half-hour from now.

"Arnold, I would appreciate your doing me a favor. That case I'm admitting this afternoon, would you mind writing admission orders? Any tests you wish. I won't be available. But I'll check with you early in the evening."

Jacobs was astounded. Although it was customary for the house staff, after consultation with the attending physician, to write appropriate orders, adding anything they thought necessary, Porter had never gone along with this. Often he wrote his own orders or else he discussed *possible* orders in an inquisitorial fashion, humiliating the house officer if he believed a suggested order was not indicated. He would allow the intern or resident to write only those orders which he specifically had approved. Here he was, however, an avuncular Dr. Porter, asking Jacobs if he would *mind* writing discretionary orders. "I'll be glad to, Dr. Porter."

"Thank you so much. And be sure to watch me make a fool of myself this morning."

"I'll be there." Jacobs left the library to return to 3 South. He wondered why Porter had sent for him. After all, the request could have been made by phone. Finally he found the reason. Porter was frightened. Even though he had been given the CPC record ten days ago, the SOB really wasn't going to be able to give a good discussion, let alone get the right answer. And what do you do when you're insecure? You make friends with your worst enemy. Yes, that was it. Shitface needed love.

Phil Wray paced back and forth. Short and wiry, he mopped at his forehead with a grease-stained handkerchief and glanced at the wall phone in the generator room.

"Come on, Sam, for crying out loud," he muttered at the

61

phone. Always a nervous man, he was at his most frayed self on those days on which he had the duty. And today was even worse than usual. He was working a double shift. His ulcer was acting up, and from six P.M. to eleven P.M. he would be alone in the engineering department. What he had noted a few minutes ago added to his apprehension and had prompted him to put in a call for March. The sudden ring of the phone sent him into a convulsive shudder.

"You have to come down here for a minute," he pleaded with March. "I know you're busy, but this will take just a few seconds. No, I don't want to tell you over the phone, it's something you have to see for yourself." Every rebuff from March seemed to up Wray's voice an octave, until a final, castrato wail succeeded. March promised to meet him in five minutes. Wray looked at his watch, finished wiping up a few oil spots on the generator-room floor, and then waited outside the room. When Wray heard March calling out, he walked quickly to meet him.

"This better be important," March said. "We're busy planning for the meeting this afternoon, so make it fast."

"This way, Sam." Wray descended the half-flight of metal stairs from the generator room to the lower level, and closely followed by March, he took the catwalk leading to the boiler area. He stopped at the door connecting the boiler room to the outside. On the far side of the door a large section of wall had been jackhammered out and was replaced by sheets of plastic visquine. "You'll see, you'll see," he said ominously to March. Then he pushed open the door, and the two men walked into the rain. The wind was so strong that Wray had to scream to be heard. "Look at that!" He pointed a bony finger toward a rectangle of hollowed-out earth, the excavation site for the new addition to the boiler room. The excavation site itself was three-quarters filled with water. Wray watched the hundreds of little splashes. "That thing's filling up. The water is only twelve inches below the boiler-room floor. It's much worse than yesterday. I don't want my boiler room all messed up. I'm alone tonight, and if it keeps raining like this, the boiler room will be flooded out."

As the wind continued to drive the rain into their faces, March motioned Wray to move closer. "Listen, you dumb son of a bitch," he shouted into Wray's ear. "Is it okay with you if we go inside to discuss this?"

Wray, feeling foolish, nodded, and the two men returned to the boiler area.

"I'll call the general contractor again. He was told yesterday to get some of his men pumping that thing out, but he's so fucking casual. If I can't contact him, we may have to call the city Public Works Department for emergency help. But the sump pumps should prevent any real damage, so don't get uptight, Phil." March shifted his gaze from the pumps to the row of large pressure-reduction valves at the end of the catwalk. These valves reduced the pressure of the steam leaving the boilers so that it could be safely conducted to all parts of the hospital through asbestos-wrapped steel pipes. That's what Wray needs, he thought. A small tension-reducing valve, a small worry-reducing valve, a small sweat-reducing valve. He visualized the all-purpose small metal valve with a wheel handle sitting inside Wray's skull, but he didn't have time to dwell on the image. He turned to go.

"I just wanted you to see it." Wray's disappointment in March's reaction was evident. He had expected to be thanked for saving the hospital.

"If there is any damage," March declared, "if there's any water damage at all, it's Swanson's ass. The hospital won't pay one damn cent. I'm sure he figured for things like this in his bid, and if he didn't, he shouldn't be in business." With that, March hurried off, leaving a still-worried Wray standing on the catwalk.

Wray looked at his watch. "I still got a little time," he said out loud. "Why I knock myself out, I don't know. Nobody gives a shit. Well, March can't say I didn't warn him." Wray chewed an antacid tablet and then headed back toward the generator room, forcing himself to walk slowly. He always hurried, but now he was going to turn over a new leaf. As he walked, he surveyed the huge plant. He felt pride in the responsbility which he had been given, but apprehension intruded itself. "Tonight I'm alone here, and nobody, not the chief, not the assistant chief, not March, nobody worries too much about this plant."

Actually, the power plant of Pacific Hospital *was* impressive, and the engineering duty officer did carry a huge responsibility. The plant had been referred to by some in the engineering department as the "guts" and by others as the "heart" of the hospital. By any standard, the plant was the most vital physical component of Pacific Hospital. Physical Therapy, the nurseries or the dietary department could be relocated or closed for renovations, even a wing of the hospital could be shut down temporarily and the hospital would continue to function. In fact, all these inconveniences and more had actually occurred during the preceding two years without noticeable repercussion. But it was different with the power plant. This part of the hospital, actually its circulatory system, delivered to all floors, via an arterial complex of wires and pipes, the lifeblood needed to keep the place running—electricity and heat.

The electrical power was supplied by the mammoth utility, Pacific Gas and Electric, which company serviced several Western states. A huge feeder line came into the hospital from underground, a 4,000-volt, 3000-ampere cable.

The underground feeder cable had performed its job faithfully throughout the years. The power it transmitted to Thornton had originated mostly in the generating plants of the northern part of the state—fossil fuel, hydroelectric, and nuclear. Some of the power came from other states, particularly from the huge hydro plants of the Pacific Northwest. So from great distances and from very great distances the power came and divided into a network of feeder cables, of which the one supplying the hospital area was only a strand of the web.

The feeder cable itself was made up of adjoining coils of copper wire, around which a sheath of lead formed an outer capsule. Between the lead sheath and the copper wire, packed paper served to help insulate the cable against leakage. A crack had developed on its undersurface, but aside from this the feeder cable was intact. Its tremendous load was reduced to usable levels by step-down transformers. The connections to these transformers were made inside a transfer vault, and what emerged were wires now carrying 440 volts, which connected to a distribution panel in the power plant. In addition to the outside power from PG and E, Pacific Hospital had the usual provision for emergency power, a generator of its own run by a diesel engine. The power supplied by the hospital emergency generator was also channeled through the distribution panel. It was not sufficient to supply the entire hospital, but was capable of supplying the load necessary to service areas designed by state code as "critical." These included emergency-exit lights, vital power-plant equipment, power for surgery, two of the eight elevators, and other life-safety systems.

Each Wednesday, the engineering department tested the emergency equipment and this was the job to which Wray now directed his anxiety.

He walked back to the generator room and unlocked the door. Inside the room he checked his watch again. Still some time.

"Hey, Phil, let me in."

Wray looked through the grillwork of the locked door. He saw Victor Bates peering in and opened the door and admitted him. "What are you doing here, Victor? I thought you had a meeting." The laundry was adjacent to Engineering, and Bates over the years had hung around the plant and become a fixture. He had struck up a friendship of sorts with Wray, both men sharing the conviction that their talents and dedication were largely unappreciated by the higher-ups. During the past several weeks Bates had become noticeably angrier because his job was in jeopardy. Today, somehow, he looked different, but Wray could not pinpoint the change.

"We had the suptid meeting, Phil. They think they're going to save the laundry. They think they're going to keep us our jobs. They think if we strike, we'll win. They don't know this hospital. I'm finished, Phil. I'm too old to be recycled. If they keep anyone, they'll keep the younger ones."

Wray wished Bates had not decided to talk about his problems. "I'll tell you, Victor, maybe they will settle. I don't want you to lose your job."

"The hospital won't settle, and the union won't win the strike. I'm no dummy. I'm not kidding myself. I'm through. I know it."

"Well," Wray said, "when it comes to a strike, if it had been the engineers, the hospital would have settled. We're too important and too small for them not to meet our demands. It would cost them more to fight us. But with your union, I don't know. You people have a chance, because the other unions may have to honor your picket line."

"You mean the power plant would close down?" Bates asked.

"No, Victor. Don't be stupid. The power plant never closes down. They got to allow an engineer to work every shift, but some engineers who do repair work and stuff like that may not cross the picket line."

"Yeah?" asked Bates. "For how long?"

"I don't know. Nobody in the engineers' union is crazy about the Institutional Workers Union, and the other unions feel the same way—the hospital painters, the carpenters, all those guys—they don't like your union either, so how many of them will cross the picket line, I don't know. My guess is that a lot of engineers will come to work."

Bates clenched his fist. "I told them that at the meeting, and Armstrong said I don't have faith. If you're not stupid, you don't have faith," Bates commented bitterly. "Listen, Phil," he said confidentially. "If I tell you something private, you promise not to tell no one?"

"Who the hell am I going to tell something to, Victor?" Wray replied. He sounded disgusted.

"Well, listen. You know about the dummy of Whitesides and the stopped-up toilets? Manuel Valdez did those things. And he told me that he's going to throw sugar in the time clocks. I wish I had his guts. I'd like to do something to really hurt this hospital."

"I think sabotage is stupid. So I don't want to hear any more about it." Wray looked at his watch. "Holy smoke! It's almost time for the generator test."

"You always test Wednesday at three. How come so early?"

"Maybe the possible strike. All I know is, the chief said eleven A.M.," Wray replied. Then he paced quickly and silently back and forth in the generator room, apparently trying to collect his thoughts. Bates had watched the procedure before and knew he had to remain silent during the test. Wray walked to the distribution panel near the generator diesel and glanced at his watch again. He picked up the phone, dialed Surgery, and alerted them that the test was imminent. Now he stood silently for a full half-minute, mentally checking everything. Then he pulled the small switch from its "line-power" position to the side marked "emergency power." Each week he dreaded this moment for what could go wrong. As the diesel generator started up, racing toward the critical speed needed to trigger the electrical transfer switch, Wray counted silently, moving his lips in concentration. One, two, three, four . . . Just before the count reached eight, a momentary blackout occurred, indicating that the load had been successfully transferred. The backup system was working.

"Very nice. Smooth as silk, Phil!" After twenty minutes in the noisy room had elapsed, he again spoke to himself aloud. "Okay, Phil, give it back to PG and E." Wray hit the switch again, starting a sequence of events to transfer the electrical load from the emergency generator to the utility company. He started to count again. One, two, three, four, five, six . . . A flickering of the lights showed that the system was back to normal operation. He wiped the sweat off his forehead, but he was smiling. Everything had gone smoothly. Then he remembered Bates, who stood there watching him. "It went real well, Victor. I get nightmares about this switching. You know, that the emergency system won't work, and then, when I switch back to outside power, something goes wrong. That's me! A natural worrier. You still on your lunch period?"

"Yeah. I'm not going to eat. No appetite. But I have to get back to the laundry. We close down at three as usual. You got the duty tonight, Phil?"

"Yup. Yours truly is in charge." Wray still felt elated from the successful test, even though it was a weekly routine. He opened the door to the generator room, and the two men stepped outside. Wray locked the door, and they walked out together to the corridor leading to the laundry.

"I'll come over later and keep you company," Bates said. "This is probably my last day working for this hospital. I might as well end it with a friend."

The doctors' lounge sounded like it was the scene of an animated cocktail party. By custom, the gathering of staff doctors there preceded the weekly eleven A.M. medical conference. Today, the Clinical Pathological Conference, or CPC, the most important of the month, was scheduled, and Asa Porter was the discussant. CPC's were teaching exercises, as were all the clinical meetings, but with a difference. This was more stimulating because it was a whodunit, a detective story in which the audience could match wits with the speaker. However, it was the latter who had to stick his neck out, giving his diagnosis after all the data had been presented. Only the assigned pathologist knew the answer.

The lounge was less murky than it had been in previous years, because so many of the doctors had quit smoking. The huge coffee urn was in constant use, and the Styrofoam cups and wooden stirrers disappeared at a fast rate. A few doctors were inspecting the mail placed in the individual cubicles of a large mailbox at the rear of the room. The TV set was silent, but had it been on, its emanations would have been obliterated by the hubbub. Bits of conversation drifted in the air.

"I told you six months ago to get liquid, Spence. You think the market's a bear? Well, my friend, it's only a bear cub. When this baby bear grows up, there'll be blood in the streets. Get out while the getting's good. You just mentioned blue chips. That's right, you finally said a few words that made a little sense. The market is *all* chips—blue, red, and white. It's one wild crap game, and listen, you're not the house. You're going to get clobbered. Temporary recession, my ass."

On a couch, Leo Vanni sat flanked by a dermatologist and a surgeon. The three of them sat quietly listening to the heated discussion.

"You know, Emil, I might think you were a genius if you hadn't been giving me this line for twenty-five years. You were liquid in the fifties and crying gloom and doom. While I had my money in good investments, you were hoarding like a senile miser, getting three percent out of some bank vault. So the last few years have been rough, so what? Someone once asked Morgan what the market would do, and do you know what he said? 'It will fluctuate, young man, it will fluctuate'—that's what he said."

"There you go again, Spence. Those days were different. Morgan was making money when the market was down as well as when it was up. You're going to be in mucho trouble, my friend. You better listen . . ."

Vanni ignored the financial complaints, relieved that something was going right for him today. His examination of the injured antique dealer, Karl Morley, had been essentially negative, and the intern Jacobs had just checked Morley and had not found anything either.

"It's like a broken record," the surgeon confided to Vanni. "Those two haven't altered their conversation since I've been on the staff. There may be a strike tomorrow, and all Spence and Emil talk about is the goddamn market!"

Now the noise in the room was increasing as more doctors drifted in. Pieces of conversation traveled through the air and reached the couch on which Vanni and the others sat.

"So she says to me, 'Doctor, I can't lose weight because I've got a glandular probelm.' You know what I tell her? I tell her it's true she weighs two hundred and seventy pounds because of a glandular problem. But then she gets mad when I tell her it's her *salivary* glands."

". . . can't sleep. I worry more and more about my patients. There's got to be a better way to make a living. Maybe I'll take a job with an insurance company and . . ."

"So there are twenty-six standing committees at Pacific and I'm on five of them. I told him no to the Credentials Committee. I attend so many meetings now that I dream about seconding the motion. I used to dream about Sophia Loren. Absolutely no I said, and . . ."

"I'm taking the family history from this man, and I ask him if his father is alive and he says no. 'How old was he when he died?' I ask him. 'Seventy-three,' he says. 'What did he die of?' I ask, and he says, 'Nothing serious.' "

". . . and Joe says to me not to take it personally but the Utilization Committee says the patient has to go home. If something happens, will the Utilization Committee get sued? You're damn right they won't. *I'll* get sued. And you know the malpractice-insurance premiums are killing me. Maybe . . ."

"This patient I'm telling you about is nothing but trouble, and a pain in the ass besides. So he says to me in this challenging voice, 'What are you going to do for me?' So I say, 'I'm going to give you a shot of penicillin.' So he says 'Penicillin? I'm very allergic to it, for crying out loud.' And then I say to him—I like this—'I don't know how to treat what you've got, but I do know how to treat penicillin allergy.' "

Vanni checked the time. Eleven A.M. Par for the course. Medical conferences never start promptly.

"You know, Leo. It's a damn crime that these negotiations have dragged on to the point where there could be a strike. I saw Whitesides yesterday, and I told him to settle. Whatever the demands, they can't be so out of line that they justify a strike. How can we even consider such a thing?" The surgeon sounded angry.

"That's exactly where you and I differ." The dermatologist talked across Vanni and directed his comments to the surgeon. "I think that if this hospital caves in to blackmail—make no mistake, this strike is blackmail and nothing less—if Pacific Hospital caves in, it will set the pattern for the other two hospitals in Thornton. We're the weak sister because we're the biggest and richest and with the most to lose. If we give in, we'll be getting permission to admit our patients from O'Brien instead of from the admissions office."

"You think the hospital should just close, then?" the surgeon said angrily.

"If necessary, absolutely," replied the other, "but it won't come to that. We'll keep operating at a low census for as long as it takes to bring the union to its knees."

Vanni started to laugh, and the two doctors sharing the couch looked puzzled. "What's so funny, Leo?" asked the surgeon.

"Just something I was discussing with someone earlier. I had been talking about self-interest, and you guys, along with me, offer a classic example of self-interest in action. You," he addressed the surgeon, "want settlement at any price. Why shouldn't you? You need the hospital. It's your bread and butter. While this hospital operates on the emergency census, all your nice elective gall bladders and hysterectomies are a no-no. And you, Charlie"—he turned to the dermatologist—"you say damn the torpedoes, full speed ahead, don't settle until you see the whites of their eyes and all that brave stuff. But—pardon a parochial pun—what skin is it off your nose? You talk about admitting patients, but how many patients do you admit a year, Charlie? Two? Your practice is practically one hundred percent office-based, and Pacific Hospital could blow away and you wouldn't be inconvenienced or feel it financially, isn't that true? Come on, admit it."

"That's not fair, Leo," the dermatologist protested. "It's the principle of the thing that I'm talking about. The entire medical system is in danger, and between the unions, the government, and private third parties, decent medical care is going to go down the drain."

"Hey, Leo," a doctor across the room was calling. "Phone call for you."

"Sorry. It was just getting interesting." Vanni elbowed his way to the phone. "Vanni here," he said.

"Righto," the voice at the other end announced. "And it's Fraser here, old chap. Calling from your friendly morgue. I'm starting the post on that patient you knocked off this morning. You wanted to be notified."

Vanni watched as the doctors began filing out of the lounge on their way to the auditorium. "Since you're the slowest pathologist in the trade, I'll be down in about forty-five minutes." Vanni paused for a second. "Be neat, Ed, be neat. And restrain yourself. Try not to drink the formaldehyde." He hung up and joined the procession.

Inside the auditorium, the noise from conversations subsided after the intern stood at the lectern. He began to present the CPC case, telling in succinct form the history of the patient, the findings on physical examination, the laboratory data, and the patient's course in the hospital from time of arrival until time of death.

Leo Vanni, with Jacobs sitting beside him, listened carefully, trying to piece together the elements of the story into a cohesive diagnosis. He preferred the unitary theory of disease, where a single disorder could explain a myriad of signs and symptoms, but recognized that at times multiple diagnoses were needed to explain the case. He watched as the intern sat down, to be replaced by a radiologist, carrying the pertinent X rays to a machine used to project the films onto a large white screen.

"In summary," the radiologist was saying, "the X rays can hardly help our discussant this morning. The changes I have described are completely nonspecific."

"If the X rays gave the diagnosis, the case wouldn't be a CPC case," whispered Jacobs, but Vanni remained silent.

Now Asa Porter mounted the lectern, having been introduced by the chief of the Department of Medicine. He stood quietly for a while, looking over the audience, smiling occasionally, and nodding to a confrere. Finally, when the auditorium had become completely silent, he stood close to the microphone and began to speak.

"My good friend Dr. Zahn from our excellent Department of Radiology has, as usual, made life difficult for us poor struggling medical men. Couldn't you even give a little hint, Julian?" he asked, smiling at the radiologist.

"I've told you too much already, Asa," Zahn replied, and the audience laughed at the banter.

"Ladies and gentlemen," Porter began, "I was not really chiding my good colleague Dr. Zahn, just now. The nonspecific findings on the X ray are entirely consistent with the nonspecificity of all aspects of this intriguing case. Neither the history, nor the physical, nor the laboratory results, and especially not the X rays," he said, smiling once more at Zahn, "point us clearly in any direction. But it is our job to weave the threads of clinical and laboratory information, regardless of how slender they may be, into the fabric of diagnosis."

As Porter continued to talk, Jacobs who was growing angry, turned to Vanni. "Why does he keep saying 'we' when he means 'Porter the Great'?" But Vanni stared straight ahead, oblivious of the remark. Something was not right.

". . . and so," Porter was saying, "we must keep this carefully in mind, we have this single factor of fever of unknown origin, this fever which manifests itself week after week. But, we may properly ask, how much of a clue does this give us? And we must in all honesty conclude, very little. For after all, fever is not a specific. It might represent an infectious process, but this hardly narrows the field of possibilities. There are sufficient infectious diseases for each of you present today to take home with you at least four apiece, and we would still have plenty of infections left."

Vanni felt a mounting agitation, the reason for which he could not fathom.

"But that," Porter continued, "is not the end of our diagnostic difficulties. For fever, as we all know, is not confined to the infectious process. We must consider other disease categories in which fever appears. We may start with malignancy, in which fever is often a prominent feature. Is it then malignancy with which we may be dealing today? But than again, fever rises to the occasion"—he waited for the laughter to subside—"in collagen disease. Is it then a collagen disease which is the culprit? But before we congratulate ourselves on finding a convenient post on which to lay our diagnostic hat, we should consider . . ."

As Porter continued on, discussing each diagnostic possibility and then ruling it out, Vanni began to tap on the side of his seat. This was the only sign of his uneasiness. A small string, taut, was vibrating in his brain, and then another. Something dimly remembered, evanescent, elusive, slipping just beyond mental grasp and then returning, only to escape again. Vanni tried to concentrate on what Porter was saying.

". . . is why we have returned to infectious disease as the cause of fever in our patient who has been so reticent to divulge to us those facts which might make our work today a bit easier. It is required that from this category we select one disease which will best fit the clinical story, enhanced by the laboratory and X ray contributions offered this morning. Perhaps I"—he shifted smoothly into singular gear—"would do better to pick up a copy of Harrison or Cecil, open the textbook at random, close my eyes, point to a diagnosis, and give it as my answer today."

Jacobs, disgusted, decided to confide his feelings to Vanni. "He went through this hypocrisy last time. And then he got the right answer. Maybe he'll miss today."

"Therefore," Porter was now concluding, "with infinite confidence that the pathology department will immediately shoot me down, I have selected as my diagnosis military tuberculosis, with lung, kidney, bone, and meningeal involvement. Now, headsman"—he tossed an imaginary coin to the pathologist—"do your best."

As Porter finished, Vanni stood up suddenly and pushed his way to the aisle, leaving the auditorium before the pathologist began to render his verdict. Vanni ran down the stairs to the basement, angry and annoyed. He pushed open the morgue door and entered the room. Ed Fraser, busy with the autopsy, did not see him at first, and as Vanni surveyed the scene, he reflected on how similar was the autopsy procedure to a surgical operation. The patient was the thin corpse lying on the stainless-steel table. A morgue assistant stood at the head of the table instead of an anesthesiologist, and Ed

Fraser, the operating pathologist, wore no surgical mask; but the knives, the lights, the blood, and the irrigating equipment all were in evidence.

Vanni remembered the anatomy table in medical school. They had gone back a long way together, Vanni reflected, as he watched the lanky pathologist at work. Not only had they shared a cadaver for dissection in anatomy, but they had been roommates as well. Their friendship had begun at the University of Pennsylvania Medical School. Leo, product of a North Beach San Francisco family had graduated from the University of California at Berkeley, while Ed Fraser, scion of an eminent New England family, had graduated from Harvard College. Fraser, a renegade from birth, finally had decided to cut loose from his stuffy family, and so he left Boston for Philadelphia. It was at least a beginning, he reasoned. When Fraser's father, a Brahmin who dabbled in commercial real estate, asked him what possible reason he had for not even applying to Harvard Medical School, Ed had replied it was "too intellectual," an answer that left the elder Fraser enraged and confused.

The first time Vanni had met his roommate, the conditions were not unlike those he had encountered earlier this morning. Young Fraser, looking very much the way he did now, was sprawled out on his dormitory bed reading a mystery story. He did not look up until Leo dropped his heavy suitcase on the floor.

"I saw the list," Fraser said, "so I presume you're Leo Vanni, Florentine mackerel eater and my new roomie. I'm Episcopal, highly religious, and unconvertible, so avoid all papist propaganda and we'll get along fine."

Leo couldn't make out Fraser at all. "We're from Genoa," he had answered, "and if the Pope needs you, we're in big trouble."

"My father feels the same way," Fraser said. "He wishes I were an R.C."

Vanni learned to appreciate his irreverent roommate from the beginning. Rarely did the young Bostonian surprise or disappoint him. Fraser had left home chafing from a warning from his father not to do anything to disgrace the family. So in early December of that first year of medical school, Fraser went to a seedy section of Philadelphia and searched for, and found, the frowiest, oldest, most outrageously dressed prostitute on the East Coast. Then he paid her generously, not to accompany him to the fleabag she worked out of, but instead to a photography studio. Inside, he donned a suit of tails he had rented for the occasion and had a photographer take an old-fashioned pose of the two of them, Fraser standing, his right arm around the seated woman, his left arm akimbo. Then he had three hundred Christmas cards made from the photo, each bearing the greeting "Holiday Cheer and Love From the Two of Us." He returned to Boston for the holidays and non-committedly received tentative worried congratulations from the many family friends who came to visit. He simply said thank you, leaving his parents to explain that it was all a joke in extremely poor taste. At the beginning of their senior year, Fraser married a nurse at Philadelphia General Hospital, and Vanni was his best man. Then they came to Stanford for internship. Leo spent many an evening with Fraser and his wife, Ellie. Ed played ragtime piano as Leo joined in with his clarinet. Ellie, very pregnant, just sat and knitted as she listened. When the baby, a son, was born, Vanni and Fraser sweated it out together at Stanford Hospital, and some of the nurses were not certain exactly which of the two men was the expectant father. Vanni and Fraser discussed the residency programs, and Vanni said that although he felt close to his family, he did not want to practice in San Francisco. Neither Ed nor Ellie wanted to settle in a big city, so the three of them decided to try Pacific Hospital in Thornton, a hospital with an excellent reputation located in a nice community—a city, to be sure, but not a big city. Fraser applied for a path residency, while Vanni wanted internal medicine. Both were accepted, and now, twenty-three years later, both were established in their respective fields. Fraser would definitely become pathologist-in-chief next June, when the head of his department would retire. Vanni, unfortunately, could not look forward to a similar appointment in his department. Asa Porter and his rich wife were insurmountable obstacles to his promotion, but Leo had a successful practice and a successful marriage and he was happy. Let Porter become chief and the hell with him. Fraser and his wife and Vanni had remained a trio, and when Leo announced his engagement to Anne, the Frasers and their children (by now there were two girls in addition to *the son) were thrilled. Ed and Ellie had unsuccessfully tried to promote a romance for their friend four or five times over the years, but nothing had come of their efforts. But then they saw Leo falling in love, and when they got to know Anne, they were glad he had held out. The week Leo told them that he was getting married, they took Vanni and Anne out to dinner to celebrate. The restaurant was new and pretentious. A maître d' indifferently escorted the four of them to a table. After he left, a waiter in a tuxedo announced, in the painful tone of one whose noblesse oblige forces him to receive orders from the hoi polloi, that his name was André and that he would be serving them their meal this evening. Fraser jumped to his feet and pumped the waiter's hand. "My name is Ed, André, and we're all going to be eating here tonight. This is my wife, Ellie, and this is Anne, and this is Leo." So Anne learned something about her fiancé's screwball friend and how he reacted to situations he regarded as pompous.*

Vanni looked at Fraser performing the autopsy on his patient Chernock. Had it really been a half-lifetime from the anatomy classroom to this morgue? It seemed incredible.

The post was half-finished. The man's scalp had been put back in place after his brain had been removed and bottled. A Y-incision had thrown open the chest and abdominal cavities, and Ed Fraser was at work removing the remaining organs, or in some cases parts of them.

"And if his right hand offends thee, cut it off. The gospel according to Saint Fraser."

"Leo, you old devil. Snuck up on me." Fraser smiled benignly in priestly fashion. "Don't tell me. You've come to face up to the results of your malefic deeds. That's good, my son, and you shall have absolution . . . strike that . . . you shall have partial absolution. Failure to adhere to the Hippocratic oath, gross neglect resulting in the demise of a perfectly healthy—"

"Okay, Ed. You're great, you really are. What I said earlier just isn't true. I *can* sell your act. In fact, if you ever give up the cadaver business, I'll go in with you. Fraser and Vanni. We'll knock 'em dead." Vanni paused and then continued. "Listen, Dr. Pasteur. I'll tell you what you're going to find in addition to bronchopneumonia. We know that he had amyotrophic, and if the Mayo Clinic couldn't pull Lou Gehrig through, you don't think that Pacific Hospital, even assisted by Vanni, was going to rescue poor Chernock. Anyway, you're going to find a big fat pulmonary embolus, and you're going to say, 'Vanni, you are a diagnostic genius,' and after you congratulate me, I'm leaving your boudoir. You're not sexy enough for me."

Fraser made no comment as he transected the trachea and excised the thoracic organs en masse. The lungs, as a result of the bronchial pneumonia, were firmer and darker in color than normal, with a yellowish cast. Fraser sliced into each one in turn, after recording the weight on a spring scale. "Aha!" he suddenly shouted. "Carcinoma of the left lung. You *really* missed this time, Leo my boy."

Vanni, who had been daydreaming, snapped out of his reverie. He moved toward the table and picked up the lung with his bare hands. He examined it closely, then put it down. "You're a no-good son of a bitch, Ed. You really are. Did you think you could fool your brilliant buddy just like that? Give me the other lung."

Fraser handed the right lung to Vanni, smiling sheepishly as he did so. Vanni looked closely at the large saddle embolus clot that proved his diagnosis correct. After also noting a pale triangular area of infarcted lung, the result of an earlier embolic episode, he returned the lung to Fraser. "Cute kid, very cute," Vanni said in his best Bogart tone. "When you're ready for the big leagues, contact me, sweetheart."

Fraser completed the remainder of the postmortem examination, weighing, bottling, labeling. When he had finished and they both were washing their hands, Vanni spoke to him in a casual, offhand manner. "Say, Ed, remember when I was making rounds on Three South about six months ago, we had a clinic patient with a very puzzling story. FUO, weight loss, the whole bit. He finally died, and you posted him. He turned out to have military tuberculosis. That was the autopsy when a cleaning woman walked in here by mistake and screamed."

"Yeah. Why?"

"Nothing special." Vanni spoke quietly. "I was just trying to recall who was watching that post when that happened."

Fraser looked quizzically at Vanni. "That's the case they had for CPC today, isn't it?"

"The very same. Who, old buddy, was there?"

Fraser thought for a moment. "Besides you and me and Pierre here,"—he pointed to his assistant—"there was an intern and a resident." He paused for a second, thinking. "Oh, yes, and Asa Porter."

PART II

Afternoon

David Raymer had been admitted for only an hour, and he felt exhausted. His roommate, a Mr. Patton, was a nonstop talker. No private thoughts of Raymer had progressed to an integrated whole without some intrusion from the garrulous man in the window bed. Now Patton was dozing and Raymer was relieved. He was glad that the operation would take place in a few hours, and he dared to hope for a chance of success this time. He knew that his wife, waiting at the motel, was as apprehensive as he was; their uneasiness had been reflected in a series of arguments that had occurred since they had arrived Monday. Yesterday they had met Oliver Lusk for the first time. He had given them confidence. Lusk was reputed to be the best corneal-transplant man in the country, and that is why they had traveled three thousand miles to see him. But it was not his reputation, it was his quiet manner that had initiated rivulets of hope. Three previous failures, each followed by unbelievable disappointment, had protected them with a covering of cynicism that no hearty words of reassurance could remove, and yet Lusk somehow had made it known that Raymer's world might not forever be black. Raymer listened to the rain splashing against the hospital window and visualized the storm going on outside.

The telephone at Patton's bedside rang, and the noise jarred Raymer. The call was for someone in another room, but unfortunately the sleep had revived Patton, who again began to talk. He had had his corneal transplant six days earlier, and now he was an authority on the procedure and on everything else.

"Yes, sir, Mr. Rymer," he began. "Nothing to it. You don't have to worry about a thing."

"Raymer, Mr. Patton."

81

Robert H. Curtis

"What's that? Oh, yes. Sorry, Mr. Raymer. Don't know why I keep calling you Rymer. Must have whiskey on my mind. Well, the only hard thing after the surgery will be keeping still. That may not be hard for you, but I'm normally a very active man and I like to keep it moving. I tell you, It's taken every bit of control to stay quiet. Outside of that, it isn't bad. Not much pain or anything like that."

Raymer became annoyed. "This isn't the first time, Mr. Patton. I've told you that I've had three previous transplants, all of them unsuccessful."

"You did tell me, and I plumb forgot. I'm sorry, Raymer. Being in a hospital does things to your mind. You said something about an accident before. You work in a factory, Raymer?"

Raymer sighed. "No, I'm a teacher, or at least I was until the accident. I was teaching a chemistry lab at the junior college." *It had been a beautiful winter day and it had snowed the night before. The air was cold and crisp in the small New England town. The sky was blue, and snow was on the ground and on the trees. He had trudged to school, enjoying even the squeaking of the snow under his galoshes.* "I stopped for some coffee and conversation in the teachers' lounge and then went to the chemistry lab." *He remembered that walk as "the last mile" and wished he had fallen on the stairs and broken his leg.* "I was walking around the lab checking experiments and answering questions. The experiment the class was working on involved concentrated sulfuric acid." *The girl was a better-than-average student with a tendency to talk to her closest friend.* "I walked up to this girl as she was starting to pour some liquid—I thought she was adding more sulfuric acid to a larger beaker with acid already in it."

"Strong stuff, that sulfuric acid," Patton commented.

"All of a sudden I realized that she was adding water, not acid," Raymer continued. "I leaned over to stop her, but I was too late." *The noise of the sputtering, followed by the explosion and the burning commingled.* "The girl screamed, and I grabbed her and pulled her to the shower at the back of the lab." *He pulled the chain and pushed her under the water and then soaked himself, feeling the burning subside, washed away by neutral H_2O. Assured that the girl was fine other than being hysterically frightened, he began to feel tremen-*

82

dous relief, when all at once he noticed that his eyes burned and that his vision was blurry. "I was just finishing my shower when I realized that my contact lenses were still in. There was acid behind them, acid that was trapped there, and it was eating away my eyes. By the time I got the lenses out, it was too late."

"That's terrible, really terrible. But at a time like that, it's only natural to forget something," Patton said.

"The result of my forgetting is that my right eye is gone and I have a prosthesis. My left eye is completely blind too. I can't even make out shadows, let alone count fingers. I was able to see for a short time after each of the three operations," he explained to Patton, "but the cornea clouded over and I was blind again. Somehow, Dr. Lusk gave my wife and me hope yesterday."

"Why, certainly everything is going to work out *this* time, Raymer. You've come to the best man, that's what you've done," Patton said. "Yes, sir, I don't mind a bit saying that Dr. Lusk is as good as they come." Patton's tone changed from possessive to confidential. "Not that I'm crazy about any of them docs. They all think they know so much." He paused, worried. "Say, you're not related to Doc Lusk, are you?"

"No, I'm not," Raymer answered.

"That's good. Well, that's certainly a tough break that you're blind and can't teach anymore. Me, I'm lucky. I got this virus disease of one eye, but the other is one-hundred percent perfect. Yes, sir, if this operation doesn't work out, I carry a spare tire right here." Patton pointed to his healthy eye. "I told you I work for the chamber of commerce, didn't I?"

"I believe you did mention that," Raymer answered.

"Yes, sir, I'm what you would call a professional booster. Nothing wrong with that. Trouble with America today is that there are too many knockers and not enough boosters. Little chamber-of-commerce joke, no offense. No, sir, you can't turn the corner without bumping into some wild-assed kid who . . ."

Patton stopped talking abruptly as soon as he heard the footsteps entering the room. "There you are, doctor," he said at once. "I'm not moving my head, just like you told me, but I can still tell when you're coming by your walk."

"I'll be right with you, Mr. Patton," Lusk said. "Just give me a few minutes to talk to your roommate." He walked to Raymer's bedside. Lusk was extremely thin and wore rimless glasses. His narrow face was topped by a shock of white hair. He leaned over to talk to Raymer, and his voice had an unusually quiet quality to it. "We're confirmed on the schedule for sometime after five, Mr. Raymer. The anesthesiologist will be here to explain his end of things. But you're an old hand at transplants. Do you have any questions?"

"No questions, doctor," Raymer answered. "You'll understand if I'm not optimistic."

"I've learned never to abandon hope," Lusk said. "I'll see you in surgery." He walked over to Patton's bed. "And how are you doing this stormy day?" Lusk asked Patton, which was sufficient to send the man into a monologue of complaints, jokes, and narratives of previous experiences. Lusk ignored all of the talk as he worked quietly, removing the patch from Patton's eye, taking off the dressing, and examining the operative site.

Patton kept talking. "Yes, sir, I know about those stitches you put in. They're fine, so fine I understand that you can hardly see them. Yes, sir." Patton's voice now had a note of challenge in it. "Well, doctor, just exactly how are you going to get out those tiny stitches? I imagine it's easy to miss a few, eh, doc? Can you tell me how you do it?"

Lusk said nothing as he continued to study Patton's eye. Patton, almost sullen, remained quiet as Lusk began the job of putting a fresh dressing over the eye. Then he taped the aluminum patch to the cheek and forehead and walked to the door. Just as he was about to leave, he turned and addressed himself to Patton.

"*Very* carefully!" he said.

"I've completed the survey," Elizabeth Scripps told Lester Whitesides and Sam March. The three of them had just finished lunch in the office of the assistant administrator. Scripps stopped talking as March's secretary, Pru, entered, collected the dishes, and left. "As you know," she continued, "our Professional Nurses Association will not recognize the strike and we will not officially recognize the picket line. The contract we signed last year specifically forbids a sympathy walkout."

"So all RN's will be on duty," Whitesides said.

"Practically all," Scripps replied. "There are three RN's who have not made up their minds, despite the contract. They come from strong union families and they don't know if they'll be able to bring themselves to cross a picket line. But essentially there is no RN problem. The LVN situation is different. They'll stay out. Even though most of them identify with the hospital, still they're members of the Institutional Workers Union."

"Can the volunteers take over?" Whitesides asked.

"That's all been taken care of, Mr. Whitesides. We have already assigned volunteers for the contingency of a complete LVN walkout. So, in summary, the strike will present problems, but at least you won't have to worry about nursing."

March nodded in appreciation. "Thanks, Liz, for bringing good news instead of a problem."

"Yes. Thank you, Miss Scripps," Whitesides added. "I wish that the Institutional Workers felt the same loyalty to the hospital as do your RN's. Pacific deserves unanimity instead of all this divisiveness. This hospital was built by love and self-sacrifice." Whitesides stood up. "I'm going back to my office, Sam. Come by at one-thirty and we can review Item 32."

"Well, what do you think? March asked Liz after Whitesides had left.

"About what?"

"About Lester." March leaned back in his chair.

"What's the problem, Sam? You've never discussed Lester Whitesides with me, and you're not about to start now. Something else is bothering you."

"You're right, Liz. There is something personal that's gone wrong in my life, but I suppose my main problem is that I'm tired as hell. I'm thirty-four going on ninety."

"You have a right to be tired." Scripps hesitated, not being certain of what to say next. "I've watched you during these last six weeks," she continued, "and you're running the show. Nobody seems to know that, but then again, I've been watching you more closely than anyone else."

"Wait a minute, Liz. Lester Whitesides is—"

"Lester Whitesides is incompetent and you know it." Something inside of Scripps was breaking loose. "He's full of pious indignation, and he might have been fine once. But since I've been at Pacific, I notice you doing the work and Lester taking the credit." She was surprised by her vehemence but could see that Sam obviously was pleased by her concern. She had been strongly attracted to him from the day she came to Pacific Hospital to assume the job of director of nursing. The man had character, which, by itself, would not have sufficed to stir the juices within her. She had known other men who were decent, responsible, and intelligent. But they had not evoked the desire to touch, to hold, to be held and loved. No, it was the totality of Sam March—the physical and emotional sum of Sam March—that had made her so attracted to him. She had, to herself, acknowledged these feelings long ago, long before the frequent meetings during these negotiation weeks, meetings that had increased the agony of these feelings. For her desire was in conflict with her own code of behavior, and Sam, she felt certain, liked her but that was it. Undoubtedly all romantic feelings he had were reserved for his beautiful and bitchy wife. He, unlike some of the other males in the hospital, was not a fanny-patter.

"Look, Sam," she said. "I'd better leave. I shouldn't have said what I did about Lester."

"Don't worry about it. It's the truth. Anyway, stay for a while and talk to me. But not about Whitesides or Armstrong or O'Brien. I've been up to my ass in meetings. Say something in female."

Liz laughed. "You've already been spoken to in that language. I was in the hall earlier when Karen walked into this office."

"That's what I mean."

"What's what you mean?" Liz was confused.

What *do* I mean? he thought. He supposed that he had taken for granted the fact that a marriage doesn't have to be much fun. He supposed he had accepted as normal the complete lack of interest on Karen's part about what he did each day at the hospital. He supposed that there were wives who occasionally at least sat down for a short time and kept their husbands company during the Super Bowl game. And he supposed that he had a right to find out for real from his wife exactly what had been bugging her these past three months. "The honeymoon is over" was the wistful complaint of some of his friends, and he felt that in this way his marriage was perhaps better than theirs. Karen had been a responsive, even enthusiastic bed partner for a while. But even this part of the marriage had soured and their sex life had stopped. Karen had blamed her unwillingness on him, on his hospital involvement at her expense. But—he had realized this much, early in the marital drought—Karen was lying. She had blamed everything on his lack of tenderness, but she had never mentioned tenderness until three months ago. Before that time, mutual lust alone was more than sufficient.

And so he changed the question he had been asking himself. When the trouble with Karen began, he had wondered if she was in love with him. Now he wondered if he was in love with her. Karen's remarks this morning had made him furious, but he was not devastated by consideration of divorce. He simply was confused by the rapidity of the disintegration of his marriage. And he was uncertain as well about his role in it. Any way he looked at it, his personal life was a mess.

"You haven't answered me," Scripps said. 'What do you mean, Sam?"

"Good question, Liz. I don't know what I mean, except that Karen and I aren't getting along. That's the personal problem I was just so fucking mysterious about. Maybe things will improve after this strike thing is settled. I've made her feel like a neglected wife."

"I'm sorry, Sam," she lied. "I hope that everything works out." Liz had disliked Karen since the first time she had met her in the medical-staff office—because Karen was Mrs. Sam March. They had been natural enemies from the start.

March stood up and walked to the window and stared out at the rain. "I don't know whether Karen and I are going to make it," he said.

Liz walked quietly and stood beside him at the window. She touched his shoulder gently. "Is it real bad, Sam?" she asked.

"Yes," he said.

"I'm sorry," she repeated.

March turned and looked at Liz. Until this instant he had considered her "off limits," a corollary of his views about marriage. But all at once he wanted to hold her. He took her in his arms and kissed her, not knowing whether he was aroused before or after the kiss. And all the feelings she had for this man came through as she responded, her lips against his, her body against his, her softness against his hardness. Then, as if to negate the long embrace, she forced him away.

"Hey, Liz," he murmured.

"Please, Sam," she implored. Tears had formed and were spilling down her cheeks. "What's happened between you and Karen is none of my business. I care for you. I'm probably in love with you. But being part of a triangle is not my thing." She started for the door and then turned. "I wish it were," she added.

"We can't walk in this weather. Besides Simeon, I feel like beating you at pinochle this afternoon."

"You've had your first good idea of the day," the other man said. "Anyway, Marian's expecting us. The money I win from you keeps her in groceries."

The two men were finishing lunch at a favorite downtown bistro. The restaurant, a popular one with the advertising, legal, and investment crowd, was lighted by amber candelabra and amber light sconces. The soft luminescence supposedly was flattering to women diners, but there were few females in sight. At lunch, almost by tacit understanding, Florio's turned into a men's club, and at the room-length bar the click of liar dice was almost lost in the hum of conversation.

Inside the main dining room the two men seated at a table resembled the other diners. Actually, they were both quite pale, although in the yellow haze it was impossible to tell this. One of them, the taller, had dark curly hair. The other one, a short man with thinning blond hair, wore horn-rimmed glasses and had on a bright plaid sports jacket. Although they were forever at each other's throats, actually they were the best of friends. Contemporaries, they had much in common, but the thing that bound them closest together had nothing to do with similar tastes or background. It was the fact that both of them were living on borrowed time. Without the weekly dialysis treatments at Pacific Hospital, neither of the men could have remained alive. The diseased kidneys of both men had failed to function; now a machine periodically flushed wastes from their bodies and prevented death from natural poisoning. Each Wednesday at three P.M. the men would report to the 3 South dialysis room, where the gigantic German dialysis nurse, Hedwig Ehrhardt, would hook them up to the machines. Two hours later they would be finished and head for home.

"Why should we go to your house today?" Paul Diamond, the taller man, asked. He was relieved that Zabriskie seemed happier now than he did at the beginning of lunch. "We've gone to your house the last two times it rained."

The other man shook his head in disbelief. "So what? I told you Marian was expecting you. And besides, it's not raining today, it's pouring, and I live close to the hospital, while you live three miles away. Did you get a look at the traffic out there? If you're going to be a stickler over reciprocity, we'll go to your place the next three times. But not today."

"Okay, you win. But no bullshit next week. There's something at home I've been saving for you."

"One of your newspaper clippings, I bet. Another one of those slanted articles that you find to try and prove me wrong."

"You don't believe anything, professor." Diamond was trying to be persuasive. "Look, if something doesn't agree with your viewpoint, it doesn't necessarily have to be slanted. Did it ever occur to you that you're wrong occasionally?"

Simeon Zabriskie looked amazed. "You know, Paul, you're a real primitive. Gauguin would have painted you if you had been alive in his day. To you the world is synonymous with finance. What's good for industry has to be good for the country."

"Aha, there you go again. Who do you think forks up the taxes which support the college which overpays you to teach? Friends of the Earth Commune? Hell, no, this country runs because of its industrial might. What would happen to Seattle if Boeing closed down? C'mon now! Even you sociologists at the state university are supposed to know that much."

Zabriskie had to laugh. "You're really something else, Paul. It must be the banking game that makes you such a great con artist."

"There you go again. You don't know anything about

banking. Hell, you don't even know anything about economics. You remind me of my nephew. I went to that kid's bar mitzvah six years ago. You know what he's doing now? He's shaved his head and put on orange robes and he's out in the street chanting all day long. He was looking for an Eastern religion. He's too dumb to realize that he had an Eastern religion that's been serviceable for several thousand years. So you chant economics, but you don't even know the tune."

"So what! So I have a different point of view from you. What's wrong with that?"

Diamond was euphoric. "Exactly. You've finally said one intelligent thing, and I'll show you why. Two months ago I visited the wild-animal park near San Diego. Close to the park entrance was a monkey cage, and I was watching one of the monkeys throw himself around. He would reach out a long hairy arm, grab a trapeze bar, and swing way the hell over, then he would curl his tail around another bar and do some more swinging. I tell you, Sim, it was one damn good performance. Finally he got tired and climbed to the top of a tree trunk inside the cage and just sat there. I thought to myself, that's remarkable. To have that muscular strength and coordination. Absolutely fantastic. That was *my* point of view. Now, get this, Sim. That monkey was watching me when I reached the parking lot, climbed into my car, and drove to Los Angeles. He thinks I was pretty remarkable. I mean, he wouldn't be able to take a key from his pocket or wherever he stores such things, place it in the ignition of a car, turn the key, and drive to Los Angeles, would he? No, he wouldn't. From his point of view, I was damn clever. So, my boy, be a little tolerant. I hope I've taught you some respect for economics."

"I don't get it."

The waiter interrupted the conversation. "More coffee, gentlemen?" He made a move to fill the cups, but both men waved him off. "Which of you gentlemen wants the damages?" He held the check out.

Zabriskie pointed to Diamond. "Give it to the industrialist. He's supporting us both." The waiter looked confused but complied.

Outside the restaurant, the two men paused under the canopy and adjusted the collars of their raincoats. The rain came down steadily, occasionally in gusts, and everywhere people could be seen huddling under awnings. Those who braved the cold rain walked quickly, shoulders hunched forward.

"It's not going to let up. We might as well make a run for it," Diamond said finally. He started out, and his friend followed. They jogged slowly, avoiding puddles when they could. Soon they reached the Financial Garage, where Diamond, an investment banker, always parked. One of the uniformed attendants spotted him before he reached the glass ticket booth and signaled that he would get the car. Thirty seconds later he pulled up with a screech of brakes that jarred Diamond like squeaky chalk on a blackboard. "C'mon, Joe. Save me a *little* lining."

Joe grinned. "That's good for 'em, Mr. Diamond," he shouted on the run. "Seeya."

The men got into the sports car, and twenty-five minutes later they pulled up in front of a white clapboard dwelling. They ran toward the entrance, but before Zabriskie could reach for his key, the door was opened by a little girl who held on to the doorknob. She smiled shyly.

"Kiss for Daddy? How's your cold?" Zabriskie leaned down, and the seven-year-old threw her arms around her father. She looked like him.

"I feel better, Daddy."

"How about Uncle Paul? Doesn't he get a kiss?" Diamond feigned outrage, and the little girl giggled, finally kissing him also.

Zabriskie took the raincoats and hung them up in the hall closet. He pulled out a card table and set it up in the living room, where Diamond was waiting. They sat down and immediately began to play pinochle. As Zabriskie puzled over his hand, his daughter, Sara, watched. While the men played, the door to the kitchen swung open and Marian Zabriskie came in with a pot of coffee. Diamond stood up and kissed her, but Zabriskie continued to study his cards.

Marian walked over to her husband. "The big banker can give me a kiss, but the absentminded professor is too busy." She leaned over and kissed him gently on the cheek.

"C'mon, Marian. Can't you see I'm concentrating? I'm trying to teach Paul how to play this game." They had rolled up their sleeves and looked very serious. Sara watched intently.

The left forearms of both men were wrapped with Ace bandages. Sara had never seen anything like it on anybody else except her Daddy and Uncle Paul. She thought it was very interesting.

The two men played with apparent concentration, yet kept up a running conversation. It was not long until they turned to a favorite subject, oil.

"You did notice what the freeze did to the East, didn't you?" asked Diamond, and without waiting for a reply continued. "So now not only is the Alaska pipeline kosher, but nobody is bitching very much about a natural-gas pipeline from up there to down here and the East. When it's between the caribou and you environmentalists keeping your butts warm at a decent price, the caribou will lose every time. It's economics, Sim."

"Economics! Dammit Paul, I'd be happy if I ever heard you admit that there is a quality of life that is independent of economics. The experts have shown that the tundra is fragile."

Suddenly the card game was forgotten as the argument became more heated. "Experts! You're always quoting experts, professor. Our experts remind me of a sign I saw at a dairy near Half Moon Bay. 'OUR COWS ARE OUTSTANDING IN THE FIELD.' Don't get me wrong, Sim. It's not that I don't have a tremendous emotional attachment to all the caribou and the whooping cranes. I do. It's just that I also think people count too."

"Aha, but which people? That's the critical thing. You completely write off people who like to breathe fresh air and see a little grass."

"Daddy . . ." Sara Zabriskie looked intently at her father. "You're yelling."

"I'm sorry, sweetie. It's just that your Uncle Paul is very stupid at times and I'm trying to help him get smarter."

Diamond motioned to the little girl. "Come here, cutie pie." Sara smiled shyly and came up to Diamond, who hugged her and gave her a kiss. "You know that your daddy is wrong, don't you? You know that your Uncle Paul is much smarter than your daddy, don't you?"

Sara giggled. She always enjoyed the show put on by her father and Uncle Paul. Just then the phone rang, and Marian answered it and called into the living room, "Simeon, it's for you. Mrs. Ehrhardt on the line."

Zabriskie looked at Diamond and shrugged questioningly as he went to answer the phone.

A minute later he was back in the living room. "We can relax for a while. Our outsized angel of mercy is going to be late today. We don't have to arrive till five. She's already called the floor, and they'll give us supper when we get there. An evening of dialysis. That's just what I've been looking forward to."

The large boardroom of Pacific Hospital was impressive. If the fifth floor was a crown of sorts, then the boardroom was its brightest jewel. Two crystal chandeliers were centered over the large table, but the functional lighting of the boardroom was actually indirect, soft, and effective. The combination of the lighting, the walnut-paneled walls, the fine, sturdy furniture, the graceful beige draperies and the thick brown carpeting presented an aura of understated opulence.

The two P.M. bargaining session of this marathon bargaining day was about to start. Gathered around the table were the five men who would participate in this final attempt to negotiate a settlement of differences and avert a strike. It had been mutually agreed yesterday that the group would be restricted to the five men present. Absent was the rank-and-file committee of the union, absent were the personnel director and the hospital attorney. Only Whitesides and March representing Pacific Hospital and O'Brien and Armstrong representing the Hospital and Institutional Workers Union sat across from each other. At the head of the table was a fifth man, Thomas Neely. Neely, the federal mediator, looked like a harassed bureaucrat. He was slightly overweight and the gray suit he wore fit him badly. His sweaty face was lined with venules, giving it a reddened appearance. The perspiration belied the external calm he had managed to project since his first participation in the negotiations. He had been trying very hard to be fair to both sides, but his position was precarious. He had no real power, and because of that fact his role as mediator was a difficult one. He was determined to see that a settlement was reached, but he was beginning to have some doubts that he could pull it off. "Well, we're all here," he announced. This was his usual way of beginning each session.

"Looks that way," said March.

"We've made quite a bit of progress to date, gentlemen. I've been working with you for several weeks now, and possibly you don't see it, but there is real reason to be encouraged. I've found in my experience that when intelligent, reasonable people sit down together, something can be worked out." As the four men stared coldly at him, he waved a protesting arm. "I'm not implying that everything has gone smoothly. We've had our squabbles, but that's to be expected. Gentlemen, I see real opportunity for movement," Neely announced heartily but without genuine warmth. "I think we're going to work it out today."

"Have you been listening to all these meetings you've attended with us," Mr. Neely?" Whitesides asked. "Perhaps I should review what has taken place and see if you are really sanguine about our progress. Under Taft-Hartley, the union is obligated to give us ten days' notice of intent to strike, and such notice has been transmitted to us by these gentlemen." Whitesides pointed to O'Brien and Armstrong. "We have now reached the final day of the ten-day period. The Central Labor Council has approved strike sanctions." Whitesides became visibly angry. "We have reached agreement on about fifty items. Which brings me to the point of my confusion over your optimistic attitude, Mr. Neely. There remain unsettled several noncost and cost items, all of them vital. What we have agreed to is minor next to what we have *not* agreed to. I personally feel that you're not being realistic."

"I think you've discounted, probably without being aware of it, all we have accomplished, Mr. Whitesides," Neely said uneasily. "All of those items you referred to—the noncost items agreed to—were not a matter of routine decision. They were hammered out by a difficult yet cooperative give-and-take, and you all are to be congratulated. I am optimistic, sir, because I feel that we can apply the same efforts to the unresolved issues and succeed in working them out as well."

"I'm glad you're optimistic." O'Brien now echoed Whitesides' line. "So far as I can see, the only real thing that labor and management agree on is that we're miles apart."

Armstrong was impatient. "I expect that we should begin

to do what we all agreed to do even if we're just going through the motions. Let's get back to Item 32, which is Article VII, Section B."

The five men picked up their copies of "Proposed Contract Modifications" and turned to the item Armstrong had just mentioned. It had been debated on three previous occasions, but debate had been suspended in order to move on to more easily soluble items.

"Staffing," Whitesides said with disgust. "That old chestnut."

"That's right," Armstrong replied. "What we've been arguing about boils down to a single word, 'staffing,' and you in administration seem to read that word differently from what poor working slobs do. I'm disgusted by the discussion we've had on this for the last three days. All I've gotten from it is that when we think of staffing, we're talking about people working, and when the hospital talks about staffing in a contract, it's talking about layoffs. It's as simple as that."

"What Jax means is—"

Armstrong glared at O'Brien, who stopped talking. Then the younger man turned back to Whitesides and March and continued. "The provision as written in the current contract gives our people no protection at all."

"And your change, your Item 32, is a bunch of bullshit," March exploded. "To begin with, it ties us to a census figure. We're running a hospital, not a yo-yo."

"It's tied to an average census figure," Neely pointed out. "I'm not quibbling with you, Mr. March, but there is a difference between 'average' and 'daily.' "

"Neely's right. It's tied to an average census figure, for crying out loud," O'Brien shouted. "Twice a year, the average census during the preceding six months is figured, and that's what it's tied to, not the day-to-day census. This gives the hospital protection, even though you don't seem to know it. You've laid off a lot of our people during the last year. Now what you got is a bunch of overtired workers. That doesn't seem to bother you, but it should. That's no good for the hospital—tired workers."

"Frank," Whitesides said, "I don't know if you're trying to make a federal case out of this thing because Mr. Neely is here, but you know very well that the hospital didn't lay off 'a lot' of your workers. Only two." Whitesides held up two fingers. "A floor-maintenance man and a wall-washer were laid off."

Neely wiped the sweat off his forehead before speaking. "It is my understanding, Mr. O'Brien, that the hospital did not act capriciously in this matter. As it has been explained, several valid reasons forced the layoffs. The purchase of new and better waxing equipment, for one thing."

"You're talking about waxing equipment, Mr. Neely, and we're talking about men," Armstrong said. "Don't you see why we're concerned? We're not interested in lifeless machinery. We're trying to protect living, breathing men— hardworking, underpaid men with families to support."

"I do understand that," Neely replied, "but rhetoric about the workingman isn't going to resolve our contract problems."

"Let's get back to this proposal," Whitesides said. "The hospital has an average census of ninety percent. We fall off during Christmas season and we're heavier during midwinter, but generally the census is constant. What Item 32 proposes is nothing less than a gimmick." He pointed a fat finger at Jax. "You place a lot of importance on semantics. Well, Mr. Armstrong, let's put the real label on your proposal— slavery!"

"That's somewhat strong, Mr. Whitesides," Neely said. "You may object to certain features of Item 32, but it certainly will not enslave you."

"The hell it won't," March replied.

Whitesides turned to Neely. "Look, the hospital would be compelled to maintain a minimum number of employees on the basis of a gimmick word like 'census'—a word that is irrelevant in the context of proposed Item 32. Regardless of other factors, our hands would be completely tied. Let me give you an example. If someone were to invent self-cleaning-and-polishing floors, the hospital would still be obliged, provided the census stayed up of course, to keep the same number of floor-maintenance men as we now have. Even your wording, 'in each job description and classification,' ties the hospital to—"

"Look," Armstrong interrupted. "Let's table this and move on to the next item. It's clear to me that all of this can't be separated from the laundry impasse. So let's tackle that tonight at six when we meet after the supper break. We better talk about jobs then, because if we don't, you don't have a prayer for a contract."

"All right," Whitesides conceded. "I agree that we can't separate the laundry plans from the staffing discussion, so I'm willing to move along. Where should we go from here, Mr. Neely?"

"Why don't we work out Item 26, which is Article IV," Neely suggested.

Papers could be heard rattling in the quiet room as the four negotiators turned the pages. "Article IV, Item 26," Armstrong read. "Changes in Employee's Health Plan."

"Let me go through this, Jax," O'Brien said. "I've made some notes, and I don't want to forget them. (1) Dental Plan. Change the benefit formula from ninety percent of the dentist's usual customary and reasonable charges to *full* payment of the dentist's usual customary and reasonable charges." O'Brien continued to read off in his gravelly voice the proposed changes in the plan. He looked at Armstrong from time to time, stating after each clause the reason that the union was insisting on the proposed liberalization. When O'Brien finished, there was quiet. Finally Whitesides broke the silence.

"Let's split the difference. Ninety-five percent. We'll give you the rest of the stuff you want for the plan. What do you say?"

Armstrong and O'Brien conferred briefly. "You've got a deal, Lester," the latter said. "Now, why don't we tie up the wage rate?"

"That's why I'm optimistic," Neely reminded Whitesides. "Both sides here are capable of being reasonable, and things can move along. What about the wage scale? Let's tackle that one." Neely reached into his briefcase and pulled out several sheets of paper, which he passed out. "Now, gentlemen, as you can see, this is a list of each job classification with the proposed starting wage. The second column shows the hourly wage rate after one year. Now, beginning with the head housekeeping aide, you can see that I suggest a start of $5.9525 and after one year a figure of $6.1525. The other classifications of housekeeping, dietary, laundry, and nursing are scaled accordingly." Neely was perspiring more profusely now, and he seemed agitated.

"Mr. Neely," Armstrong said, "we can proceed with this thing if you wish, but you understand, of course, that any agreement we reach is only tentative. Unless we solve the laundry situation, this is an academic exercise. Now, do you still want to proceed on that basis?"

Before their eyes, as they were looking at him, the four men noted an alarming change in Neely. His face, wet from perspiration, was no longer red. Instead, Neely had become pale, grayish pale, and he was pressing his left hand against his chest. "I don't feel well, gentlemen. I don't feel at all well. Would someone please call my doctor, Leo Vanni."

As the young transplant technician walked toward the hospital, gusts of wind traveling horizontally collided with gravity and sent rain into her face. She was glad to reach the lobby, and once inside, she took the stairs to the basement and entered the morgue.

Pierre, the morgue attendant, was sitting at a desk as the girl entered. He smiled when he saw her. "I heard you were coming yourself. It's been a long time," he said to her in a slightly accented voice.

"I took the call when it came into the transplant bank, Pierre. I was coming to the city anyway, so I said I'd do it myself. The drive wasn't bad."

The transplant bank was located sixty miles north of Thornton, and although the highway was good, she had expected more traffic on a day like this. "So where is Mr."—she looked at a sheet of paper she had taken out of her purse,— "Chernock?"

"In this one." Pierre opened one of the four stainless-steel doors and pulled out the frame bearing Mr. Chernock's body. "Do you want him on the autopsy table?" he asked.

"Right here is fine," she replied as she unpacked her equipment. "Do you know it's been a year since I was here?"

"Has it been a whole year?" Pierre was surprised. "I hear that you trained all the morticians in the area so they can take the eyes now."

"You heard right. We had to. We just don't have enough technicians to go trotting all over the state, and luckily, the morticians are darn good." Now she donned a white jacket and stood alongside the refrigerator. The girl looked at Chernock. He had such a kind face. He must have been a good man, she thought. She picked up a speculum from the line of instruments she had just placed on a sterile towel and held it absently in her right hand. "Do you know how long they've been doing corneal transplants, Pierre?" she asked.

"No, I do not," he answered. "Not very long, I would think."

"For over seventy years! Isn't that amazing?"

She looked again into the eyes of the corpse before beginning the procedure of removing them. The eyes, complex beyond comprehension. Working as a team in the closest biological cooperation, two small portions of the human mechanism, which itself is the finest, the most complex biological commune extant. Eyes—the body's tiny cameras. But it is the visual cortex of the brain which develops the pictures. The brain sees, and eyes and ears and other sensory organs are outposts of the brain, sentries getting the first messages and passing them on. Rays of light pass through the transparent part of the eye, the cornea, and from there through a diaphragm, the iris, colored brown or blue or sometimes green, the iris with two tiny muscles which contract or dilate its center, the pupil. The rays move past the iris, move through a watery fluid called the aqueous humor, move through the lens of the eye, move beyond through jelled fluid, the vitreous humor, and finally reach the back of the eye, the thin membrane called the retina, whose cells contain rods and cones, rods for dim vision and cones stimulated by bright light and responsible for color vision, rods and cones hit by light bringing news of the outside world, and then the chemical messages transmitted from the retina via the optic nerve to the brain. And all those connections inside the brain itself, all those connections that help keep balance, judge distance, respond viscerally to shocking scenes, provide the "blur" that permits discrete images to meld into movement.

The technician's hands operated mechanically, doing what her eyes and her brain, with its connections, commanded her to do. She deftly inserted the speculum, an instrument that looked like an eyelash curler, so that Chernock's eyelids were spread apart. Then, using a small forceps and scissors, she freed the eyeball from its conjunctival covering. Next, with the help of a small hook she cut the six muscles which were attached to the outside of the eyeball and moved it. Six tiny muscles, connected to the brain by three cranial nerves, six tiny muscles which made the eyes move together, conjugate deviation, which made the eyes move upward and downward, sideways and combination directions, tiny muscles that, like so many other parts of the body, unknowingly obeyed the brain. Now the last muscle was cut and she reached down for the forceps. Grasping with the forceps the stump of the muscle nearest the nose, she lifted the eye and severed its last attachment, the optic nerve. After removing the eye, she put some germicidal drops on the cornea and then she placed the eye in a special bottle into which she had injected some bacteriostatic solution. She repeated the process on the other eye—this cornea would go to a different patient—filled the now-empty orbits with cotton, put in place two tan mortician's eye caps, and closed the lids. She transferred the bottle into a blue Styrofoam box filled with ice.

"Sometimes I wonder," she said, turning to Pierre, "what would happen if I ever got in a car accident. I carry all sorts of things like eyes, and placentas, and cartilage, and bone from the transplant bank to various hospitals. With stuff strewn all over the highway, what would the cops think?" She looked down once more at the corpse. Thank you, Mr. Chernock, she said silently. Good luck, Mr. Raymer, she said silently. "Take care of yourself, Pierre," she said aloud.

"What's he got?" Leo Vanni pointed to an old man walking in the corridor outside the coronary-care unit.

Jacobs watched the wide and slapping gait. After raising each foot, the man would clomp it to the floor so that the noise of his footsteps resounded. "I can't figure that out, Leo," Jacobs answered. "I've never seen anything like it before."

"I'll give you a hint. Penicillin has made it practically extinct," Vanni told the intern.

"Tabes?" Jacobs ventured.

"Very good. You're watching a man with neurosyphilis—

tabes dorsalis. Notice that his position sense is gone? He doesn't know where his legs are in space."

"I guess those spirochetes have eaten the hell out of his spinal cord."

Vanni watched the man for a few seconds more. "He's doing better now than at night, because the light helps him know where he is in space. He has pains in his legs which are worse today because it's wet. After the storm, he'll feel better. Okay, let's see how Tom Neely is doing."

The doctors entered the unit and went to the chart rack. The CCU was an impressive place. On entering it, a visitor was at once aware of several unique features. The first was the absence of noise. Even for a hospital, the quiet here was constant and pervasive. The carpeting, the thorough sound-proofing, but most of all the sight of the seriously ill patients combined to extract whispers from visitors, as if they were in a church.

Second, the visitor would notice the six large rooms arranged peripherally around a central working area. Each room was isolated from the rest of the CCU by floor-to-ceiling glass-panel sliding doors. It was only after being in the unit for a while that the visitor would notice a third feature of the CCU, the complex electronic equipment used to monitor the heart action of the patients. Today, three of the cubicles had patients in them.

The central working area contained a large desk where charting was done; at its far end, oscilloscopes and the cardiograph machine were placed. At periodic intervals the EKG machine printed a record of each patient's electrical heart activity. The squiggly black marks on the paper often gave a verdict of life or death.

After reviewing the chart, Leo Vanni and Arnie Jacobs entered Room 2. Tom Neely, a monitoring electrode attached to his chest, was lying quietly. He was receiving oxygen by nasal cannula, two prongs at the end of the clear plastic tube fitting into his nostrils. An IV was running slowly.

Vanni watched the steady drip from the IV and made a small adjustment to the rate. The intravenous pathway could be used for rapid administration of drugs, but that had not been necessary so far. Now Vanni turned his attention to the meter measuring pulse rate. Located alongside an oscilloscope screen, its small red indicators were set on the 60 and 100 marks. If the pulse varied from these limits, a warning buzzer sounded, alerting the CCU staff. Now the pulse was 86.

"Well, Leo, how am I doing?" asked Neely.

"Better than when you arrived here, Tom."

"Are you sure this is a heart attack? There's no more chest pain. I don't know what's going to happen to the negotiations without me."

"There's no doubt whatsoever, Tom," Vanni answered. "Forget about the negotiations. You've been working twice as hard as you should, and pleasing everybody is a strain. Nature steps in once in a while to make sure people like you get a little rest. Why didn't you tell me about the chest pains you've been having the last two weeks?"

"I thought they were indigestion, Leo," the mediator said. His voice was weak.

Vanni listened to Neely's heart and lungs and then checked his legs. They were covered with white emboli stockings to prevent clots from forming and breaking loose. When he had finished, he motioned to Jacobs. The intern went through the same procedure, except that he listened for a long time to the right lung base. Then he helped Neely return to a recumbent position.

"Anything wrong down there?" Neely was apprehensive.

"No," Jacobs answered. "I just needed a longer time than Dr. Vanni."

"Do me one favor, Tom," Vanni said. "Don't goose the nurses. Just get some rest. I'll be back later."

Neely managed a tired smile and closed his eyes as Vanni and Jacobs slid the door shut and walked to the desk.

"Those enzymes come back yet?" Vanni asked the nurse.

"I just checked with the lab," she answered. "Ten more minutes. They'll phone the results. I can page you, Dr. Vanni, or if you're not in too much of a rush, there's some coffee for Arnie and you."

"I'll wait," Vanni said, and he and Jacobs went into the small back room, poured themselves some coffee, and sat down.

"Better get a central venous pressure going soon," Vanni told Jacobs. "Well, what did you hear?"

"Crepitant rales at the right base, Leo. They didn't clear

with coughing." The rales were crackling little noises, signs of fluid in the lungs and early heart failure.

"That's right, and with a blood pressure of ninety over sixty, we got trouble," Vanni said. "Our old tightrope is stretched out, and poor Tom Neely is walking it."

"Incipient shock and early failure," Jacobs continued with the thought. "We give too much fluid, and the failure gets worse; we give too little, and he goes into deep shock. I know the prognosis is bad, but do you think there's a chance he'll make it?"

"I think *all* my patients will make it," Vanni said. "I'm not kidding," he continued when Jacobs smiled. "You won't find it often in textbooks, but attitude makes a big difference. Both doctor's and patient's. Physical factors affect the heart, no question. Cold weather combined with exercise is a killer, for example. But these physical things—diet, smoking, heredity especially—all of these aside, never underestimate emotion. Look what emotions can do. We blush, faint, retain fluid, or, like Neely, have heart attacks. The problem is, I'm not sure you can teach sensitivity to anyone." Vanni sighed at a recollection. "I remember back in my internship days, there was a young girl with acute leukemia. One of my colleagues was taking a family history and then he said to the girl, 'Well, you'll be joining your ancestors soon.' Could anybody ever teach a guy like that about other people's feelings?"

"That's pretty extreme, Leo."

"Right, and that's lucky. Now, you asked me about Tom. I have to believe that he'll make it, because I really don't know, and neither does anybody else. It's a more subtle thing than Pascal's gamble. If I *think* death, I won't have to say it; Tom will know it, and is that good for him?"

"I saw Susan a little while ago." Vanni's talk about morale had brought the young diabetic to Jacob's mind. "She's starting to wake up. At least the surgery is over."

"A courageous woman," Vanni commented.

The nurse stuck her head in the doorway. "The enzymes are back and they're incredible," she said. She handed Vanni a slip of paper. Jacobs looked over his shoulder.

"I guess this one is a new world's record," Vanni said. He pointed to another result scribbled on the paper. "We're just catching the rise on this thing."

"Over half of his left ventricle must be injured," Jacobs said. Vanni nodded, and Jacobs continued. "Do you want him digitalized?"

"No, his heart is going to get irritable, and I don't want to make things worse. Stick with the diuretics, and don't let him have any pain." Vanni glanced toward the cubicle and saw Neely dozing. "The Valium is working," he said to Jacobs. "I'll see you later. I'm going to check Karl Morley."

"Before I start report, I want to check again about your status. Miss Scripps wants an up-to-date survey." It was three P.M. and the outgoing charge nurse on 3 South was about to give the current status of the floor to the oncoming afternoon shift. She turned to the four LVN's sitting together on a couch in the nurses' lounge. "Have you changed your minds?" she asked. "Will any of you come to work if your union calls a strike tomorrow?" She looked at each of the LVN's in turn, but no one raised a hand. One of them, an older black woman, appeared close to tears. "All right, then," the charge nurse continued, addressing the entire group of RN's and LVN's. "I hope that the labor difficulties are settled and we can continue with our ordinary headaches." She picked up a sheet of paper. "301A, Susan Royal. She went to surgery this morning and she's in ICU now."

"Tough break," someone said, echoing the general sentiment.

"303A, Karl Morley. Dr. Vanni's patient admitted this morning from the E.R. Auto accident but X rays are negative. He doesn't look so hot, but his last blood count at one-thirty was the same as the admission CBC. There's an order for some more lab work in a little while. He complains a lot."

"You can say that again," one of the younger nurses responded. "He's gross."

"305A, you all know her, the eighty-seven-year-old lady with left hemiplegia and carcinoma of the esophagus. We've just started bottle number twenty-eight of five-percent dextrose in half normal saline. Her condition is poor. 305B . . ." The nurse continued giving the report. She was tired and ready to go home. She thought about the long bus ride ahead of her. It would be a hassle.

Harry Albright washed his hands and went to a table to finish his notes on the last case. The morning and early afternoon had been busy, but aside from an old woman who had slipped on the wet pavement, no fractures had come to the emergency room. Albright, expecting a series of accident victims, was surprised once more by life's inconsistencies. He had just put his pen away when Marilyn Latimer sat down next to him.

"Welcome respite, isn't it?" she asked.

"Yes, it is, Latimer," Albright replied. He looked at her, and the familiar feeling of pleasure flowed through him. It always surprised him to find her so appealing.

"It hasn't been too bad, the storm considered," she continued. "When I was coming to work, I heard a screech of brakes near the hospital. Dr. Albright's next case, I thought, but you know what happened? Those two cars, going at right angles to each other, skidded to a stop about six inches from contact. How's that for luck? Me, I just look at my car and another dent appears."

"Latimer, let me tell you: bad luck, real bad luck, is more than a matter of a few dents. Ending your practice in an emergency room with a sewing kit, that's bad luck. Losing a practice because people can't tolerate honesty, that's bad luck that leads to bad luck."

He had lived on dreams for years. Essentially frightened from childhood into a retreat within himself, he camouflaged his inner terror with a gruff manner. His imperious parents were long gone, but until recently his fantasy world had remained intact. But the day came when reality could no longer be ignored. There were not enough patients left in his practice to pay the bills. He had to give up private practice and seek employment.

"Maybe I don't understand," she replied, "but it sounds like you're saying it was your honest approach to patients that made you lose your practice."

"Of course you don't understand. Here, people come in because they think they have an emergency problem. Maybe very little is wrong, but they're scared anyway, and they're desperate to see anyone who can help. But out there"—he pointed to the world beyond Pacific Hospital—"out there, it's reassurance and pampering they want, that's all."

"Everyone needs to be reassured. What's wrong with that?"

"Are you purposely being dense, Latimer? There isn't a damn thing the matter with reassuring patients who have nothing wrong with them. What I said was sweet talk is *all* the public wants. They want to be given a clean bill of health and told all the unhealthy things they do are fine and they shouldn't change a thing." Albright had been raising his voice, and he checked himself. "I should have given the public what it wants, and I'd have been a rich man today instead of a boy scout."

"You do good work here. I'm really surprised that you're not happy."

Albright ignored her observation. "When those fat women came in munching their chocolates, I told them to stop. I pointed out that there aren't many fat people who reach old age. It did a hell of a lot of good. I should have encouraged them to eat even more. 'You're only two hundred and twenty pounds today. That's not good enough for a woman who is five-foot-one. But I can see you're trying. Let's see if you can get up to two hundred and forty in a few months.' "

"That's ridiculous and you know it. I doubt if any woman faulted you for telling her that obesity was unhealthy. Really, don't you think that the *way* you told them might have been the real problem? At times you're far more blunt than is necessary. It seems to me that you're really taking out your personal problems on the patients."

Albright, stung by the remark, struck back. "I should have realized how much you resemble my ex-wife. I don't mean that you look like her, only that you dislike me so much. However, she at least voiced her feelings more directly. Sorry you have to work with a has-been you can't stand."

"You've succeeded in making me quite angry, but I don't happen to dislike you," Latimer said. "If it makes any difference, during the time I've worked here I've gained respect for you. But I've never seen a man who felt as sorry for himself as you do," she continued, facing him once more. "You're intelligent, capable, and in good health. You've got a good job. But do you talk about any of that?"

"Should I say that I'm happy when I'm not?" Albright was taken aback by the tone of her voice. "I suppose I should lie and say everything is just wonderful."

"No, you don't talk about any of that," Latimer continued. "When you're not insulting patients, you're moaning about how tough life is. Do you think you're unique? Do you think that only you suffer the slings and arrows? That you have been singled out? Well, dear Dr. Albright, we all suffer pain, even problem-free me. I've had my share, plenty of it—no more than anyone else, but no less either. But I don't spend all day moping the way you do. 'I'm so old, I'm such a failure, life's given me a bum deal.' That's all I hear from you, day after day."

Conflicting emotions were confusing him. He was furious, but at the same time, he became aware of an elation he had not felt for years.

"Miss Latimer . . ." The emergency-room ward clerk had come over to the desk. "There's a mother with her little boy. He swallowed pills. They're in Room Five."

"Did you hear that?" Latimer asked him. She had calmed down. "I'll go in."

"I'll go with you," he said. They walked together, somewhat ill-at-ease with each other, and entered the examination room.

"I'm so frightened, doctor," the mother said. She was stammering. "About ten minutes ago I noticed that Clifford wasn't himself. He's always high-strung but not like this."

The little boy was overtly agitated. He could not remain still. He ran from one end of the examination room to the other, grabbing pieces of equipment and putting them down.

"What happened?" Albright asked the mother.

"I found Clifford holding this empty bottle. He took all of the capsules. I have colitis."

Albright took the bottle and looked at the label. It was a belladonna type of prescription, a commonly used medication to reduce bowel spasm. "How many pills were in the bottle, and when did he swallow them?"

"The bottle was only a third full. There were thirty capsules when I had it filled."

"When did he swallow them?" Albright repeated.

"It was a half-hour ago. He took the capsules during a commercial in the *Jason's Corner* show. Thank God the hospital is near."

Albright looked at the treatment sheet. "Clifford is three and a half?" he confirmed.

"Yes, doctor. I'm so scared. He's never done anything like this before."

"At least you brought the empty bottle," Albright said to the mother. Then he turned to the boy, who was still running around the room in underwear shorts. "Come here, Clifford," he ordered. "I want to check you over."

The little boy ran to Albright, who hoisted him onto the examination table. The boy could not sit still, shifting his head from side to side.

"Why did you take the pills?"

The little boy's mouth was dry and he had trouble speaking, but he managed to talk. "Candy." He tried to jump off the table, but Albright grabbed him.

"I have to examine you," Albright said, and quickly proceeded with the examination. He noticed the widely dilated pupils, the rapid pulse, and the dry skin. The boy's temperature was one hundred. Albright asked Latimer for syrup of ipecac and gave the little boy a teaspoonful. Five minutes later, the child gagged a few times and then vomited into an emesis basin.

"It's atropine poisioning, but he'll be all right," he said to the mother, "no thanks to you. Was your bottle placed where Clifford could reach it?"

"Yes, it was on the bottom shelf of the medicine cabinet, but he's never gone in there before."

"He's not blind. He's watched you, and he watches people taking pills on television. Do you tell him it's like candy when you have to give him medicine?"

The mother nodded, afraid to say anything.

"In the future, madam, keep all medicine out of reach—well out of reach. He's less than four years old. He doesn't know better, but you should. And stop telling him that you're giving him candy when you give him medicine—aspirin or anything else. Drugs are dangerous. We're not supposed to enjoy them. We take them only because we need them. Is that clear?"

The mother nodded. She seemed numb but managed a quiet "Thank you, doctor."

Albright patted the little boy, by now terrified of him, on

the head and returned to the desk. Ten minutes later, Latimer rejoined him.

"Dr. Albright, he seems a little calmer. His mother is keeping an eye on him, and I'll recheck him in a little while." She paused, and when Albright looked up, she spoke. "I just want to tell you I'm sorry. I had no right sounding off like that."

Albright was almost prepared to forgive her. She had made the appropriate sacrifice to his pride. When he started a half-hearted reassurance, she shook her head.

"Let me finish, if you don't mind. I'm not sorry for what I said. I meant every word, and I'm not apologizing for that. I'm sorry only that my tone was so strong."

"Don't let it worry you, Latimer. I'll accept your labels of self-pity and rudeness. You're not telling me a damn thing I don't already know. I'll even give you one more label—coward."

"That's nonsense," she said.

"The hell it is. I complain about doing minor surgery, but I couldn't hack it if anything more serious than a boil or a laceration came through the door." Latimer tried to interrupt, but he continued on. "I'm not saying I was always this way. Once—it was a long time ago—I knew I could lick the world. But something funny happened on the way to the fight. The world was a little tougher than I thought, and it could rabbit-punch besides."

"Dr. Albright, you seem to enjoy putting yourself down."

"Latimer," Albright said, "I'm sure you've heard the maxim 'Silence is golden.' Why don't you try to stop talking for a while?"

"Mr. Morley. I was told you wanted to see me. I'm Miss Scripps." If the young director of nursing thought that her smile would help matters, she was wrong.

"The hospital owes me as much respect as it does any patient, and from what I gather, that isn't very much."

"I'm not sure of your complaints. I'd like to help you, Mr. Morley, but I have to know what's wrong."

"To begin with, it's demeaning to be a patient here. This hospital is run like a fiefdom, and we patients are peasants, the serfs of your manor. Condescension is the rule here rather than the exception. I don't patronize my clients. They pay my bills, after all."

"I'm sorry you feel that way, Mr. Morley," Scripps said. "Nobody deserves to be put down, particularly when they're worried. Fortunately, other patients feel differently about Pacific."

"Let me be more specific," Morley continued. "I was told to rest, but rest is the rarest commodity in this place. I was ignored until I fell asleep, but once I achieved that almost impossible task, a barrage of nurses woke me up to take my blood pressure, take my temperature, and generally take away my tranquillity. Are your room rates, perchance, too low to indulge patients with a modicum of decent treatment?"

"Look, Mr. Morley. What can I say?" Scripps asked. "I'm sorry you're so unhappy, really I am. I'll see to it that the situation is remedied." She smoothed the covers of the bed reflexively. "If things don't get straightened out, call my office again, okay?"

"You can be assured of it," Morley replied.

As Scripps left the room, Vanni entered it. "What was that about, Karl?" he asked, pointing in the direction of the departing nurse.

"I wish to go home," Morley announced. "This hospital is doing me absolutely no good. And when I'm home, nobody will disturb me."

"Forget it, Karl. You'll rest right here," Vanni said. "Just be grateful that you have no broken bones. You have to stay twenty-four hours for observation, and that's that!" Vanni noted the dark circles under Morley's eyes, and the patient's increased irritability did not escape him. He proceeded with his examination, spending a long time checking Morley's left upper abdomen.

"What did you find?" Morley asked. He was clearly conscious that something was wrong.

"I'm not sure, Karl, but I'm going to ask our chief of surgery, Dr. Madden Chase, to have a look at you."

"A surgeon! Not on your life, Dr. Vanni. Are you saying that I need an operation?" he added as the implications of Vanni's statement hit him.

"No. I'm not saying anything like that. The consult is

purely a precaution. You told me yourself that your stomach hit the steering wheel hard. I want to make sure that everything is okay."

"No surgical consult," Morley announced "They're all knife-happy. One of their tribe killed my brother on the table during an unnecessary hernia operation. I don't want any of them near me."

Vanni stood for a while without saying anything. "Karl, let me ask you something, and I want you to be completely honest with me. Do you want me off the case? Would you rather have someone else take over? You've been fighting me since you arrived."

"No," Morley said. "You don't understand. I trust you and I do not want anyone else taking care of me."

"But you're not letting me take care of you," Vanni answered. "Madden Chase is not beating the bush for patients. He's extremely busy because he's good. He is not someone who rushes people to the OR."

Morley seemed in great conflict. He started to speak several times but stopped. Finally he spoke to Vanni in a tone the latter had never heard him use—an almost imploring one. "Would this be all right with you? Asa Porter takes care of my elderly aunt. Let him check me over, and if you both agree that this fellow Chase should see me, I'll go along with it. Is that fair enough?"

Vanni shook his head in resignation. "Karl, you've managed to convince me that you have faith and don't have faith in me at the same time. All right. I'll call Dr. Porter." He picked up the bedside phone and made his request to the operator.

"I think Dr. Porter is on Three North, Dr. Vanni. I'll try to get him. Hold on a minute." Mabel Catlin's sharp voice was almost painful to listen to on the phone. "I have Dr. Porter for you. Go ahead."

"Hello, Asa. This is Leo Vanni. Listen, one of my patients, Karl Morley in Room 303, was in an auto accident today."

"Sorry to hear that." Porter suspected what was coming.

"He's the nephew of one of your patients. I'd like Madden Chase to take a look at him, but Morley wants you to see him first. If you concur, then I'll call Madden in."

"Flanders Ainslee."

111

"What?"

"Flanders Ainslee. That's the name of Karl Morley's aunt. Her place is filled with his antiques."

"I'd appreciate it if you could come down right away," Vanni said. "I'll wait for you in the room."

Six of one and a half dozen of the other, thought Porter. He would have preferred that the consult request would have originated with Vanni himself, but at least the son of a bitch had been forced to seek his opinion. And not one word of congratulation about the CPC. These parvenus are always jealous. He looked at his watch. "All right, Leo. I'll be right down, but I have to leave soon." After he hung up the phone, Porter clapped his hands together. Maybe the hotshot is beginning to realize that he's not so hot after all, he thought.

Twenty minutes later at the bedside, Vanni began to feel very uneasy. The longer Porter spent examining Morley, the more Vanni's apprehension grew. Porter's deliberate examination did not please him, because its studied intensity was caused by something other than getting a clinical picture. It was this something else that had Vanni worried. Finally Porter finished, and in the hall he again reviewed the chart, including the latest laboratory results. Then he turned to Vanni.

"I think you're a little overanxious, Leo."

"What?" Vanni asked.

"I said that I find no need to press for a surgical consultation at this point. I find nothing alarming either in the physical examination or in the laboratory studies, and that is what I think you should tell Morley."

Vanni tried to hide his anger but it showed through, to Porter's enjoyment. "Look, Asa, since I've been following the patient and since I'm uneasy about him, how can you possibly object to Madden having a look at him?"

"Are you purposely being naive, Leo?"

"I don't know what you're talking about."

Porter smiled indulgently. "Let me spell it out, then. The patient has some rights too, and he objects to a surgical consultation. I can't say that I blame him. You know as well as I do that surgeons take a 'what-do-we-have-to-lose' attitude. Well, we have a patient to lose, that's what. The laboratory confirms that no further bleeding has occurred. Look at this." He pointed to the lab sheet. "Hemoglobin 12.5 grams, RBC

3.8 million, hematocrit 39—that was 40 before, and the slight drop, as you know, is well within the limits of laboratory error."

"Thanks for the lesson, Asa. Incidentally, his red count is normally 4.5 and his hematocrit is normally 45. You do admit, at least, that he had a bleeding episode?"

"Of course, Leo. No one is denying that. You should listen to what I said. I said that no *further* bleeding has occurred. Why"—he smiled again, and his smile was reproving—"do you feel so desperate about rushing in?"

"You should listen too. I'm only trying to get a surgical opinion, not rushing Morley to the OR. I don't like the way he looks. It's as simple as that."

"You find the lab work of no significance?" Porter sounded incredulous.

"Don't tell me about the lab work, Asa. I know it by heart. As I told you at the bedside, I felt a spleen. He could have injured his spleen or liver."

"I don't know what you felt, Leo. *I* certainly did not feel a spleen," Porter said. "If I had felt a spleen, I would tend to doubt my physical examination. Did you find any evidence of a ruptured spleen? Did you hear the patient complain of pain in the left shoulder? That's Kehr's sign, you know."

"Don't patronize me, Asa. Kehr's sign isn't always present. Just let me ask you one question. Do you ever believe in a *clinical* hunch?"

Porter felt the insult. "I believe in *my* clinical hunches, not yours," he snapped.

"Okay. Let me ask you another question. Will you take over the case?"

Porter looked grim. "Under no circumstances. For all intents and purposes, I was called as a consultant. I have fulfilled that role and given you my opinion. Anything else is between Karl Morley and yourself."

"Look! I saw no need to call you. It was Karl's idea, and he deserves to hear in your own words that we disagree." Vanni paused and looked directly at Porter, then continued. "Or are you uneasy about giving your opinion without a script?"

Porter reddened and seemed for a short while unable to speak. Vanni kept looking at him, and the steady gaze was a stimulus, because Porter finally spoke. "I'll be glad to tell Mr. Morley what I think," he said.

The two men stepped back into the room.

"I want you to understand that this is not the customary procedure," Porter began. "Usually your doctor gives you the consultant's opinion, with the consultant chiming in to amplify, but Dr. Vanni wishes *me* to tell you what I told him." Porter noticed that Morley was hanging on every word, and his tone changed from annoyance to kindliness. "I must speak with complete honesty to you, Karl, because I know of no other approach that would be fair. The point is that Dr. Vanni and I completely disagree, and strange as it may be, I find that I feel exactly as *you* do rather than the way your doctor does. I find nothing alarming in either your physical examination or in the laboratory results. I believe, as you do I'm sure, that careful observation is necessary, is mandatory, but after all, you're lying in a Pacific Hospital bed, not on some freighter in the middle of the ocean. I find myself under no duress to rush in with a kitchen knife, despite the earnest concern of my good colleague here. That's all I have to say. If Dr. Vanni would like me to see you later, I'll be happy to comply."

After Porter's departure, Vanni seemed rooted to the floor. Finally he spoke. "I don't like the position I'm now in, Karl. I'll stay on the case because I don't abandon patients, but no more interference. You better understand that if you get even the slightest bit sicker, I'm calling Madden Chase."

Karl Morley, relieved, nodded.

Jacobs looked at Susan Royal's stump again. It was covered with dressings and swaddled in bandages. While the intern was relieved that the amputation was over, Jacobs now had a new problem. Susan had not come out of the anesthesia the way she should have. She had partially awakened, remained drowsy, and then slipped into coma. "Where are the lab tests, Nina?" he asked the charge nurse. "We've got a damn sick patient."

"The lab said ten minutes. I'll give you the results just as soon as they come in."

Jacobs didn't move from the bedside. Instead, he surveyed the unit. There were six patients in all in ICU. Besides Susan,

114

there were three post-op cases, one of whom was a woman who had had a lung removed that morning. Her chest was being suctioned. The other two surgical patients were almost ready to be discharged and returned to the floors. The fourth and fifth patients were on respirators. One of them was a woman of twenty-five who had overdosed and was beginning to respond. The other patient was a middle-aged man who had had a stroke that morning. His condition had rapidly deteriorated. Now he was essentially dead, and only the machine kept his heart beating. Jacobs looked at Susan once again. Then he said to the nurse, "Damn that lab! I'm going down myself."

In the clinical laboratories he hurried past banks of working technologists until he reached the rear section where the chemistries were done. "What's holding you up?" he asked the young man standing by the flame photometer.

The technologist did a few calculations and scribbled some numbers on a piece of paper. "You won't like it," he said, and handed the slip to Jacobs.

"Blood sugar—1,000 milligrams percent!" Jacobs exclaimed. He looked sick. "Are you sure this is right?"

"Positive. I checked it twice."

"I'll need more tests soon, so don't even go out to take a leak."

"Good luck," the technologist called out, but Jacobs was already out of earshot.

Back at ICU, he saw Vanni looking down at Susan. Jacobs shook his head from side to side, and then he handed the lab results to Vanni, who studied the piece of paper. "This happens sometimes," he said to the intern, "and we don't know why."

"I didn't know that the blood sugar would be ten times normal, and the low potassium was also a surprise, Leo."

Vanni looked at the IV and then said to Jacobs. "Give her one hundred units of regular insulin intravenously stat and add some potassium to this bottle. Don't give the potassium too fast, and don't forget the bicarbonate. Keep on top of this with lab tests, because she's going to need a lot of insulin. I've got to see Neely, so you're in charge here."

After Vanni left the unit, Jacobs studied the young woman. The IV was running well, and an indwelling catheter led from Susan's bladder through tubing to a collection bottle on the floor. All that was fine. But her appearance frightened him. She was drawn and slightly shrunken now, and she was breathing rapid, shallow breaths with tremendous effort. In her unconscious state, her body seemed to have called into use every muscle in her chest and neck, and she strained for each respiration like a high-school miler at the tape. It occurred to him quite suddenly that she might stop breathing at any minute.

"Dr. Simpson should be here soon now, Sheri." Herbert Johnson leaned over and kissed his wife. "She'll probably give you something to start you going again, honey."

Sheri tried to smile and reassure her husband the way he was reassuring her, but she was very nervous. Her contractions, which had been strong and regular when she was admitted, had faded and finally stopped completely several hours ago. Everything had been going so well at first, and then . . . Sheri wondered if their baby would ever come. Perhaps—and she would never mention this to Herbert—they would have to perform a cesarean section. She had read that even if labor was active, sometimes the baby was just too big to be born the usual way, and an operation was needed.

"Herbert, you know something?" Sheri said.

"What, Sheri?"

"I love you, that's what." Now Sheri did smile. With Herbert as her husband and Anne Simpson as her doctor, everything *had* to be all right.

The Johnsons were silently holding hands when Anne Simpson entered the room. "Nothing yet?" she asked.

Sheri shook her head. "Not even one contraction since you last checked me, doctor."

Anne Simpson pulled the curtain around the bed. She put on a sterile plastic vaginal glove and squeezed some K-Y jelly onto its index finger. After spraying the vulval area with an antiseptic solution, she began a vaginal examination, feeling upward toward the cervix. The uterus was now a balloon filled with the Johnson baby, and the tip of the balloon, the cervix, was barely dilated but effaced. It would have to open completely before the baby could be born. Anne disposed of the glove and washed her hands. Then she spoke to the prospective parents. "You two have been very patient, and so has the little one here." She touched Sheri's abdomen. "We better give you some help. I'm going to induce labor and see if we can't speed things along." She left the room for a few minutes and returned with a nurse holding an IV bottle, along with a set of tubing. Anne inspected the label on the bottle and then checked a small glass vial. Satisfied, she broke the lid of the vial, emptied its contents with a syringe, and injected them through the rubber stopper of the IV bottle. Then she took a piece of tape with the word "pitocin" written on it and pasted it on the bottle. She hung it on the stand at the head of the bed after attaching the IV tubing. Next she tightened a tourniquet around Sheri's left arm and carefully pushed the needle at the end of the tubing into Sheri's vein. She lowered the IV bottle below the level of the vein, and blood flowed into the tubing, showing that the needle was properly placed. She lifted the bottle back on the stand and adjusted the flow rate of the IV solution. "Now, let's see if we can begin to get some action around here." The nurse left, and Anne sat down. She watched the drip, which was proceeding at a rate of ten drops per minute. She had not wanted to worry Sheri, but she was concerned about the polyhydramnios, the excess amount of fluid in which the baby was floating. It was safer all around to induce.

Herbert watched the drip anxiously. "Is it going all right, doctor?" he asked.

"It's going fine," Anne answered. "I'll be back before long." She stood up, but before she could leave, Herbert touched her arm.

"Dr. Simpson?" he asked timidly.

"Yes, Herbert."

"We were wondering, if it's all right with you, could we name the baby Anne?" He quickly added, "If it's a girl, that is."

Anne Simpson checked a flip response. She looked at the Johnsons, waiting nervously for her approval. "I'd be honored," she answered. "I hope it is a girl. Anne Johnson," she mused aloud. "It has a nice ring to it."

Asa Porter felt exhilarated as his sports car raced toward Ferndale, the town twenty miles from Thornton where his boat, the *See-Sick* was berthed. The wet road was deserted and Porter could see in the rearview mirror the mini-wake from his tires as he headed eastward. It had been a good day generally, particularly his brilliant performance at the conference. He wondered if Vanni's crack about a "script" implied that Porter had known the answer in advance. He frowned for an instant at the memory but recovered quickly. Porter's capacity for ego maintenance had grown since his marriage had given him social and career insurance. His pleasure from the results of the Morley consult, at which he had humbled Vanni, had more than equaled his CPC triumph, and now, the culmination of his day was close at hand.

He passed the small general store of Ferndale, a town barely more than an intersection of two country roads. He kept heading east, and soon he could see the river and the metal roof of the small marina which accommodated only the fishing boat of its owner and the *See-Sick*. It assured Porter of the privacy he needed. Soon he turned into the marina parking area, now mired by the rain, and eased his car to a stop. He made a run for the dock, and after boarding his boat from the ladder near the stern, he opened the cabin door and stepped down.

Inside, the curtains had been drawn, and as he turned and opened the door to the master bedroom, he felt the usual anticipatory excitement. He was not disappointed. Karen March was sitting on the bed smoking a cigarette. She was wearing a transparent black nightgown and nothing else except her I-think-I'm-going-to-be-very-nice-to-you-this-afternoon-smile.

Porter smiled back but said nothing as he completed his survey of her. The blond hair cascading down to her shoulders, the long legs, the small breasts and pink nipples visible through the black lace, presented him now, as they had for many Wednesdays, with his most engaging landscape of the week. "You are lovely, Karen," he said finally. "There simply is no other way to describe you. Lovely."

"I think you're saying something more, Asa," she teased, "but I'm not exactly certain of what it is."

She is different from all the others, he thought. She is classier and sexier and more beautiful than all the others. But then, he reminded himself, he always felt that way for the first three months. "Try to guess, beautiful," he said, and leaned over and kissed her. She opened her mouth slightly, but before he could insert his tongue, she closed her lips and pulled her head away. "Let's not rush things today, Asa," she said. "Sam told me last night that the labor talks will probably go on till nine tonight. So I want to talk to you at least for ten minutes." She noted his disappointment and added, "I won't be able to stand waiting longer than that. See." She guided his hand up the inside of her thigh and held it against herself. Then she removed his hand. "Sit over there for a minute." She pointed to a chair. "I have to tell you some news, and I can't concentrate if you're any closer."

Porter reluctantly sat down in the chair at the foot of the bed. *What* news? he wondered, and became apprehensive. Had Sam March gotten another post and would they be leaving Thornton? No, Beulah would have told him something like that. "You tell me your news and I'll tell you some of my own," he said.

Her heart began beating faster. Maybe this is it, she thought. "I know how you feel about women's lib," she joked. "After you, Asa."

"Very well. Two things. First, and not terribly important, your admirer scored satisfactorily at the conference today. I was lucky, but the obscure diagnosis I offered was right on target."

"Oh, Asa. I'm proud of you," Karen exclaimed. "Every time you do something brilliant, you ascribe it to luck. You're too modest." Say the important thing now, Asa, she said to herself. Say it.

"As I said, that was of minor importance, but this is good news for us both."

Now, finally! Karen thought.

"I am quite sure—I can't promise, but I almost can—I am almost certain that Beulah and I have reached an agreement that will make you very happy."

Now I'm happy, she thought. "I'm happy now, Asa. But I'm anxious to hear all about the agreement."

"I have just about convinced Beulah to take a three-week cruise with her sister in June. I'll be chief of medicine then, and she understands that my new responsibilities will prevent me from traveling for a while. But, of this I can assure you, Karen, they won't prevent you and me from having the wildest three weeks in history. I'll see that Sam is kept very, very busy. I may even send him to the National Administrators' Conference for a week. We can live on the boat. Well, what do you think? You don't seem very enthusiastic."

"It's not exactly what I thought you would say. I thought it would relate more to the news I have for you." Now she smiled, relieved. Of course, that was the reason. How could he say more, when she hadn't told him anything yet? "You want to hear it?" she asked brightly.

"Of course I do."

"I broached the subject this morning," she announced.

"What subject?" Porter was confused.

"Divorce, Asa. I finally got up the courage—*you* gave me the courage—to tell him that the marriage wasn't working and that we should strongly consider divorce. I didn't tell him that I had made my mind up already. That will come soon. But I've put in the opening wedge."

Porter's thoughts raced. He was determined to handle this thing right. Something similar had happened five years ago, and he had worked out of it gracefully. But first he had to know. "Karen," he said softly, "I'm not sure what you meant when you just said that *I* gave you the courage."

"Oh, Asa. You're being modest again. Don't you think I've been listening to what you've been telling me these wonderful months? Don't you even have any idea of the effect you've had? I knew you wanted me to ask for my freedom but you weren't certain that I wanted to. You are just too fine a man to try to force me into a decision like that. Well, darling, you're not forcing me. This is something I want as much as you."

"Did you tell Sam about us?" Porter ventured. He held his breath.

"Of course not. You're such a boy in many ways, Asa. No woman tells her husband that she has fallen in love with a man with whom she's been having an affair and now that man and she want to get married. First the divorces, then the decent interval, then the marriage."

No, he had not misunderstood. She had confirmed it all with the single word "divorces." Now he must be careful. Too easy to mess things up. "Karen, I can't express to you how touched I am. You've just showed me that you know how much I care for you. You are very precious to me, and that's why I can't do anything to hurt you."

"I don't understand. You've been telling me how much you love me, so why would you have to hurt me?"

"I'm a lot older than you, and I can tell you that breaking up of two marriages would hurt you a great deal." Karen tried to say something, but Porter held up his hand. "Bear with me, Karen. Let me tell you why I know what I'm saying is right. Certainly I would like to marry you, but it's impossible. I thought you understood that. I'm a father and a grandfather, and regardless of my relationship with Beulah, I could never hurt my entire family by such a selfish move. But more than that, you would soon come to regret such a happening. Oh, I'm not talking about your own marriage. You've been very honest about the fact that you and Sam don't get along. I'm sure that there is a good chance that you may divorce him someday. But you are young and you haven't really given yourself sufficient time to be certain of the way you feel. And I do know something else." He spoke cautiously but without halting. "What we have between us is something special, something to be nurtured and protected. Karen, if we did what you suggested and announced that we wanted to get married, a stain we could never eradicate would spread over our relationship, and that stain would, yes, sully it. No one would really understand, and the community would regard what we have treasured as merely a sordid affair. No relationship, not even ours, could sustain such inference. What we have means too much to both of us to ruin everything by an act of foolishness. The only way we can keep the love we have for each other is by doing exactly the opposite of what you suggest. What we have is too personal, too private to be understood by anyone else. We have something that will last a lifetime, and I don't want it to all go down the drain."

What was going down the drain was simply everything that Karen had planned so carefully. She had no particular feeling for Porter, but she had envisioned a life filled with exciting social engagements, a life where money was plentiful—money for trips, money for clothes, money for anything. And now it was all gone. She was too smart a girl to think otherwise. She got off the bed and began to get dressed. Porter came over and tried to place his arm around her. "Get away from me, you dirty old man!" she said. She quickly finished dressing and left the boat.

When Asa Porter heard Karen's car start up and drive away, his first reaction was one of relief. This had been a closer call than he had envisioned. Why do some of them get so serious? he asked himself, and then realized that the question was rhetorical; he knew the answer. He was attractive, he was brilliant, he was successful—in short, he was a damn good catch. Karen's last remark to him had stung him, but her anger, he philosophized, was understandable. She was desperately in love with him and wanted all of him, up to and including a marriage certificate. She had not wanted to share him with Beulah. Well, she was just another foolish girl. A luscious one, he had to admit, and he would miss her, but there had always been luscious girls. It wasn't at all like streetcars, he thought, remembering a college consolation. He wouldn't even have to wait for another one to come along. He had already selected the next recipient of his attentions. But for now he would remain for a while on the boat. He would relax completely. He turned on the hi-fi and went to the bar and poured himself a double Scotch.

Zabriskie and Diamond sat in their reclining chairs in the dialysis room. They had finished their supper and were waiting for Nurse Ehrhardt to arrive and start the dialysis. They turned their heads to the windows as a flash of lightning created a fraction of a second of daylight. Finally, several loud thunderclaps completed the cycle.

"I wish she'd get here," Zabriskie said. "We can't start without her. These babies"—he pointed to the two dialysis machines—"can't do it by themselves. They need her just like we do."

Diamond looked up quizzically. Zabriskie sounded very depressed, and it was obvious that this duel with death was affecting him.

"I'm not enchanted with our dependence on those robots either, but what the hell, Simeon, everybody is dependent on something. Neither of us is a candidate for a transplant, so we need the machines, but so what? Everybody needs air to breathe and everybody needs farmers to grow food. I know a guy who is dependent on sex. No kidding. He says if he doesn't get laid every day, he'll go crazy. Every time I see his wife, I look at her funny and I think she knows what I'm thinking too. So *we* need the machines."

"It's not the machines themselves. It's the restriction. You know how Marian and I love to travel and what a hassle it was for us to take that vacation last summer. It was very hard to get other dialysis centers to give me a treatment, and it's not getting any easier. You know that, Paul." Zabriskie sighed.

"Yeah, Sim, that part's rough, but I'll make a prediction. Those smart engineers will work out a small portable unit someday just for traveling."

"Someday," Zabriskie said, and sighed. "I'll tell you one thing—that guy you know is lucky. I wish I had to get laid every day. I wish I *felt* like getting laid once a month."

"You're dreaming, pal, you're dreaming. Don't you know that men reach their peak of horniness at eighteen and it's all downhill after that?" Diamond, pleased that his friend looked less sad, continued. "So you see, Sim, don't blame the kidneys when it's the old pecker that's pooping out on you." His tone became confidential. "Of course, I'm the exception, and my wife thanks me for it. Actually, that guy that gets it every day is really me. I hate to make you miserable, but honesty, as old Abe said, compels me."

"Bullshit!"

"Okay. So I lie a little. No reason to get sore."

There were footsteps in the corridor, and both men turned toward the door. They could hear the *clump-clump-clump*, accompanied by heavy breathing. Hedwig Ehrhardt was about to arrive, and Diamond and Zabriskie waited intently. During these weekly encounters with Ehrhardt, they ribbed her mercilessly, but always there was the awareness that their lives were literally in her hands and they were grateful for her cultural thoroughness.

She huffed into the room, and Zabriskie and Diamond raised their arms in protocol salute. *"Sieg heil,"* they said with one voice.

"Hans and Fritz. I vas hoping you should stay home today, but you two bad boys haff to spoil my whole night." Ehrhardt took off her raincoat and shook it vigorously, scattering drops of water over her two patients. After she hung up the coat, she looked at the men, an expression of long-suffering endurance on her face. "How many times do I haff to tell you boys I did not like that paperhanger? Still you keep giving me that crazy salute. Ach, I don't know why I walk through *Donner* and *Blitzen* for you two bummers."

"Because we turn you on, Hedwig. Admit it!" Diamond started to laugh as he spoke, and Zabriskie joined in. "You don't get enough at home and you're after our bodies, right?"

Ehrhardt walked to the washbasin and returned with a bar of soap. She held it up for her patients to see. "Go ahead. You say more fresh words to me." She paused and smiled, showing that there were no hard feelings. "Then I vill teach you bad boys just like I teach my little grandson Gunter." She brandished the bar. "I wash out your mouths."

Zabriskie and Diamond looked at each other, temporarily subdued. Neither was absolutely certain that Nurse Ehrhardt would not keep her promise. They watched as she gathered the equipment—plastic tubing with special connections—she would use to attach them to the machines. Although a physician was in charge of the dialysis unit, Ehrhardt had been on the job for ten years and needed no supervision. She worked quickly and efficiently, tending first to Zabriskie. He had an older type of connecting device, a shunt. Plastic tubing had been sewn into the large artery and vein of his arm. During the week, the arterial and venous tubes were connected, forming a U over the forearm. Now Ehrhardt opened the connection, hooking up the arterial cannula to long tubing going to the artificial kidney and using a return plastic tubing to connect to Zabriskie's venous cannula. The result was a larger U, the machine being the closed part of a U whose two arms were now the tubing coming from and to the patient. When Ehrhardt had finished with Zabriskie and his machine was turned on and the dialysis was under way, she directed her attention to Diamond. He had a newer arrangement, a vein graft. Some vein from his leg had been sewed to connect arm artery to arm vein, and now Ehrhardt inserted needles connected to tubing into both sides of the U-shaped graft. Zabriskie's shunt had become infected several times during the past two years, but Diamond's vein grafts were beneath his skin, which protected him against this hazard.

Now both dialyses were under way and the men watched the lights and listened to the buzzers on the two machines. There were green lights and yellow lights and red lights, most of them steady but several of them blinking. And there were legends printed behind some of the lights, legends that read "Heat Control" and "Recirculating Pump," and others to show that the mechanical components were operating properly. Now the plastic tubes from the men to their machines were filled with blood, some on its way to the machine and some on its return trip to the patient. The machine acted like the patient's own kidneys were supposed to—as a strainer, keeping blood cells and proteins intact while waste products diffused or were excreted into the urine. Here, however, instead of the walls of the millions of capillaries acting as filters, a plastic membrane inside a coil in the machine did the job—a semipermeable membrane permitting the patient's wastes to filter into a solution which would be discarded after the dialysis, and the patient's blood would be cleansed temporarily. The discarded dialysate fluid was the patient's "machine" urine, partly artificially prepared fluid and partly the natural waste products that had diffused into it.

"You know what frightens me about her?" Diamond asked Zabriskie. He was playing the old game of pretending Ehrhardt wasn't there and waiting to get a rise out of her. Ehrhardt ignored him, checking the dials on the machines, noting the thermometer readings, the blood flow, and the pressure readings. "She comes from Transylvania, Dracula country, and she might decide to make the blood flow a one-way proposition."

Zabriskie said nothing, but Diamond continued on. "You can tell by the eyeteeth, Sim. They're longer than the average, and more pointed. Don't look now, but later, when she smiles, you can take a peek. But how do we get her to smile? She's such a mean lady."

Now, to Diamond's delight, Ehrhardt acknowledged the conversation. She turned to face her patients, hands on her hips. Then she smiled broadly, so that her teeth became very prominent. "I tell you something, you boys haff nothing to worry. Vampires take blut from nice people, not from bad boys. Und you dumpkopfs don't know yet vere iss Transylvania. Iss in Rumania. I haff cousin there."

"Thank you, Hedwig," Diamond said, feigning relief. "Ve're safe, ve're safe."

"Vampires do not come from Silesia," Ehrhardt said, "but famous war hero, Baron Manfred von Richthofen, vas born in Breslau. My papa vas his friend." She paused. "I think I told you boys. Silesia, iss very sad, Silesia iss now Polish."

Diamond was delighted. "Hedwig is maybe your aunt, Sim." Then he turned to Ehrhardt with a puzzled look. "Baron who?"

"Manfred von Richthofen. Der Red Baron." She stopped talking to search for a word and found it. "He vas an *ace*. You boys know better. Don't kid me."

"We believe you, Hedwig." Diamond became sincere. "We never heard of any Red Baron, but we're not saying you're lying. You might be telling the truth. Did you ever hear about Major John Wayne?"

"Who you say?" she replied.

"You want us to know all about your heroes like that baron fellow, but you don't know anything about ours. Major John Wayne only happens to be *our* World War Two hero." Diamond shook his head in reproval before continuing. "He fought everywhere, in the Atlantic, in Europe, in Japan, in the Pacific, everywhere. And you never heard of him? I bet you never heard of General Eisenhower, either."

"Why don't you knock it off, Paul. I'd like to get a little rest," Zabriskie said suddenly. Then he closed his eyes, pretending to be asleep.

Diamond, taken by surprise, started to say something but stopped before the thought emerged. In two years, Zabriskie had never spoken this sharply to him. They had argued incessantly, but it was at the level of banter, not real annoyance. Diamond looked at his friend for a moment and then returned and watched his machine with its blinking lights.

"I've remained silent while listening to all of you for the last ten minutes," Beulah Porter whispered to Whitesides, who sat to her right at the negotiating table. "What I've heard is the word 'strike' thrown around by both sides. Every time they mention strike," she said to him, "you and Sam threaten retribution. That's a waste of time. Nobody wants a strike. The union and the hospital both want an equitable settlement."

"I disagree with you, Beulah," Whitesides whispered back. "They don't give a damn for what is equitable." He pointed across at O'Brien and Armstrong. "You people are for the union first, second, and third, and if you kill the hospital in the process, that's okay too."

"What you are saying is that the people who work for this hospital are no part of it, right?" Armstrong's tone was icy.

Whitesides glared at Armstrong. "There isn't a prayer for settling this dispute."

"Lester," Beulah whispered again, "please be clear about this. I wouldn't have insisted on joining this meeting after Neely got sick if I believed that there was no possibility of settlement."

The discussion around the negotiating table had heated up again. For a while after Neely had been taken to the coronary-care unit, labor talk had ceased, replaced by speculation over what had happened to the federal mediator. Whitesides had received a phone call, left for a few minutes, and returned to the room accompanied by the chairperson of the board of directors. Beulah Porter had announced that in view of what had happened to the mediator, she wished to join in the negotiations. She clearly was not a neutral, she admitted, but pointed out that she was familiar with the workings of Pacific Hospital and that time was short. O'Brien and Armstrong had decided to caucus privately about this. At first they had questioned having another avid hospital advocate join the negotiations, but then Armstrong had second thoughts. He pointed out that Whitesides was intransigent and that this lady had both money and power. Finally they agreed that they had nothing to lose. When they returned to the table, they publicly objected to her presence but stated they would go along with it for a while.

But surprisingly, Beulah Porter had been a moderating influence. Now, with an argument in full swing, she remained calm, and hers was the only voice that had not been raised in anger. As a matter of fact, she was concerned about Whitesides' demeanor and thought that the hospital would have a better chance if he could remain more in control of himself.

For the moment, she would content herself with ensuring that Lester did just that.

"Beulah," Sam March said, "Lester and I don't want a strike, but I'm not buying your observation that they don't either." O'Brien started to reply, but March kept on talking. "Listen, I've been telling these guys about the permanent scars that come after a strike," he said to Beulah, "but these stupid bastards just laugh. Let me tell you something that happened this morning. This mainly concerns you, Jax, because possibly you can understand why the woman was so upset."

"What woman?" Armstrong asked.

"She's an LVN in this hospital, and she's black. I'm not telling you her name because you people would take it out on her, but she came up to me crying. 'Please settle this dispute, Mr. March,' she said, 'because I don't want to strike against this hospital. Pacific has been good to me. Here I'm a *professional,* Mr. March. I have responsibility and dignity.' You can write this off as bullshit if you want, but it's true, and she is not alone in her feelings."

"Do you think we object to this nurse having dignity and responsibility?" Armstrong asked. "What we want is the same rights for all of our workers, including those who work in the laundry. And one more thing—you can't live on dignity. You need security and bread, man. That's money."

"There is only so much money that is available," Whitesides said. "You talk loosely about 'hospital profits' and say the government should put a ceiling on us. But all the unions scream at the mention of wage control."

"When national health insurance comes in and the government puts a limit on hospital costs," March added, "you can be goddamn sure that health care will be rationed. The hypochondriacs will clog up the system because it will be for free, and the union people with that nice medical- and hospital-insurance plan will suffer along with the rest of us."

"Gentlemen," Beulah Porter interjected, "we're getting way off the track. All this talk about health-care rationing is theoretical—in the future. Right now, we had better get back to the present and our agenda. Seniority is next on the list. Mr. O'Brien, I believe you wanted to speak to this point."

Armstrong looked at Beulah Porter. She was sounding like

a moderator, almost like Neely, and this made Jax apprehensive.

O'Brien began to read aloud: " 'In the case of a vacancy occurring on the same shift, employer shall use the criterion of seniority, provided such vacancy be permanent, as described in Article III, Section C, Subheading (i).' This is the paragraph we want added to the old section."

"You know our objections to this," Whitesides said. "You're trying to bind us to seniority and tie our hands. The next senior employee may be as competent as the one who is leaving. If so, we'll give him the promotion. We always have. But if we don't think that the most senior man—"

"Or woman," Armstrong added.

"Don't quibble! If we don't think the most senior man or woman is the best replacement," Whitesides continued, "we damn well won't be forced to give him or her the job. Now, Administration has talked this over, and we're aware that there is no mention of seniority in the article as it is presently written. We don't want to be unreasonable, so we're willing to go this far, and I think, Mr. Armstrong, that you and Frank will agree that this is fair. Change the wording to 'In the case of a vacancy occurring on same shift or another shift, employer will give *consideration* to seniority,' et cetera, et cetera. In other words, we're promising to fill a permanent vacancy on the basis of seniority whenever possible, but we're reserving the right to have the last word. Is that satisfactory?"

Whitesides sat quietly while O'Brien and Armstrong conferred in whispers. This was a charade, and everybody knew it. Finally Armstrong nodded to O'Brien. The game was being fully played out. O'Brien spoke. "Lester, this sounds fine on paper, but suppose that you don't act in good faith. Now, I'm not suggesting that you don't always act in good faith, just giving something in theory. What can we say if every time this happens, you fill the job with someone you want and then tell us you gave 'consideration' to the senior employee but the senior employee couldn't really do the job?"

"Come on, Frank," Whitesides said. "If you find that we're being unfair or unreasonable, you know you can use Article IX, Grievance Procedure. We meet jointly to work things out, and if we can't agree, the article commits us to accept binding arbitration."

"You know that it's in both our interests to get the best man for the job, Frank," March added. "You can't lose. We're giving you what you want on this one, so just have the decency to say thank you."

O'Brien, after checking again with Whitesides for the new wording, wrote it in and initialed it. He pushed the document across the table, and Whitesides added his initials.

"Looks like you're a good influence," Armstrong said to Beulah Porter. He and O'Brien were surprised that the seniority item had gone through easily. They had anticipated a fight, but they had gotten what they wanted without significant change and with practically no opposition.

"I want to talk about something that is not specifically on our agenda but relates to this whole negotiating process, to the entire relationship between Pacific Hospital and your union." Whitesides pointed a finger across the table at O'Brien and Armstrong. "I'm referring to the 'for-cause' case."

O'Brien groaned. "You know that that matter is still under investigation, Lester. Why the hell bring it up here? We got enough to do. We're working to prevent a strike, and frankly, you don't have the time to—"

"Don't tell me how much time I have! We can stop negotiations right now if that's the way you feel." Whitesides was furious.

Beulah Porter decided to let this go on for a while and not intervene.

"That's fine with us," Armstrong said. He started to get up, then eased back in his chair as the administrator continued.

"You know, grievances are supposed to work both ways," Whitesides said, ignoring Armstrong and continuing to raise his voice at O'Brien. "You spoke about good faith a minute ago. You met during working hours in the laundry. The contract specifically forbids that. And another thing, you've been dragging your heels for three months on this, so who is guilty of bad faith? Well, Frank, you want to tell me about good faith and bad faith?"

The problem concerned a security guard about whom there had been many complaints. The hospital had tried to fire him, but the matter had ended up with the Grievance Committee, and the case was still being discussed there.

"Lester," O'Brien replied, "the union is not acting in bad faith. I don't think that now is the time to talk about this, but since you're hot about it, I will. We're not crazy about him either. Your people on the committee know that. But we got legal problems to consider. The hospital isn't the only one who needs a lawyer."

"This man has been surly to patients and employees, he reports in late frequently, people have seen him asleep on the job, and we think he's moonlighting. The contract says that the union is supposed to stop that sort of thing—what more do you need?" Whitesides glared at O'Brien and Armstrong.

"We know what you're saying," Armstrong said, "and Frank and I agree with you. We're just waiting for something concrete. We want to pin something that will stick, and then he'll be out on his ass. What have you got now? Nobody who has seen him asleep has been willing to testify. You just said you 'think' he's moonlighting. That may be the case, but thinking isn't enough. Do you know what he could do to us if we agreed to fire him at this time?"

"What about Pacific Hospital? Have you people any interest in Pacific Hospital?"

"Just let me give you our position," Armstrong continued. "Under NLRB, the union must, is *legally obligated* to, give him fair representation. If we don't have the goods on him, he can sue the hell out of us, and that wouldn't be good for us, and to answer your question, it wouldn't be good for Pacific Hospital either. He's been warned, and we're keeping an eye on him."

Beulah Porter had remained silent during the exchange. Now she spoke quietly to the administrator. "Lester, I'm going to be blunt. What you've brought up has very little to do with the items we have to discuss. We would all do better to avoid this kind of digression in the future." Then she spoke to the entire group. "Gentlemen. If it's agreeable with you, I think that now is a good time to break for supper."

She looked around the table, and the four men nodded in turn. Then everyone stood up and stretched before filing out of the boardroom.

PART III

Evening

"Where does it hurt, Mr. Morley?" Madden Chase asked as he pressed the patient's abdomen. He had just been called by Vanni, and the two doctors were completing their examination.

"Everywhere!" said Morley. He winced every time Chase prodded him. "You might try being a little gentle."

"I am being gentle," Chase replied. "I think it's your spleen that's being unkind. You hit it pretty hard in the accident, and I think it's bleeding on you."

He motioned Vanni away from the bedside, and the two men conferred quietly. "The latest blood count has dropped, and I'll bet it's even lower now," Chase said. "Are you agreed that we should take him up for exploratory surgery? There's no doubt in my mind that he's bleeding."

"No question, Madden. Take him up. I'll be in CCU if you need me for anything. I'd watch the surgery, but I have a patient there who's in bad shape."

A nurse came in with a large syringe. Chase drew blood from Morley and filled two tubes. "These go to the lab stat for blood count, PCV, and type and crossmatch for three units," Chase said to the nurse. "Have someone take Mr. Morley up to the OR now." He scribbled on Morley's chart and handed it to the nurse. "Here are the pre-op orders. Give these stat. Also, get him to sign the permission slip for surgery."

Morley called from the bed, "I heard that. Why should I give permission? You're all knife-happy." His voice was too weak to be convincing.

"Look, Mr. Morley," said Madden Chase. "If you wish to continue selling Duncan Phyfe chairs, just sign the permission slip and allow me to get moving, please."

135

Outside the room, Chase spoke again to Vanni. "What the hell was the matter with you, Leo? You had this man in for several hours. Why did you wait so long to call me?"

"No excuse, Madden." Vanni quickly told Chase about the Porter consult and the events leading up to it. "I was wrong and I went against my judgment and decided to mark time," he concluded. "Porter wanted to make a horse's ass out of me, but I've done it all by myself, at Morley's expense."

"You know," Chase said to Vanni, "there are basic flaws in Porter. Judgment and something else. Look, would he purposely jeopardize a patient just to spite you? What you said about his wanting to show you up doesn't entirely make sense, Leo. He would want to cover himself. We both know that things go sour rapidly, as they have, so why not be on the safe side and get a surgical opinion? No, there's something missing in Asa's character."

"Karl might have listened to me had I forced the issue," Vanni said.

"You should have," Chase replied. "Next time, call me right away. I don't mind a good bedside fight."

Sam March sat in his office munching on a sandwich as he studied a folder prepared for him by the director of personnel. He was hoping to find something new, some logical bit of insight that might help with the negotiations. He looked again at the pages entitled "Retraining." This might just do it, he thought. He put down his sandwich as his office door burst open. Karen was standing in the doorway. "I told you I'd be late tonight. I'm supposed to call you when the meetings end. What are you doing here?" March was still angry.

Karen closed the door and walked to the chair in front of her husband's desk and sat down. "I wanted to talk to you, Sam," she said. "I've felt awful ever since I left you here this morning. I realize that we've been under a lot of strain since these labor talks began, but that's no excuse for the way—"

"There's been a lot of strain *before* the negotiations ever started," March reminded her. "Don't try to pin a bum rap on me, Karen. You've been a fucking bitch—strike that— you've been a bitch for months, and I don't know what the hell has made you that way."

"I don't either, but I'm sorry. I came to apologize. I guess

I've realized all day how much you mean to me and how much I've loused things up. I've done a lot of thinking, Sam. Sometimes fighting can be helpful. It helped me at least to appreciate you. I guess I always took you for granted, and then, after I mentioned that awful word this morning . . ."

"What word?"

" 'Divorce,' Sam. I was stupid and I said something about divorce, but I want you to know I didn't mean it. I'm sorry I said it and I'll never say it again. I'll make it up to you, I promise."

"You confuse me, Karen. For two months you don't give me the time of day, and suddenly everything is peaches and cream and you're all smiles, showing me, I guess, that the precious shrine between your legs is now available. I just don't get it, Karen. Explain it to me. Did you get some real bargains on your lousy shopping spree today?"

"Sam, you don't have to be vulgar. I said I'm sorry for everything, and I really am." She lifted a shopping bag she was carrying. "As a matter of fact, my shopping was successful. There's a nightgown inside the bag that I bought when I thought about you. I plan to model it for you tonight when you come home." She walked over to March and kissed him. "C'mon, Sam. Please tell me everything is okay. Please."

"Just like that," March said. "After all that shit you've been shoveling at me for the last two months? And your talk about divorce this morning?"

"I'm cured, Sam. Cross my heart. My bitchiness is exorcised."

"Everything is definitely not okay," March said.

Karen decided to defer further explanation. "What time do you think you'll be coming home, Sam? I have a lot of making up to do. You won't be disappointed!"

"I have no idea. I do know that I'm not thrilled about rushing back to you. Leave me the car keys and take a taxi home. I'm not trying for a cab tonight in weather like this."

Karen sighed. She had anticipated, considering her earlier conversation with Sam, that there might be much difficulty in obtaining his forgiveness. Still, on the drive from the boat to the hospital, she had hoped for an immediate resolution to the fix she had gotten herself in. It was not to be. She should have been wiser, more patient and certain before beginning the break with Sam. And with Porter, she might at least have entertained the possibility that he viewed her only as a superb lay. In the future, she would be less naive and far more clever. She was battle-wise now; the next Porter would not get away. Concerning the present, it would take a little longer to reconcile her differences with Sam and buy herself some time. So what! He was essentially a simple man. She would require a few days, at the outside, to convince him that everything was going to be fine. The disharmony of the past months had been caused by a series of mutual misunderstandings. That was good! Mutual misunderstandings. She toyed with these thoughts as she absently reached down in her purse and felt the plastic tag. She tossed the keys to March. The keys sailed through the air, and March caught them. Karen reached down to close her purse and panicked. The car keys with the purple plastic boxing gloves were still inside her handbag. "Sam, those are the wrong keys," she said as calmly as she could. "Here are the car keys."

March did not answer her. He stood for long seconds looking at the key in his hand, a key with a plastic float and a plastic name tag attached—a name tag that read *See-Sick*. He didn't want to comprehend what he was seeing, but he couldn't help it.

"So this was your shopping trip," he said finally. "Your Wednesday to get things. Did you pick up anything catching? How many men are you fucking besides Porter?"

"It's over, Sam. I can't explain how or why it began, but it didn't mean anything." She was stumbling over her words now. Nothing sounded right. "There's never been anyone but you really. Asa Porter was more like a father to me. You were yelling at me a lot, and he was sympathetic when I went to his office. That's how it started. But it never meant anything. Really." Karen brightened slightly as she remembered something. "I told Asa this afternoon that it was over. We didn't go to bed. I told him that I finally realized I loved you and the affair was a stupid mistake."

March had remained silent during his wife's recitation. Now he reached over and took the car keys from her hand. He looked at the plastic boxing gloves for a second. Then he walked to the door. He opened it and threw the keys to the *See-Sick* into the hall. "I don't know whether your affair is over or not," he said, "and I don't give a shit. Our marriage is over, though. I'm moving out tomorrow."

Suddenly Karen looked desperate. "I don't blame you for the way you feel," she said, "but try to understand me. I was lonely, and I didn't realize how much I loved you. So I was tricked into a meaningless relationship."

"Who tricked you?" March asked.

"Asa. He said I needed affection and he could give it to me without anyone knowing. He said nobody would get hurt." She clenched her fist and hit the wall. "I was so stupid, Sam."

"That you were," March said.

Karen sensed that she was on the right track. "Asa was unfair to both of us."

March looked at her without responding.

"He implied to me," Karen said, "that it would be good for your career if I were cooperative. That's what he said. Really."

"So you were a philanthropist," March said. "You gave your all for your husband. That's very touching. Thank you."

"It sounds so awful the way you say it, Sam," Karen argued. "I was mixed up and I—"

"That's enough, Karen," March said. "I'm not interested in hearing any more." He walked to the door and turned toward Karen. "Screw yourself to the throne of England if you like. I'm not sticking around to watch." Then he walked toward the boardroom.

The ICU gave Phil Wray the creeps, and he hated to come into the unit. He didn't like to be reminded of illness and death. Didn't they know he was a sick, nervous man? "It's all fixed." He pointed to the oscilloscope screen. "It was only a loose wire. Why can't you learn to use the biomed engineer? This is his job. I have enough to do."

The charge nurse, Nina, in turn pointed to all the tubes connected to the patients. "I'm busy too, or hadn't you noticed? You waste a lot of time complaining, Phil."

He felt his stomach tighten but decided against taking an antacid pill. He looked at his watch—6:39 P.M. and time to get out of this depressing place and back to his home in the basement. He felt better in the bowels of the hospital. Wray opened his tool kit and replaced the screwdriver he had used for the repair job. Then it happened.

The underground feeder cable, which eventually supplied the hospital power plant, followed a mostly linear path. However, at various points under the manholes in the street the cable would make a bend, where switches hyphenated the flow of current it carried. During the day, the cable handled its load without sign of effort, but each evening when the inhabitants of the city returned home, the cable responded to their commands for more power to turn on more lights, more television sets, more dishwashers. At these times, the cable reacted to overwork. It overheated and expanded, and this daily stress manifested itself mainly at the bending portion of the cable. Here, under a manhole at the side of a street a few blocks from the hospital, a tiny crack appeared on the underside of the cable. The process, started eighteen months earlier, continued, and within a year the minute break in the lead sheath had deepened, to make the fracture of the sheath complete.

Nothing of consequence resulted because the paper insulation still was protecting the cable against leakage. But then, three days ago, with the onset of rain, the paper began to absorb moisture. The wetness had dried out and recurred, dried out and recurred, until this instant, when water poured from the street into the manhole. Now, at 6:40 p.m., the feeder cable shorted out. After a muffled explosion, the lights in the area went dark and the switchboard at PG and E lighted up.

When the lights in ICU went out, the unit became silent as well as dark. The background noise of suction machines, the sounds of respirators, the beeps and buzzes of electronic gear—all this electrical chattering was stilled.

Wray ran to a window the instant the lights went out and looked around. The entire area was black, excepting the headlights of the cars whose beams reflected the rain. Now, as he had done earlier during the generator test, he began to count. One, two, three, four, five . . . please let it happen . . . six, seven . . . Thank God! At the count of seven, power to the ICU was restored. The usual noises sounded reassuring, as once again they filled the unit. Wray looked at the street once more. What he already knew was confirmed: this was an area blackout, and for a while—a very short while, he hoped—the hospital would be running on its own auxiliary power. Wray grabbed his tool kit and raced for the stairwell. As he ran, he noted that the critical lights were working as they should.

In the basement, he heard the familiar whirring of the diesel engine. He opened the generator-room door and quickly checked out the engine and the generator. He was pleased enough—the Herz values were sixty cycles and the switches and voltage indicator were okay.

The phone rang and he picked it up. It was a security guard calling from the lobby. An elevator was stopped between the second floor and the lobby and some visitors were stuck in it. They were pounding on the door.

Wray knew at once what had happened. With the power failure, mechanical brakes were automatically applied to prevent the elevators from falling. "I'll give you power to Number Five, Joe. Watch it and let me know when it reaches a floor." Wray, holding the phone against his ear, moved to the distribution panel and pulled a switch.

"Okay, Phil. She's at two," the voice in the phone said.

Wray cut the power to Five. "Listen Joe, run like hell and give me a reading on numbers One, Two, Three, Four, and Six. Call me right back!"

Wray paced nervously. He wanted to phone PG and E but was afraid to tie up the line until he heard from Joe. He looked at his watch and cursed. What was taking so long? Finally the phone rang.

"We're in luck, Phil," the voice announced. "One, Three, Four, and Six got stuck on floors with their doors open or partially open." The guard sounded out of breath. "Everyone is out on those floors, and also they got out of Five when you moved it to the second floor. Now, can you give power to Number Two? That one's stuck between floors."

Wray was pleased. He was getting off easier than he might have. "You got it," he said after pulling another switch.

"Okay. Cut it!" Joe said. Wray pulled the switch again. "It's on three. I'll run up and check it," Joe announced.

Again there was a wait. This one was brief. Forty-five seconds later Wray learned that the passengers from Number Two elevator had all disembarked safely on the third floor. Now all the nonemergency elevators were out of service, and they were all empty. Only Seven and Eight, the elevators designated as "emergency" by the state, were now in service, powered by the hospital's auxiliary generator. "Put signs in Seven and Eight, Joe," Wray told the security guard. " 'Emergency use only.' " He hung up and after a brief interval picked up the phone again. He dialed O. He tapped nervously as the muted rings sounded in his ear. "What took you so long, Mabel?" he complained. "Look, make an announcement to use the stairs until the blackout is over; elevators Seven and Eight are for patient emergencies only. Now, get me PG and E."

He again waited impatiently until he finally got through to the service department. "This is Phil Wray at Pacific Hospital. What's going on?"

"Who are you again?" The voice at the other end was friendly.

"Phil Wray, the watch officer on duty at Pacific Hospital. We're operating on emergency power, and I want to know what's going on."

"We're not sure, Phil. We've sent an emergency crew to the scene. It's this damn storm. We think a twelve-thousand-volt feeder blew. Your whole sector is out."

"How long?" Wray asked.

"A while. Listen, I gotta go." The man hung up.

Wray muttered, "Thanks a lot, genius." Now he noticed that the lights that were on were flickering somewhat. This was a signal that the rpm's were varying, causing the diesel engine to override the governor setting. He thought of trying to regulate the engine speed manually, but at that moment the governor seemed to take hold, everything stabilized, and the readings were steady. He wanted to call PG and E again but realized that it wouldn't be of any help.

"Hey, Phil!" There was a figure outside the door. "Let me in."

Wray could see Victor Bates through the grillwork and admitted him. "Don't touch anything, Victor. We're on emergency power."

"When'll the blackout be over?" Bates asked.

"I called PG and E. They don't know their ass from a hole in the ground. You know what the guy said when I asked him? 'A while.' " Wray walked over to the rpm meter and looked at it a full minute. "At least this thing's settled down," he said. He pointed to the governor and told Bates about the trouble he had noted a little while earlier.

"That federal mediator had a heart attack," Bates announced. "I wish it had been Whitesides."

Wray looked at Bates curiously. He sounded more vengeful than he ever had before, and Wray decided not to respond.

The phone rang, and it was Mabel. "I have Mr. March, but before I connect you, Surgery wants to know why the lights flickered and when the blackout will be over."

"PG and E doesn't know. Why the hell should I? Tell surgery that when all the lights come back on, the blackout will be over. Now, give me Sam."

The voice at the other end sounded faint but audible. The connection was poor. "I just wanted to find out how things are going, Phil," March said.

"Can you come down for a few minutes, Sam? Before the blackout, I had to mop up near the boilers. The damn wind was blowing water in, and the excavation site is almost filled. Swanson never came." Wray had wondered, not entirely illogically, why the power plant was so deep in the ground, since his miseries about water were compounded by the fact that the hospital was built on a hill. Besides rain coming in through the visquine, water was also cascading down the steep concrete steps leading to the other outside entrance to the power plant. "And listen, Sam. PG and E doesn't know when they'll have power back on."

"I'm in the middle of a meeting, Phil. Emergency power is okay. These things usually last less than an hour. Any problem with the elevators?"

Wray told about his evacuation success and was immediately sorry he did.

"Good, Phil. Call me if there's anything more. I'm available if you need me," March said and then hung up.

Wray stood up for a second, holding the receiver. Everyone was hanging up on him. Finally he replaced the receiver on its hook. "The son of a bitch won't come. I only wanted five minutes of his time, but he's too busy. Can you believe that, Victor? We're having a blackout, and he's tied up in some stupid meeting."

"I can believe anything about this hospital," Bates answered.

"Listen, Victor. I got problems. It's six-fifty-five—already fifteen minutes. Water is coming in through the evacuation site. We're on emergency power, and when the blackout started, a safety secured the boiler. I have to reset the safety and light-off the boiler. This is too much for one person. I'm here all alone. Just think what would happen if something goes wrong with the emergency power before those assholes at PG and E get things fixed."

"I wouldn't want to be in your shoes, that's for sure," Bates said. "Look, you got a lot on your mind. I'll come back in an hour when everything is okay again." With that, Victor Bates turned and departed, leaving an anxious Wray to ponder over exactly what to do next.

Dr. Oliver Lusk stood in the locker room in his underwear and surgical shoes. The operation on David Raymer would be a very tricky procedure. He neither sighed nor frowned in contemplation of his task. Lusk simply did his very best at all times, and the knowledge that this was so was helpful to him. He was not a temperamental surgeon who yelled and threw instruments, but neither was he a relaxed man.

Lusk took a size "small" green pants from the shelf and quickly put them on over the operating shoes. Then he pulled a short-sleeved green shirt over his head and sat down on the bench. "As I told you earlier, Dr. Cheney," he said to the eye resident, "this one is touch and go."

"Acid burns," commented Michael Cheney, shaking his head.

"His right eye is enucleated, gone. And three surgical failures on the left eye in the last five years. We can do no more than guess what it feels like to be deprived of vision four times in five years," Lusk said. "Well, let's get started."

Accompanied by Cheney, Lusk walked from the dressing room to the scrub room adjoining the ophthalmologic-surgery operating room. He went immediately to the double sink and began the scrub. Cheney, standing next to him, also began the cleansing procedure. The spray from the shower-head faucets splashed over their hands and forearms as they worked the germicidal soap into a lather. They washed off this lather and then began the soaping process all over again in a continuous soaping-and-rinsing cycle.

"What are the chances for another immune reaction, Dr. Lusk?" Cheney asked.

"I'm more concerned with the technical aspects of the surgery. We can't be certain exactly what caused the clouding after the other operations. Yesterday in the office I pointed out to you just how little healthy cornea remains to work with. These chemical injuries are the worst. In addition to the usual problems, you get drying because of tear-duct scarring and loss of lubricating mucin. This can lead to corneal ulceration. The point I'm making is that if we can succeed in the technical part of the transplant, I think we can avoid an immune reaction or at least control it until it subsides." Lusk shut off the faucet by placing his thigh in the horseshoe-shaped stainless attachment and pushing it to the side. Then he stepped on the floor pedal, releasing more soap on his hands, and continued the scrubbing process, using a small, stiff handbrush.

He wondered how many times he had been through this scrubbing procedure. The estimated figure had come to over fifteen thousand several years ago, and yet this and every other phase of eye surgery exhilarated him. He loved his work, and although extremely sensitive, he was strong enough to accept the personal pain of failure while keeping in perspective his outstanding successes and the resultant adulation he received daily from patients and colleagues. "You asked about immune reactions, Dr. Cheney, and I never answered you. The figures aren't too bad. Clouding over after chemical burns occurs in about twenty-five percent, and half of these reactions can be controlled by medications. If we can get firm attachment of the donor cornea, I think Raymer will have his sight back." As he talked, Lusk took an orangewood stick and worked the soap under his fingernails again and again, pressing hard to remove any residue of dirt.

"I've never seen anyone scrub as long and as hard as you do, Dr. Lusk. Never!" Cheney commented.

"Always retain your respect for bacteria," Lusk replied. "It's indecent to get a bad result from infection when five extra minutes with soap and water will prevent it. Now, in Raymer's case . . ." The surgeon stopped talking as the lights in the hospital suddenly went off. "Stay where you are and don't break scrub!" he commanded. In a few seconds the lights came back on. "I wonder what that was all about," he commented, and then continued. "With Mr. Raymer, where there has been so much tissue damage, infection is likely and must be avoided." He looked at Cheney. "Are you set?" he asked the resident, who nodded. "All right, let's go."

Lusk, holding his arms up, used his foot to push open the swinging door into the operating room, and held it open, allowing his young assistant to precede him. Raymer had been transferred from the gurney onto the table, and one surgical nurse was finishing laying out the instruments on a tray. A second nurse helped Lusk and Cheney don sterile gowns, after which she tied the gowns in the back. Then she stretched open the rubber gloves for Cheney. Lusk operated without gloves. The nurse noticed him looking at the lights, which flickered slightly.

"Do you know we're having a blackout, doctor?" she asked. "We called, and every place within a mile of the hospital is dark. We're on emergency power, and that's why the lights are acting up a little."

"We'll try not to let it distract us," Lusk said. "I suppose that every time an elevator starts to go up or down, we'll get some flickering. The lights dimmed each time Cagney got the chair at Sing Sing."

He walked over to a square table on one side of the operating room and sat down, Cheney taking the seat across from him. Then Lusk reached for the white plastic container and opened it. He removed the eye and placed it on the table in front of him. A tiny piece of optic nerve remained on the posterior surface of the eye, giving it the appearance of a cherry with part of a very thick stem still attached. He placed the eye and held it against the table so that the eye looked at the ceiling of the operating room.

The first phase of the corneal transplant was about to begin. Lusk, assisted by Cheney, placed some holding stitches in all four quadrants of the donor eye. Then he turned to the nurse. "Trephine," he said, and she handed him a small instrument with an adjustable circular cutting edge. He began his circular cutting around the periphery of the donor cornea. "Gentle treatment of tissue is largely responsible for success in this work, Dr. Cheney," Lusk commented as he worked. "Never treat tissue harshly in any surgical procedure. Now, in this operation we are essentially transplanting one layer of cells. One vital layer of endothelial cells. Never become so certain of yourself that you become careless." The trephine had scored a circular mark on the donor cornea, and now Lusk dropped some fluorescein dye onto it. The dye outlined the mark, and besides, stained the entire cornea, giving it a beautiful green iridescence. He used a small scissors to cut along the scored margin, and soon he had separated the donor cornea from the donor eye. He placed it in a small container filled with a salt solution. Cheney felt a mounting apprehension, although the responsibility was not his. The young eye resident realized that the first phase of the transplant procedure had been completed without incident, but this was routine. The most difficult part of the operation was about to begin.

Lusk stood up and walked to the operating table. "You stand right there, Dr. Cheney"—he pointed to the opposite side of the table—"and don't let Dr. Woo there give you a hard time. He thinks all young assistants are hot pilots who need taking down a notch." The anesthesiologist merely smiled in response.

The levity was over. Cheney looked down at Raymer's eye and dreaded once more what he viewed. What was left of the original cornea was not cloudy from disease alone. It was horribly scarred and opaque. There was practically nothing left of what once had been a clear window for light rays to penetrate on their way to the retina. An immune reaction had transmuted the clear, even "glass" of the latest transplant into a milky and irregular cover laced with small ugly blood vessels.

Lusk began to dissect, explaining to Cheney as he worked. "What I'm doing now is cutting the adhesions between the eyelids and the globe."

Coming from another eye surgeon and on a different case, Cheney would have resented such explication of the obvious. Not from Lusk, however. The man never said anything that wasn't important, and Cheney knew the remarks were not to elucidate anything routine. He listened carefully as he assisted.

Lusk turned toward the scrub nurse, who anticipated his wants. She handed him another sponge, a tiny tapered yellow cigarettelike, specially designed sponge, and the surgeon dabbed at a bleeding point. "You notice all the bleeding we're encountering from the superficial and deep corneal vessels. Chemical burns always cause vascular overgrowth," he said as he continued to dissect. "We're lucky that Raymer hasn't developed secondary glaucoma or cataract." He moved his scissors and snipped twice. "There. We have it."

Again the scrub nurse acted without command. She handed a trephine to Lusk, who adjusted it to the diameter he wanted. "This is very tricky," he told Cheney. "Look at how little spare cornea is left for attachment." He stood quietly, the trephine in his hand. "The prognosis," he said softly, "is guarded. And you know, Dr. Cheney, one can sense when someone has decided that enough is enough. Raymer is a courageous man, but this is the last chance he'll give us." The surgeon took a deep breath and then held the trephine over Raymer's eye, centering it. As he had done with the donor eye, he etched a circular mark and outlined it with a few drops of fluorescein. Using the dyed groove as a guide, Lusk took the tiny scissors which had just been handed to him and began to remove Raymer's own cornea by cutting along the perimeter of the scored circle.

In the boardroom, all lights went out suddenly, and immediately March ran to the window. "It's an area blackout," he announced to the others, who remained seated around the table. "I'll be back in a few minutes."

While March was gone, Beulah Porter went to a cabinet and took out two candlesticks with long white candles, used by the board for its formal dinners. She lit them, and the glow from the candles supplemented the emergency incandescent lighting, which had come on again after a few seconds of complete darkness.

"Everything's okay," March announced when he returned to the boardroom a few minutes later. "I checked the third and fourth floors, and the emergency power is working fine. Why does this son-of-a-bitch blackout have to hit in the middle of our meeting?" he grumbled. March sat down at his place at the table and picked up a phone. He spoke to Phil

Wray, and after he hung up he told the others that PG and E didn't know how long the blackout would last. "All right," he finally said. "Back to the laundry. Let's solve that, and we can all go home happy."

"You've *given* us your idea of how to solve the laundry problem," Armstrong said. "No matter how you sweeten it, you're talking closing. And we don't go for that. Do I make myself clear? Close the laundry, no contract, strike. That's our bottom line."

"What Jax means—" O'Brien began.

"Damn it, Frank, when I need a translator I'll ask for one. What I mean is exactly what I say, and if it's not clear to everyone, that's not my fault. Do you want me to repeat it for your benefit, Frank?"

"There's no sense continuing these talks," Whitesides said to Beulah. "You heard him."

"We're in this meeting to discuss options, Jax," Beulah Porter said, "so why don't you listen to the data about our laundry costs first and see if you can't understand our situation. Now, these are the figures I remember—correct me if I'm wrong, Sam. We use twenty-one pounds of linen per patient per day, and currently it costs us twenty-one cents per pound. With a patient load of two hundred beds—and I'm using a low census figure—that comes to forty-two hundred pounds per day or a cost of $882 per day, which gives us an annual cost of $322,000."

She doesn't use notes, March thought. I never knew about her memory before.

"Now, Jax," Beulah Porter continued, "subcontracting out the laundry will save us some fifteen percent, which is an annual saving of over $48,000. You've been talking about management inefficiency, gentlemen. It would be gross negligence and unfair to the community if the hospital did not take advantage of this saving. That's our point of view. Now, we can understand your feelings about the jobs involved, and we're going to do something about them. The hospital is not going to throw good, loyal laundry workers out on the streets."

"If you're about to mention retraining, Mrs. Porter, don't," Armstrong said. "The laundry stays open, that's it."

"Let's at least hear what the plan is, Jax," O'Brien pleaded.

"We'll probably turn it down, but what harm is there in listening?"

"Mr. Armstrong isn't here to listen, Frank," Whitesides said to O'Brien. "His aim—and I think yours as well—is to shut down the hospital. I mentioned the 'for-cause' case earlier not for itself but to point out the deterioration in labor-management relations that has occurred in the past three or four years," Whitesides continued. "We've sat in these negotiations week after week, and I don't mind telling you I don't like what I've been hearing. Don't you know what it costs to run a hospital these days? Don't you people have any idea? You seem to think that we in administration control all finances—that we have all the say—and if we want money, we snap our fingers and a genie delivers it."

"Maybe you'd have more money," Armstrong suggested coolly, "if you administrators and some of the high-priced doctors your hospital employs took a cut in salary."

"That's typical of the kind of irresponsible thinking that has us in trouble now," Whitesides answered. "All the salaries we get, combined—*you* know what they are Mr. Armstrong —if they were completely done away with and we all worked for nothing, it would be a tiny drop in the bucket of expense, and you know it."

"You have to have the fanciest and the latest equipment, like a CAT scanner, don't you?" Armstrong asked.

CAT was an acronym of "computerized axial tomography," an amazing technique of taking serial "slices" of tissue. The entire body or any part of it could be visualized in this manner, the penetrating X rays scattering and the tracks they made being gathered, sorted, and printed by a computer. The net result was an entirely new sort of X ray, one that resembled a photograph of an actual anatomical slice, showing soft tissues as well as bone, soft tissues badly discerned, if at all, by a conventional X ray. It was revolutionizing diagnosis.

"Only the most expensive—nothing but the best for good old Pacific Hospital," Armstrong continued. "You want a CAT scanner, you go out and order one right away. You don't let it worry you that the medical school already has one. You don't worry about spending $750,000 for it. Instead, you worry about important things ilke saving money on workers' wages—not about three-quarters of a million."

"That's plain stupid, Jax, and you're not a bit stupid, so don't play games," March answered. "The cost of the CAT scanner is a capital expense. Comparing direct operating costs of the laundry with purchase price of the scanner is apples and oranges."

"If you want to talk about the capital expenses of buying the new equipment we would need if we intended to keep the laundry open, I can give you the figures on that," Beulah Porter said to Jax.

Armstrong looked at Beulah Porter and recalled a strange aspect of this discussion. It was a memory of when he was five years old. His grandmother was a laundress for several of the Sealawns' households, and Jax remembered trudging the area with her the year before she died. He thought that Mrs. Porter had been one of her customers but he couldn't remember for sure. "It's irrelevant, Mrs. Porter. You can marshal all the statistics you want, but the issue remains. You're not denying, though, that the medical school has a CAT scanner?" Armstrong turned to Whitesides. "In the future, the HSA—that's Health Systems Agency, Mr. Administrator—will prevent you from buying every toy you want. You won't be able to waste money duplicating facilities that neighboring hospitals or the medical school already has. You won't—"

"The medical school is *twenty-five* miles away, don't you know that?" Whitesides' interruption was almost a shout. "This community," he continued, "is growing, don't you know that? This is a voluntary, a *community* hospital, don't you know that? You can't kid me, Armstrong. The big issue here is hospital survival, and we all know it. Who's kidding whom? We can't afford the laundry"—Whitesides' voice was getting angrier—"but we can't afford *not* to have the best equipment for this community. You people are talking about a strike. Who do you think owns Pacific Hospital? I'm not asking you who paid to have it built or enlarged, because over seventy percent of the construction money was privately raised or donated, but who owns this hospital?"

March placed a restraining hand on Whitesides' shoulder. "Take it easy, Lester."

"Well, goddammit," Whitesides shouted at Armstrong and

O'Brien. "who owns Pacific Hospital? Don't you experts know?"

"How the hell do I know?" O'Brien answered angrily. "Probably Mrs. Porter and the rest of your rich board of directors."

"The community owns this hospital!" Whitesides screamed. "You're part of this community, and so are your families."

Beulah Porter had become alarmed as she watched Whitesides. His face was scarlet.

"Take it easy, Lester," March said again. "You'll end up lying next to Neely."

Whitesides looked at March and nodded. "I'm sorry," he mumbled. "I need a slight break. I'll go down and see how Tom Neely is getting along."

After Whitesides had left, Armstrong addressed himself to Beulah Porter. "The concept that Administration doesn't seem to understand, Mrs. Porter, is that the hospital is like a family, and you don't deal with family in terms of dollars and cents alone. There are obligations for devotion and loyalty. I don't know many things that should be more intimate than the way a hospital looks after its sick patients. Care has become impersonal enough, but when you begin to subcontract out, you lose part of your hospital family."

"Who's guaranteeing that if the laundry is subcontracted out, that Janitorial and Dietary won't be next?" O'Brien added.

Armstrong glared at O'Brien. "The laundry should not and will not be subcontracted out, Frank. That is the point I was trying to make," he said.

"But, Jax," March urged, "listen to what Frank is saying. He's worried. All right, forget the laundry for a minute. We can guarantee you that the hospital has no plans to subcontract out any other divisions of your union. We'll even put it in the contract so you're legally protected for three years. And we'll relocate every single laundry worker. Every last one." He opened the folder from Personnel. "Now, here's how the retraining program will work."

Anne Simpson saw Sheri grimace, and placed her hand on Sheri's abdomen. She felt it contract, the muscles tightening beneath her hand. "That was another strong one, Sheri. If

152

your cervix is listening to the rest of your uterus, we're in business. Let's see."

Once again, as she had done so many times during the day, she examined Sheri Johnson. This time she smiled with relief. "You're doing it, Sheri. Your cervix is dilated to nine centimeters. Time to move you up to labor and delivery. Are you ready too, Herbert?"

"Yes, doctor," he said. "I knew things were going to be all right. Sheri has been having one hard contraction after another." Despite his nervousness, he suddenly clapped his hands with excitement. "It's coming now," he said. "Our baby is on its way."

"That's true, Herbert," Anne replied, "but there's some work to do first. I'll be right back." She left the room and returned a few minutes later, followed by an orderly who pushed a gurney into the room. "This is Noel," Simpson said to the Johnsons. "He loves to push pregnant women around."

"Oh, stop it, Dr. Simpson," the orderly, a jolly, epicene man replied as he helped Sheri onto the gurney. "We won't pay any attention to her at all, will we?" he asked the Johnsons. "We'll just have us a nice ride to the elevator." He spoke to Sheri as he pushed the gurney toward the elevator. "Is this your first?"

Sheri grimaced from another contraction, and when it subsided, she nodded. "I can always tell," Noel announced with satisfaction. "After a few times, the ladies all get that 'here-goes-again' look. Real bored like. You don't have that look at all, Mrs. Johnson."

"My wife's ready," Herbert said as he walked beside the gurney. "We're both just ready."

They reached Number Seven elevator and Noel pushed the button. He looked at the indicator showing the elevator was still on the main floor. "Isn't that a bitch?" he said. "This elevator is supposed to be for emergency use, and some silly ass has it tied up in . . ." He watched as the indicator hand began to move. "Here it comes now, Mrs. Johnson," he said, no longer petulant. The elevator stopped and the doors opened. Noel reached inside and pushed the gurney into the elevator so that Sheri's head was toward the back. Herbert stood to her left next to the IV pitocin drip, which was running slowly.

"One lady with a baby coming up," announced Noel as he released the stop button and pressed Four. Just as the doors were closing, he remembered the chart. "Oh, my God!" he exclaimed, grabbing the doors and holding them. "Mr. Johnson," he said, "hold onto these for a second. I've got to get your wife's chart at the station." Noel ran toward the nurses' station as Herbert held the doors open. Sheri, very jumpy, looked at her watch. It was almost 7:05 P.M. She suddenly realized that the way things were going, today would be her child's birthday. While she was thinking this, she began to have another strong contraction. Her hands tightened against the sides of the gurney, and she let out an involuntary cry. Herbert quickly turned, letting go of the elevator doors. His wife obviously was in pain. "Are you all right, honey?" he asked, gently wiping the perspiration from her forehead. She nodded to show that the contraction was lessening. Just at that moment, the elevator doors closed and the elevator started to climb. Inside it were three persons. Sheri Johnson, her baby, and her husband.

Liz Scripps looked distracted as she headed for an inspection of the ICU. She felt confused about everything, and about her life in particular. Damn that Sigmund Freud, she thought. He was probably right. She had fallen in love with her father. Sam March of the fair face, Sam March of the uncompromising honesty, Sam March of the contented state, was a younger edition of Marcus Scripps; and all of that would have been fine if her blue-eyed wonder were not married and unavailable. The situation she found herself in was ludicrous, but she could not manage even a sardonic smile; she hurt too much. Sam had described his marital setup as "bad" before he kissed her, but he had a naiveté about women, she surmised. That bitch Karen, she felt certain, would contrive to remedy whatever had seemed to Sam to have gone wrong. She would manage to patch things up, and Sam would not be the wiser. He would not recognize the rottenness underneath; Karen's skillful surface patch would be all that he would see. Liz sighed. If Sam's marriage was giving him a temporary rash, she had no intention of being the salve. But suppose that something were really wrong, suppose that there were unpatchable things about which she could have no knowledge but which nevertheless had started an inexorable crumbling process? . . . Impossible, she concluded. Karen was too clever to ever let a husband like Sam March escape. And why did she, Liz—her mind uttered a not-uncommon plaint—why did she have to fall in love with a man who wasn't available? Why had she found unappealing those men in her life who had been both serious about her and free to marry her? The answer to that, she supposed, returned her to Sigmund. They did not fit the image of the man she wanted, and life was too short to attempt to compromise unyielding feelings, feelings that were well-developed before she had graduated from high school.

She had been born and raised in the Sunset district of San Francisco. She had always wanted to become a nurse, as far back as she could remember, and in some way, she thought that this desire was related to her mother. It was not that her mother required nursing care; no, her mother, though confined to a wheelchair because of childhood polio, was the most independent of women. But seeing her mother make a life for herself and her family must have made her wonder about other disabled people who were dependent on a great deal of outside support to survive. What would happen to them if no one cared? Perhaps it was as simple as that explanation, or perhaps it was something far more complex—she could not be certain. But she did remember that even in elementary school she had wanted to know all about sickness and she had wanted to help sick people wherever she could. Her father, a practicing idealist, encouraged her, and after a year of college she had decided to enter the nursing program at that part of the university closest to Thornton. She could accomplish two things by the move: get her RN along with her BS degree and establish a certain distance between herself and her folks, a geographic distance which was not too far but which was sufficient to allow her to test her wings. Her parents concurred in this decision.

She had been apprehensive when she had first started nursing school. Perhaps, she feared, she would not find the profession as much to her liking as she had anticipated it would be. But she need not have worried. She loved the academic part of her schooling and she enjoyed even more the clinical experience at University Hospital and at Pacific Hospital in

Thornton. Excelling in her studies, she also was popular with the other students and she was elected president of her class in her senior year. After graduation she went to work on the floors of University Hospital. Within a year she was a charge nurse on Pediatrics, and six months later she joined the nursing-school faculty, advancing to the position of assistant director of education. When the job of director of nursing at Pacific became available, she was chosen from many applicants because of the superb letter of recommendation she received from the university. At Pacific there were some ruffled feelings at first among some of the nurses who had taught her during her student-training days. Although a firm administrator, she nonetheless was gentle in the way she assumed authority, and the fears of those other nurses were soon allayed. She was a pleasure to be around and was neither wishy-washy nor condescending in the performance of her administrative duties. Within a few months of her arrival she had the complete loyalty of the nursing staff.

Her life at Pacific had been a full and uncomplicated one until a few hours ago. Why did one lousy kiss have to upset her ordered world? she wondered as she walked down the half-darkened corridor. Sam March, she said to herself, why did I have to fall in love with *you*?

Everything was quiet in Operating Room One, the only other OR in service this evening at Pacific Hospital, other than the one Lusk was using. Dr. Madden Chase, the chief of surgery, was not humming the way he usually did. A thin man with graying temples, his face obscured by the surgical mask, Chase looked anonymous, another look-alike surgeon garbed in the green uniform of the surgical team. His presence, however, was unique. The chief was a leader in the operating room. Deft, forceful, brilliant, he was the consummate artist and technician. Surgical residents and interns vied for the chance to scrub with him. Every operation under his tutelage was a learning experience. But now Chase was not gently ribbing the surgical resident for a slight gaffe the latter had committed yesterday. Instead he stared at the large operating-room light with its bright beam converging on the operative site, Karl Morley's abdomen. The patient himself lay quietly. All of the others in the room also seemed concerned with the light, but the two operating-room nurses continued to fuss with their respective territories. The scene here was similar to the ophthalmology OR; the scrub nurse busied herself with the instruments, rearranging one of them from time to time. The other nurse retested the electrical coagulator, the Bovie unit, and then walked around the room adjusting the suction outlet. Twice she left the room on some errand related to the imminent surgical procedure. The resident, standing on the opposite side of the table wearing mask, green cap and gown, and surgical gloves, appeared like a mirror image of his chief, and as if to emphasize the effect, he too stared fixedly at the light. The anesthesiologist sat on a stool behind Morley's head, and from time to time he took the patient's pulse and blood pressure and wrote them on the chart he used to keep a running record of the operation. Altogether, there was an uneasy mood of expectancy. The lights had briefly gone out and come back on again, but until a short while ago their intensity had varied every few seconds. Chase had delayed the onset of the operation, hoping things would stabilize.

Now the light was steady, and as if by signal, the operating room became absolutely quiet. Chase nodded to the anesthesiologist. Pentothal induction was started through an IV, an endotracheal tube was inserted, and a drug to relax the muscles of the abdomen was given. Two minutes later the anesthesiologist signaled the start of the operation with the announcement: "He's ready."

Karl Morley lay on the table asleep and Madden Chase worked as quickly as he could. Despite the transfusion in progress, Morley's blood pressure had started to drop and his pulse had become rapid. While some of these changes were secondary to the anesthesia, Chase knew that internal bleeding was chiefly responsible. He glanced at the X-ray viewing box at the far end of the operating room. Two views of Morley's abdomen were held in place by clips, but the films gave no clue to the probable site of bleeding. They were both negative. Chase had cut through the skin, using a left rectus incision, and now he cut deeper toward the peritoneum, the thin covering of the abdominal cavity. With each knife movement, small severed vessels bled, and Chase and his assistant immediately stopped the flow of blood. They used either the Bovie unit, which congealed the cut ends of the vessels by literally frying them, or else they clamped and tied them. Chase felt tyrannized by the pale color of the blood, and with a sense of increased urgency he exposed the glistening peritoneum. He glanced at the wall clock—7:02 P.M. Only five minutes had elapsed since the start of the operation, but it seemed like hours. Chase etched his knife across the normally white layer of peritoneum beneath which was the abdominal cavity and all the abdominal organs. Now, however, the peritoneum looked blue because of the intra-abdominal bleeding. This was the critical moment, the culmination of the exploratory phase of the operation. As Chase cut, blood gushed out of the incision and was suctioned out. If the spleen was the lacerated organ, at least it was bleeding slowly, because after the suctioning, there was only slight oozing from the area.

Chase separated the cut edges of the peritoneum by placing a large flat holding instrument, a retractor, in the incision. As the resident pulled on that instrument, Chase put his hand in the abdominal cavity and began to palpate the various organs, looking for the one that was bleeding.

As the man inched his way along the rear catwalk, he realized that his plan faced two obstacles, and both of them were serious. In the first place, Wray might not come back to the boiler area. Then, even if he did, he might lock the door to the generator room behind him. This would waste valuable time. Clouding everything was a third barrier the man did not want to admit even to himself—the possibility that the area blackout itself might end too soon. He simply assumed that PG and E would not be able to find and fix the trouble right away—that he would be allowed sufficient time to inflict major damage.

He moved as silently as he could, even though the machinery noises would have drowned out the sounds of any misstep he made. Now he had almost completed the back circuit to the boilers, and as he neared the site for the new addition, he noticed the water running under the plastic visquine. He gripped the foot-and-a-half-long iron pipe as he moved. At last he reached his destination and carefully climbed over the catwalk railing, crouching in the semidark.

The light was not sufficient for him to see the time, and he struck a match—7:01. "CAN YOU DRAW?" the cover asked. I can do better than that, he answered. Wray was due here now. The man was apprehensive; no alternate plan was likely to succeed as this one was. His anger began to rise again. Was even this final blow against tyranny to be denied him? Then he heard noises, and he held his breath. They were footsteps, and they were getting louder. He crouched lower, trying to hide himself almost completely, with only his eyes and the top of his scalp above the catwalk. He felt relieved as he recognized Wray approaching. Obstacle number one removed. Things beginning to go his way.

The engineer walked quickly. The fail-safe system had shut down the boiler on the line, and before Wray could relight it, he would have to check to make sure the boiler firebox was purged of trapped gas; otherwise an explosion would occur. He walked back and forth past the end of the huge boiler, so close that the man could feel the breeze. Finally Wray stopped. The man knew immediately what Wray would do, and he was ready. As Wray bent over and peered through the boiler peephole to double-check, the man, grasping the catwalk railing with his left hand, sprang forward, wielding the pipe with his right hand. Wray felt his head exploding. Time turned into slow motion. Slowly, oh so slowly, he was turned by some force, helpless in the periphery of some mysterious vortex. Slowly, oh so slowly, he felt the painless impact of the left side of his chest against the catwalk railing, and clearly and oh so distinctly he heard some ribs cracking, and he assumed they were his own. And slowly he drifted toward the metal deck, impacting, softly he thought, against the ribbed, unyielding surface. Then time stopped moving for Wray and he lost consciousness. He rolled over once, and as he did so, the metal ball-point pen in his left shirt pocket plunged vertically into his chest.

The man waited for an instant, making certain that Wray would not move. He held the iron pipe aloft, ready to strike again, but it was not necessary. He looked at the motionless Wray and felt a momentary sadness. He wished it had not been necessary to use violence against this engineer he liked. He saw the trickle of blood coming from the back of the engineer's head, blood resulting from his own direct blow. In a moment of tenderness he reached in his pocket for his handkerchief and dabbed the wound, hoping that it was not serious. But there was no time to spare.

He pulled himself over the railing and walked steadily toward the generator room, retracing Wray's steps. He listened and watched as he moved, making certain that his presence was not detected. Relieved now that he knew he was alone, he mounted the steps to the generator room. The door was ajar. He would not have to search the unconscious Wray for the key. He had not miscalculated. Forget obstacle number two. It had just canceled itself out.

Now he was inside the generator room. He grabbed a chair and placed it alongside the diesel motor, just behind the generator. He stood up and looked at the governor. Then he began to swing the pipe against the governor linkage. As the fourth blow landed on the mangled linkage, the diesel engine raced in overspeed and the emergency power shut off. It was 7:05 P.M. Pacific Hospital was in complete darkness, and the silent power plant echoed with Lester Whitesides' heavy breathing. The union had been planning to slowly strangle Pacific Hospital. Now Armstrong and O'Brien would receive full credit for this quick murder.

Argument in the boardroom stopped as the lights suddenly went out. The flickering reflection of the candles played on the four anxious faces, but only March knew the full implication of the blackout. He picked up the phone and told Mabel to ring the generator room—he wanted Wray now! March listened as ring after ring went unanswered.

"What the hell is happening?" O'Brien asked March, but the latter, listening for Wray, remained silent.

"I'm going down," March announced, grabbing a flashlight. "The son of a bitch doesn't answer." He pointed to O'Brien and Armstrong. "You two come along in case I need help."

The fallout from the power failure had already begun, he knew, but he had no time to contemplate the effects. He cursed the elevated location of the boardroom as they maneuvered the five flights. They all could feel the silence as deadly as the blackness. The generator-room door was open, and March called out for Wray, but there was no answer. They entered the room and March quickly shone the beam around.

Nothing wrong here! A chair was neatly in place against the opposite wall, the diesel engine and generator were intact, the distribution panel seemed untouched. He had the feeling of being on some ghostly ship, alone with an unfathomable mystery. Instantly he thought of trying to start the engine, but checked his impulse. Wray would have done that. There was some reason not to touch the engine for the emergency generator. He had better first locate Wray and get an explanation, but fast. His mind was racing now. He reconsidered. Screw the explanation! What did he have to lose anyway? The starter switch for the diesel engine was in the "auto" position. March turned the switch past the "off" setting to "manual start" and prayed. The unit started, picked up the emergency electrical load, and then kicked out in overspeed. March now knew that there must be a problem with the governor. Then he remembered something else and felt a wave of nausea with the recall: a few weeks ago, Wray reminded him that it was time to replace the batteries used to start the diesel engine. They had been in service three years. Was this the opening round of Murphy's Law? he asked himself. If anything could possibly go wrong, would it? His mind, disciplined to priorities, considered what should be done if the engine failed to start on the next attempt. He wondered how long it would be until area power was restored by PG and E. March thought about calling the utility company, but decided to hold off until he talked with Wray. He pointed his flashlight at the starter switch and told O'Brien to get ready. Then he moved to the manual speed-control handle of the diesel engine. "Okay, Frank, do it."

As O'Brien pushed the switch, March held his breath. RRR RRR RRR. The three men in the generator room knew what the sound meant. Every one of them owned a car. Something clicked in March's mind and lightened it for an instant, but the thought was preempted by another, a terrible possibility: Wray had relighted the boiler too soon, March speculated. With the blackout, the fail-safe system had operated to shut off the boiler, but Wray had not sufficiently purged it. March could visualize flames and gas shooting out of the fire register as if propelled by a gun. "I know where Wray is!" he announced. "Follow me." He walked down the half-flight, and when he reached the catwalk, he stepped into water, ankle-high. "Damn Swanson," he cursed. The excavation site had filled with rain, he realized, and it was spilling into the basement. He had his answer about Murphy's Law.

He sloshed ahead, leading the others, and as he approached the boiler, he saw Wray's inert form. He shone the light on the engineer, who was semiconscious and moaning. The back of his head was bleeding, but at least he was alive.

There was no sign of any explosion. No apparent damage to the boiler, not even any soot on the outside. He turned his light 180 degrees and saw the water pouring in under the visquine covering the addition site. He reached for the wall phone. "Mabel. This is Sam March. Get two security guards down to the basement. It's an emergency! Send them to the generator room." He hung up. "Let's go. We're wasting time."

Back at the drier level of the generator room, March asked Armstrong to wait outside and to direct the guards to the boiler area and tell them to get Wray to the ER when they arrived. He dialed Mabel again. After she told him that the security guards were on the way, he asked her to ring the fire department.

"Engine Company Six. Kamler speaking."

"This is March. I'm assistant administrator here at Pacific Hospital and we have an emergency." March heard Armstrong's voice directing the guards, who had arrived. "We've got a flood in the power plant. We knocked out a wall for an addition to the boiler area, and water is pouring in. Our auxiliary power is out, so the sump pumps aren't working. The water level is rising, and if it reaches the critical elements of the boiler, the cold water could rupture it. That means evacuation. We need portable pumping equipment now. How fast can you get here?"

"The streets are a mess," Kamler said. "We'll make it as quick as we can."

As March hung up, he could hear the guards returning. He shone his light and saw the first one, a tall burly black walking with the semiconscious Wray draped over his back. The guard had Wray in a fireman's carry and was moving quickly, considering all the water.

"Can you get him to the ER by yourself?" March asked as the guard got closer.

"No problem, Mr. March."

"Good. Keep going! Anders," he shouted to the other guard. "You and Jax come up here." When they reached the generator room, March spoke to Anders, Jax, and O'Brien. "Here's the situation. First we have to slow down the water coming in, or it's good-bye hospital. We're going to have to drag down some mattresses."

Armstrong spoke up, "You have your master key? The last time I worked here, there was a small storeroom around the corner. There were a bunch of old mattresses piled up. Maybe they're still in place."

March reached for his keys and handed them to Armstrong, the master key extended. Three minutes later Armstrong returned. "The mattresses are in the storeroom," he reported. "I left the door open."

'Good. Anders, move your ass upstairs and bring down ten men as fast as you can," March directed. "Orderlies, guards, patients, anyone. Have each man pick up a mattress from the storeroom on the way here."

Anders ran down the corridor, and March explained to Armstrong and O'Brien, "The batteries for the diesel motor are dead. We need batteries, and fast. The system is thirty volts, so we can get auto batteries and hook them up in series." He handed a wrench to Armstrong. "You and Frank run outside. Lift the hoods of parked cars and take the batteries."

The two men left, and March, alone now, tried to think out the situation. Something was wrong, and he didn't know what it was. Wray probably tripped, because the alternate explanation was untenable—there was no evidence of a flareback. But he wouldn't have been heading for the boilers if the emergency power was out. What March couldn't figure out was *why* it failed. The dead batteries were stopping him from starting the emergency generator, but it was probably running when Wray left the generator room. March suddenly remembered that the lights had flickered when the area blackout first occurred. Now he had a working scenario. The governor had been temperamental for a while, he guessed. Wray had controlled it manually and had assumed it was okay. Then he went to check the boilers and slipped. After that, the governor got temperamental again and cut out in overspeed.

That was the missing factor, but a governor slightly out of adjustment could be manually controlled again. What was needed now were the batteries and the fire department. Newer cars had twelve-volt batteries, so with luck, three would be enough. Three twelves, or two twelves and a six.

March shone his light and noted apprehensively that the water level had risen to a new high. He realized that if the fire department didn't arrive within fifteen minutes, it would be too late. Turning back to the diesel, he thought for a moment of starting it with compressed air or a portable gasoline engine. That would take too long, and he had no choice but to wait for the auto batteries. He shone the flashlight beam on the box containing the dead heavy-duty batteries. As soon as O'Brien and Armstrong returned, they could disconnect these mothers and hook up the new ones. March decided in the meantime to inspect the governor. He hoped that whatever was wrong with it would be minor; maybe its oil level would be low. He started to pull the chair from the wall, but as he did so, he saw what appeared to be a rag on the floor. He looked at it and put it in his pocket. Then he moved the chair alongside the motor and stepped up on it. He shone his light on the governor with its coat of bright yellow paint. The beam stopped on the smashed linkage.

"Goddamned son of a bitch!" March cried out.

Lift with tiny forceps, snip with tiny scissors, lift with tiny forceps, snip. Oliver Lusk completed the final cut; Raymer's cornea was completely free of his eye and the last anchoring tissue was gone. It was at this moment, the point of no return in the operation, that the lights went out and the operating room became black.

In the ophthalmology operating room, an infrared photo would have given the impression that everybody was playing the game Freeze. Lusk's command "Nobody move!" was still reverberating off the walls. Only Raymer, asleep on the operating table, appeared to be breathing.

"Carol. Where are you?" Lusk spoke to the roving nurse.

"Here, Dr. Lusk."

"Get the battery-pack light. Call outside and tell them to stay out of this OR. Then come over here very slowly and light the field. Don't bump into me."

When Carol reached the operating table, Oliver Lusk still held the diseased cornea in the small forceps. The hand, the forceps, and the just-excised cornea were all motionless a foot or so above Raymer's head. She shone the light on the operative field.

Lusk slowly replaced the diseased circle he had just severed, placing it back in the center of the eye. "Now shine the light so that Inez can prepare a moist gauze pad." The light beam changed direction toward the scrub nurse, who took a piece of gauze moistened with saline and handed it to Lusk. He in turn placed the gauze over Raymer's eye. "This is to protect his lens and iris," Lusk explained to Cheney. "We'll just wait a few minutes until power is restored." He turned to Carol again. "Shine the light so Dr. Woo can get some data."

Woo, the anesthesiologist, reported that pulse and blood pressure remained stable. All was fine from his point of view.

A minute passed, and then two. There was no sign of power return this time. Three minutes, five minutes, Lusk made the decision to continue. He removed the protective gauze and then lifted the old cornea, placing the gauze and cornea on one of the drapes covering Raymer's chest. "Get me the donor cornea, Carol."

The nurse walked to the small table on which the donor cornea, moistened by saline, rested in a glass container. She brought it to Lusk.

After retrieving the new cornea from the container, Lusk gently eased it into place in the center of the eye. Now he began the critical last stage of the transplant. Taking a curved needle loaded with almost invisible suture material, he placed a stitch in the periphery of the cornea and brought the tiny needle back through the remaining rim of Raymer's own cornea. Skillfully he pulled until the two edges came together; then he tied a knot and snipped the suture just above the knot. He repeated the process 180 degrees from the initial stitch. Then in rapid succession he placed sutures at the other two quadrants, anchoring the graft firmly. Now he began to place the intervening stitches in, each one only a millimeter from its neighbor. When Lusk had completed three-quarters of the stitching, he worked more slowly.

"No, this one won't do," Lusk said as he pulled up on the

tiny stitch he had just completed. Using a small forceps for traction, he snipped the suture and pulled it out, discarding it. "Let's try again," he said to Inez, who passed him a new suture.

"This part of the remaining recipient cornea and adjoining sclera is terribly thin, Dr. Cheney," he explained as he completed the resuturing. "We have to be especially careful. We must avoid leakage. The blackout makes it harder, but the field is small and the light is sufficient."

Cheney had to ask the question burning inside him. "Because of all the adverse factors, the scarring and the thinness, do you think there will be a bad result, Dr. Lusk?"

Lusk kept working, apparently ignoring the question. Then, after he had placed two more sutures, he spoke quietly. "No, I think there will be a good result. This was a borderline case, but the technical aspects worked out. Tomorrow Mr. Raymer will be seeing the world again."

It had been several hours since Karen had left, and Asa Porter, lounging in a chair on his boat, was ruminating over the events of the day. He had escaped from a deeper involvement than he had expected, and his manner of handling the situation pleased him immensely. Again he remembered Karen's striking out at him when she finally realized that he had absolutely no intention of marrying her. The woman had to be slightly daft to think that he would cast himself loose from a respectable marriage to spend the rest of his days with her; she had only one thing to offer. No money, no position, no real breeding. Just a superb capacity to enjoy and give enjoyment in sex, hardly enough to justify her expectations. And yet, he couldn't blame *her*, looking at things from her point of view. She *was* entirely justified in wanting him so desperately. Her mistake, he acknowledged, was her inability to be objective, to understand that her capacities were quite limited when compared to his own. No, he couldn't blame her for lashing out in fury at him. Perhaps in time she would wish to resume their dalliance on a more realistic basis. One thing for certain, he told himself. He would set the ground rules clearly, and Karen would have to understand and accept them. He possibly could sweeten the pot a bit. He had not given Karen any presents, and for that he was remiss.

Porter stood up and stretched. He walked to the side of the cabin and pulled the curtain. It was completely dark, and the rain was still falling. He listened for a while to the raindrops splashing into puddles, and then closed the curtain and returned to the bar. He fixed himself a light Scotch and sat down again in the chair. Sipping absently at his drink, he continued to ponder. Something was disturbing him beyond the Karen incident; that scene had been merely an uncomfortable annoyance. What was it? Suddenly he felt a wave of apprehension, and then he recognized the source of his discomfort. It was Vanni's remark during the Morley consult. What was it exactly that the assured bastard had asked? 'Are you uneasy about giving your opinion without a script?' That's what Vanni had said to him. The implication was clear. Vanni was insinuating that his, Porter's, diagnostic triumph at the conference had happened because he had been present at the autopsy some six months earlier. Why, of course he had been there, he now remembered, but he had not paid that much attention to the findings. He would have gotten the correct answer even if he had not seen the post. That was something Vanni did not realize. But Vanni would learn to be more respectful. When Porter became chief of medicine, Vanni would learn to toe the line or else leave Pacific to join the staff of one of the other hospitals. That probably would prove to be the happiest solution. Force the bastard out of the place. It might take some time, but he had time.

Porter stood up again. He was becoming restless. It was that consult thing again. It was terribly important right now for him to confront Vanni—to have him mumble an apology about undue haste in deciding to rush a relatively healthy Karl Morley to the operating room. It was important that Vanni acknowledge error in failure to recognize when a patient's condition had stabilized. "Clinical hunches." That was another thing Vanni had said. Porter smiled with satisfaction. It was time to return to the city.

As the lights went out in ICU, Jacobs left Susan's bedside and headed for the other end of the unit. His decision was instantaneous: Susan, unattended, probably would not die in the next several minutes, but the young woman who had taken an overdose of sleeping pills would. By the time he had reached her, the nurses were already in action, and as always, he was impressed working with them in an emergency situation. Now the diorama was played almost silently under flashlights. They were working on the young patient, whose life depended on assisted respiration.

"You'll be able to quit that soon," Nina, the charge nurse, said to another nurse, who was giving the young woman mouth-to-mouth resuscitation. Implicitly neglected was the other respirator patient, the man who had suffered a massive stroke. His brain was electrically, irreversibly dead; and now, without oxygen, tissues which could neither think nor feel were completing the process of cessation of vegetative life. The blackout, Jacobs thought, was not without its blessings.

Jacobs helped the second nurse complete the attachment of an Aires bag to an adapter connecting to the woman's tracheotomy tube. "All set," the nurse said. Now she began to squeeze hundred-percent oxygen from the bag every few seconds. This manual pressure forced the vital gas into the girl's lungs. It was an effective stopgap measure.

"We'll spell you in about ten minutes," Nina said.

Jacobs noted the ominous silence of the ICU. With its machines stilled, the absence of familiar humming, beeping, and suctioning was almost palpable; noise was an integral part of the unit.

While one nurse was left pumping oxygen with her hands, the other two and Jacobs moved to attend to the needs of the remaining patients. "I'm afraid we got to him too late," Nina said to the intern, composing then the official story about the stroke victim. Nobody would be sorry; family would be relieved, but just the same, intentional neglect was still not legally acceptable.

In the middle of the unit, the woman who had had chest surgery that morning needed suctioning. Quickly Jacobs detached the rubber tubing from the glass suction machine and hooked up a fifty-cc syringe. Within seconds, manual suction was effectively clearing the patient's pleural cavities, giving her more breathing space.

Now Jacobs returned to Susan to maintain his uneasy vigil. He had been standing only a minute, checking vital signs, when suddenly the noises began. The sounds of Susan vomiting mobilized Jacobs.

"Nina!" he shouted at the charge nurse. "She's choking!" Together they rolled the girl on her side. Jacobs lifted the girl's head from the small pool of vomit and placed a towel under it. He and the nurse swabbed out Susan's mouth, using a damp washcloth.

Jacobs shone his flashlight on Susan's face and checked her eyeballs. "They're still soft," he said. "She looks lousy, doesn't she?"

"There's no real change, Arnie," the nurse answered. She shone her light on the IV. "She's getting insulin, salt, potassium, and bicarbonate. Keep your fingers crossed!"

She's getting insulin, Jacobs thought, but she's not getting better. He visualized the injected insulin molecules circulating through Susan's bloodstream. These molecules were supposed to act like little keys and open the body cells so that sugar could get in. But Susan wasn't recovering the way she was supposed to, and Jacobs was frightened.

They could hear people racing down the hall. The swift movements in the dark added to Jacobs' apprehensions about Susan. "I wish the damn lights would go on so the lab could function," Jacobs said. "I don't know where we are with anything. Let's see what the urine is doing." He took the tubing attached to Susan's catheter out of the collection bottle and let a few drops of urine spill onto two paper sticks used to check sugar and acetone. "They're both still four-plus," he reported. "Even with dilutions, they're not giving us much help at this level. I have to run another blood test."

Nina handed a rubber tourniquet to Jacobs, who tightened it around Susan's arm. He drew ten cc of blood into a test tube. "I'll be in the small lab if you need me. I should be back in five minutes."

He clutched the tube of blood to his chest. He didn't want it to splatter in some silly collision, and he beamed his light ahead. Inside the lab he shone his flashlight on the bottles of reagents on the shelves and pulled down the trichloroacetic-acid and the sodium-hydroxide bottles. He had run the test one-half hour earlier, and the deep orange color characteristic of very high blood sugar had appeared. This time he hoped for a deep yellow color. It would mean that although the blood sugar was still very high, it was on its way down.

Jacobs filtered the blood, letting the filtrate drip into two empty tubes. He took the first of these and carefully added the sodium hydroxide solution to it. Then he put a glass bead in the tube and placed the tube in a holder. He struck a match and turned on the gas valve to the Bunsen burner, adjusting the burner so that it gave off a blue flame. Next he held the Pyrex tube in the flame until its contents began to boil. He allowed the solution to boil for approximately a minute and then held his breath. His shone his flashlight on the tube, and his heart sank. Once again, a deep orange color was present. Jacobs had little hope that the test for acetone on the other tube would be any better. He expected that the purple ring would be just as intense as before. Why in the hell wasn't Susan responding? he wondered.

Harry Albright followed Latimer into Examination Room Three of the ER. Phil Wray, lying on the table, groaned from time to time but was more alert than he had been when he was brought up from the basement.

Albright shone his flashlight on Wray's scalp and looked at the cut in the occipital area. It was oozing slightly. "No problem here," said Albright. "A routine job for the seamstress." He talked directly to Wray. "Just a bad bump on the head. You're lucky. You really took a fall when you slipped."

Wray, still groggy, said to Albright, "Did I slip? I thought somebody hit me over the head." He tried to sit up. "Who's taking care of the basement?"

"Sam March and some others are down there," Albright answered, "but you're out of action, so don't even give it a thought." Welsh, the orthopedic technician, held a flashlight in the dark room as Albright proceeded with the examination. He felt the skull area carefully. "I don't think you've got a fracture, but we'll get some X rays later when the power goes on. The skull films aren't of any value, but we have to get them for legal reasons." Albright noted the bruises over the left chest, but it was a small circle of dried blood that alarmed him. That was where the ball-point pen had penetrated. The pen had come out while Wray was being placed on the examination table, and no one had seen how far in it had been. Albright concluded that the chest wound was not serious and continued the examination. He palpated the ribs, feeling for crepitus, the sensation felt when two ends of a fractured bone rub together. After completing the exam, he was satisfied that Wray was in good shape, considering the fall. Albright sewed up the skull laceration and left the room, leaving Latimer to apply the dressing.

The ER was quiet for the moment, and Albright sat down at a desk. He was still angry over Latimer's earlier remarks to him, and he had continued to sulk since she had made them. Relations between the two were strained. Only a few minutes had passed when Latimer approached with a flashlight.

"Dr. Albright," she said. Her voice was anxious. "You better have another look at Phil Wray. His pulse is faster."

Albright picked up his flashlight from the desk and followed her into the examining room. He shone the beam on Wray's face. It was bathed in sweat, and even in the poor light Albright saw the cyanosis, a slight bluish cast to the color of Wray's skin. The man was not getting enough oxygen. The pigment giving blood its red color, oxyhemoglobin, had been replaced by the bluish, reduced hemoglobin, and Albright sensed the reason and hoped he was wrong. He had listened to Wray's lungs a little while earlier. He listened again. The breathing was now fast and labored, but Albright could find no evidence that oxygenation was being impeded by the lungs themselves. There was no sign of pleural effusion, no sign of severe embolus, nothing primarily wrong with the lungs. He wished he had a chest X ray.

"What's the blood pressure, Latimer?"

She rapidly inflated the cuff and began to deflate it, the familiar hiss of air signaling the start of the search. "Seventy-eight over sixty! It's dropped more," she reported.

"Look at his neck veins," Albright said.

Latimer looked, and they seemed to distend before her eyes, bulging without respite.

Albright put his hand to his chin, and as he did so, his flashlight reflected the anguish on his face. He returned the beam to the tiny, blood-crusted mark on Wray's chest. Albright placed his stethoscope on the chest, listening to Wray's heart sounds at the four valve areas. It was the same everywhere. The heart sounds were faint, muffled. He reached for Wray's pulse. The pulse was rapid, thin, but every time Wray took a breath, the pulse disappeared.

"He has cardiac tamponade!" Albright announced. "Some bleeding from the heart is filling the space between the heart and the pericardium. The heart simply isn't filling well." Albright went to the wall phone and called surgery. "Is any surgeon up there?" He sounded desperate. "This is Harry Albright in the ER."

"Dr. Lusk is finishing a transplant, and Dr. Chase is working on that case you saw this morning—Karl Morley."

"How long till Dr. Chase will be finished?"

"There were some complications. I guess about twenty minutes more, at least."

"Don't let him leave the floor," Albright said. "I have an emergency here." He hung up the phone. "At least twenty minutes," he said to Latimer.

"Can you wait? I mean, can we get him to the OR now and have him ready?"

Albright shone the light on Wray's face again. The face was bluer, the veins more distended, the effort to breathe greater.

"He's going to die if I don't do something soon," Albright whispered. "But I don't want to kill him. Maybe if we wait he'll still make it."

Latimer knew he didn't believe it. "Do what you have to do," she implored. "Whatever happens, it will be the right thing. Trust yourself."

"It's been so long since . . ." Albright stopped talking. He had made his decision. "We'll tap him now. Get me a long seventeen or eighteen needle. And have someone bring in one-sixth grain of MS and some procaine. Hurry!"

Latimer was out of the room before he had finished talking. In a few seconds Welsh came in with two syringes filled with the drugs. He held his flashlight as Albright injected the morphine intramuscularly. Then Albright percussed the heart area, determining where resonance turned to dullness, where outer heart edge met lung. He swabbed the chest area with Zephiran and infiltrated procaine into the fifth intercostal space a little less than an inch inside the border of cardiac dullness. He watched Wray's labored breathing with growing apprehension. Death seemed much closer. Would it be by his own hand? He began to perspire. He put on surgical gloves and placed sterile towels over the chest area. When Latimer returned, she tore the paper wrapping off the syringe and Albright grasped the plunger end. "Got a seventeen on this?" he asked.

"An eighteen," she answered.

"No time for any rubber tubing. I'll go in directly." Albright poised the syringe, contemplating for one last second the implications of what he was about to do. He visualized the coronary arteries and prayed that the needle he began to push toward the heart would not rip into one of them. He advanced the needle slowly, and as Latimer held the light, she noticed that his hand did not shake, and she marveled at it. She herself was shivering with fright.

At two centimeters he pulled back on the plunger. Nothing. He advanced the needle. Two and a half. He pulled the plunger again. Still resistance, but nothing else. Slowly he pushed farther in. It was now well over an inch into Wray's chest. Again nothing.

Wray was breathing faster now. His mouth was open and he was gasping for air. Two minutes to live, guessed Albright. He pushed once again. He felt something give as he pushed. He hoped he had passed through the pericardium. Once more he tested aspiration. *Success!* Blood was coming back into the syringe as he pulled. Albright had a terrible thought. Had he penetrated the heart itself instead of its fibrous capsule? He kept pulling. "Give me that forceps!"

Latimer pushed a small tray toward Albright, who picked up the forceps. He clamped it at the junction of skin and exposed needle so that the forceps would prevent the syringe and needle from accidentally going deeper.

Suddenly Wray's breathing was easier. His neck veins were going down. "Marilyn, give me a BP reading."

"One-twenty over seventy." Albright could not see the tears in her eyes.

Holding the syringe and needle clamped in place with his right hand, Albright reached for Wray's wrist with his other hand. He felt the pulse, which was now full and responding properly to respiration. "No more paradoxical pulse. Okay. We'll need some help. We're going to carry Wray to the OR. Madden Chase can sew up the cardiac laceration." Albright's next remark to Latimer was tentative. "When we're through tonight, I want to buy you the best steak dinner in town at an all-night joint I know, okay?"

"No," Latimer answered. Albright was glad his disappointment didn't show in the dark. "I have a better idea," she continued. "I'm going to cook you the best steak dinner in town."

Since 6:40 P.M., when the area blackout began, Liz Scripps, flashlight in hand, had been touring the hospital. Although emergency power lighted the corridors and nursing stations, the patients' rooms were dark. She noted ambulatory patients standing at the doorways of their rooms, talking nervously to each other. Scripps told the staff to check the patients confined to bed, since they were the most apprehensive of all.

Liz already had been to Pediatrics, the neonatal ICU, the ER, CCU, and ICU. Everything in those areas was under control. During the tour, some obviously anxious patients and visitors had stopped her to ask what was going on. She had explained that there was an area blackout, which should be fixed soon, but in the meantime, the hospital was using its own emergency power; there was nothing to worry about.

She reached 3 North just as the hospital totally blacked out at 7:05 P.M. She was filled with panic as she realized that something had happened to the hospital's own power. She dialed Mabel, thankful that the telephone and paging system operated in emergencies on an independent battery system that would last for four hours. "Mabel, what's happening?"

"Phil Wray's not answering his phone. You're not the only one calling, honey. The whole board's gone crazy."

Scripps hung up and headed for 3 South. As she arrived at the dark station, a beam of light traced an irregular path toward her. Holding the flashlight was a breathless orderly. "I'm glad I found you," he said. "The elevator just went up with only the Johnsons, and now it's stuck between floors. She's having a baby!"

"Slow down, Noel," Scripps said. "Why are they alone?"

"My fault. We waited for the emergency elevator a long time. That was during the area blackout. Finally the elevator came and I pushed Four. Then I realized I'd forgotten her chart, and I told Mr. Johnson to hold the door for a second.

I guess Mrs. Johnson got a bad contraction, because her husband let go of the door. The elevator started up to Delivery, but now it's stuck."

"Who's the doctor?" Scripps asked.

"Anne Simpson," the orderly replied.

"Locate her and tell her what happened," Scripps said. "We can't do anything about the elevator until power is restored. The doors lock for fire prevention." She shone the light on the large ring of keys she was carrying, took one off, and handed it to the orderly. "After you've notified Dr. Simpson about the Johnsons, go down to the storeroom and get a box of flashlights and batteries. They're on the first shelf as you enter. Distribute them to any staff or patients who really need them."

Noel left for the delivery room, and almost immediately Scripps heard a commotion nearby. She and the charge nurse ran to the room. They shone their lights on a terrified patient, a man who pointed to his IV. "I got scared when everything just went dark," the man said. "They told me to watch it, and I was afraid that if it ran out, I would get air in my veins."

The charge nurse explained to him that nothing would have happened even if the IV bottle had emptied itself.

Scripps left the floor and continued to tour. She noted now that more people, anxious patients and visitors alike, were congregating in the black corridors, and there was more confusion than earlier. She heard the sound of glass shattering but did not stop to investigate. Instead, Scripps changed course and went down to the PBX room. Mabel and an assistant operator were busy at the board.

"I want to make an announcement, Mabel," Scripps said. She sat down at the board, put on a headset, and pressed the Page button. "May I have your attention, please. May I have your attention, please. This is Elizabeth Scripps, director of nursing. Efforts are being made to restore power to the hospital as quickly as possible. In the meantime, nurses will be checking every room regularly. All patients and visitors please return to your rooms if you are not in them now. Please return to your rooms and remain there until further notice. Thank you."

When Scripps had finished, Mabel came over and plugged in a line. "Lester Whitesides for you, honey."

"Yes, Mr. Whitesides."

"That was good thinking, Liz," the administrator said. "The announcement was a good idea. I'm here in the boardroom with Mrs. Porter, and I want you to know that the blackout may last longer than we thought it would. Sam March phoned to tell me that he's trying to fix the emergency power system. If power is not restored by eight P.M., we'll implement the Internal Disaster Plan. Mrs. Porter wonders if you want her with you?"

"Not right now, Mr. Whitesides."

"Good. We'll remain in the boardroom and use it as a command post. Call if you need help."

The anesthesiologist broke in sharply. "His pressure has just dropped to eighty over sixty, Madden. He looks lousy!" With these words, the surgeon, Chase, noted with horror the blood welling up in the abdomen and spilling over the edge of the wound. And almost simultaneously the lights in the operating room went out, leaving the room in total darkness.

"Get a light!" Madden Chase ordered. Only seconds, he thought. Only seconds before Morley goes into irreversible shock. Probabilities. The abdominal cavity is filled with blood, and this man is dying. Before the lights went out, I felt around and looked, but there was no obvious bleeding site. Some oozing, but from where? Now the blood dam has burst, but where is the hole? Probabilities. Auto accident. Vanni felt spleen, Porter didn't, I wasn't sure. BP near shock. Have to go for it now.

Chase's reflections were racing but orderly. In the pitch-black operating room, he made his decision. His left hand felt through the blood and reached upward. He squeezed as hard as he could.

"I've got the ligament and I'm close to the hilum." The hilum was the portion of the spleen where the major blood vessels entered and left. He turned toward the scrub nurse. "I'm going to need a Péan clamp. Feel around for it. Where's the light?"

One of the nurses had made her way to the far wall of the operating room, searching for a battery-pack light. Chase continued to squeeze with his left hand, hoping he was compressing the splenic artery enough to stop the flow of incoming blood, and just as important, that it was the correct organ, that it was indeed the spleen which had poured out its blood, that it was indeed the spleen that without intervention would kill Morley. Now Chase's right hand moved high against the left side of Morley's abdomen, up against the left side of the diaphragm, grasping the spleen, tearing it loose from its attachments above, delivering it upward as he used his fingers as dissecting knives. The organs were warm to the touch. He could feel the colon, he could feel the stomach, he could feel the left kidney as his hand moved. Each of those organs had left a developmental indentation in the spleen's surface. But he was not worried about *those* three organs. What concerned Chase was a different organ, the pancreas, giver of digestive enzymes and insulin. The tail of the pancreas inched up next to the spleen. Soon Chase would clamp the hilum and run the risk of squeezing the pancreas in the unrelenting grasp of the Péan forceps. Then, later, if this happened, there was the high risk of another killing complication, a subphrenic abscess. But the risk of bleeding to death was greater, and furthermore, it was immediate.

"Péan." Madden turned to the scrub nurse. He assumed that she had found the instrument in the dark, and she had. She reached out tentatively, feeling for where his hand was, placing the forceps firmly into his hand instead of the customary slapping handoff.

Now the instrument was in his right hand, and he quickly pushed it into place above his left hand, which had been squeezing the ligament connecting kidney and spleen. He closed the clamp firmly until the ratchet mechanism engaged; then he let go. Blood still filled the abdominal cavity, and the life-or-death question now was whether the blood was old, pre-clamping blood, or whether new blood was being pumped into the area from some other site. If that was the case, Morley was a dead man. Chase now could only wait and pray.

"I've got it, Dr. Chase!" The nurse had located the portable wall light and flipped the switch, advancing, beam of light in front of her, toward the operating table. She pointed the beam at the abdomen, at the pool of blood.

"Suction!" ordered Chase reflexively.

"It's out, doctor," reported the nurse. The lights had not come back on and there was no electrical power for suction.

"Let's get some ABD's and mop this stuff out." Chase, using his hands, began bailing out the blood and clots which had formed. The scrub nurse handed the surgical resident the abdominal pads, and the young assistant used them to soak up the pool of blood, which began to subside. Chase searched carefully for another source of bleeding. Aside from some oozing from the splenic bed, there was none. No artery hidden in the depths of Morley's abdominal cavity was robbing him of blood.

"Shine the light on the spleen!" Chase's order was again crisp. As the light beam played over the surface of the spleen, Chase fingered a deep laceration. "Here it is, boys." Chase's triumphant exclamation echoed throughout the OR. "This thing must have clotted, later oozed, and then when we opened him up, the clot broke loose. This was a close one."

"His pulse is about one-twenty." It was the anesthesiologist. "I need a BP right now."

All at once, everyone realized that the danger was not over. Before the lights had gone out, Morley's pressure had dropped rapidly. As Chase pushed compresses into the splenic bed to stanch residual bleeding, the nurse directed the light to the head of the table. The anesthesiologist quickly pumped up the cuff. "Seventy over fifty," he announced.

Chase continued the packing operation. "Take another reading, Bert," he said to the anesthesiologist. There was no panic in Chase's voice, although there might have been. Morley's blood pressure was at shock level.

"Seventy-two over fifty-four." It was that last-minute call announcing a reprieve, a spared life, and they all were greatful.

"All right, Bert, let's pour some blood into this man." Chase's voice was lighter, more relaxed now. "You know what?" he asked rhetorically. "We didn't nip even a little piece of pancreas. We have in this clamp"—he pointed down at the Péan —"exactly what we're supposed to have." He turned to the anesthesiologist. "You wouldn't object if I proceed with this splenectomy, would you?"

"No objection, Madden," said Bert. "Proceed at will."

Hedwig Ehrhardt shone her light on the electric wall clock—7:05. Ehrhardt quickly shifted the flashlight beam to the dialysis machines and her two charges connected to them. Zabriskie appeared to be dozing, but Diamond was awake and talkative.

"I told you, Hedwig. I told you last week and you didn't believe me," he said.

"What you told me?" the big nurse asked.

"I told you not to lose your cool, Hedwig. Don't you remember? I said, 'Hedwig, if you ever really got mad, your face could stop a clock.' Now you'll listen when Paul Diamond tells you something." He hesitated and then risked talking to Zabriskie. "Hey, Sim, she actually did it. She stopped the clock, and the whole damn power system to boot."

"What time is it, Paul?" Zabriskie asked. He had not been asleep.

"Five minutes after seven, Sim. What I'm curious about," Diamond continued in the dark, "is whether the reverse is true. If Hitler's girlfriend were to beam a Teutonic smile at the clock, would it start up again?"

"I don't know," Zabriskie answered. "Look," he continued, "I'm very tired and I want to sleep."

Diamond, confused by the rebuff, returned his attention to Nurse Ehrhardt. "Hedwig, mein darling," he called out. "There is something I have to tell you. Something important you have to know."

"Don't bother me," she answered. Then she became curious. "What you haff so important?"

"I thought you'd never ask," Diamond replied. "Come here." Ehrhardt moved toward him. "Closer, Hedwig, do you think I can tell the whole world?" She took another step forward and leaned over. Diamond whispered in her ear, "The machines have stopped running, Hedwig."

"Dumpkopf! You think I don't know that? I just gave heparin to your friend, and now I fix some for you. If lights don't come on in fife minutes, dot's alles for tonight. I want no clots in coil." She had prepared a syringe with the anticoagulant and now injected the contents into the tubing attached to Diamond's arm. Then she shone the light on her wristwatch. "You boys haff until seven-twelve for the hospital to fix itself up. At seven-twelve, no lights, no more dialysis. You boys come back tomorrow."

"Tomorrow, Hedwig!" complained Diamond. "I have plans for tomorrow."

"Too bad," Ehrhardt replied. "Tomorrow vas little Gunter to spend the night mit me. I change plans, you and the other bad boy change plans too. What's gut for the goose is gut for the gander." Ehrhardt laughed heartily, pleased with her application of the recently learned proverb.

Diamond looked at his watch, which glowed in the dark. He hoped that the power would return soon. Enough of his life centered around dialysis, and it wasn't the dinner party he would miss tomorrow night that upset him; it was the same frustration that was bothering Sim—complete dependence on dialysis.

Now Ehrhardt shone her flashlight on Diamond's machine. The blood had stopped moving, and like the clock, was in suspended animation. Ehrhardt, a thorough and orderly woman, was annoyed by the blackout. She was affronted by the stupidity of it all, and she shook her head from side to side in disapproval. It was now 7:11. One more minute of darkness and she would terminate the dialysis. She knew Diamond and Zabriskie would be disappointed, and she felt sorry for them. She did not really object to the banter of the two men of whom she was so fond.

The minute passed. "Dot's it," she announced. "I disconnect you first," she said to Diamond. As she walked toward him, she skidded and almost fell. She shone her flashlight on the floor, and they both gasped at the same time. The slippery liquid was blood, and its trail led to Simeon Zabriskie. He sat in the chair dead, his eyes open. He had disconnected the arterial connection to the machine. In the dark, he had opted for suicide by exsanguination, and he had succeeded. Diamond began to cry as Ehrhardt screamed uncontrollably.

Suddenly the elevator carrying Sheri Johnson and her husband up to the delivery room stopped and became dark. For a moment Herbert Johnson was paralyzed by confusion. He stood in his tracks, not knowing what had happened. It was Sheri's scream that startled him into a realization of their dilemma.

"We're stuck, Herbert!" she shouted. "And the baby's coming soon! Press the buttons! Get the elevator to go up!" Sheri was terrified, and so was her husband. Herbert pressed all the buttons he could feel, but nothing happened. He tried to keep his voice under control. "They know we're in here and they're fixing what's wrong right now." Herbert placed his hands flat against the elevator doors and tried, without success, to press them open. He was unable to budge them. Then he pounded on the doors with his fists and yelled, "Help! Help! Is anyone out there?" There was no answer. He took off a shoe and pounded again.

Sheri's cry rang out in the darkened elevator. "I'm having another one." Her voice, impeded by the contraction, echoed her panic and discomfort. Herbert made his way to her side and held her hand tightly during the contraction.

"I'm scared," Sheri said after her uterus relaxed. "They're coming faster now. You've got to do something. Please do something!"

Herbert went to the front of the elevator and again hit the doors while shouting for help. This time there was an answering pounding from above. Herbert was overjoyed. He knew now that rescue would be only a matter of minutes. "They're out there, Sheri," he shouted at his wife. "They're right out side." He yelled, "Can you hear me? Can you hear me out there?"

The answering voice was faint. Herbert could not make out what the man was saying. A telephone inside the elevator began to ring. He moved quickly toward the sound. His hand felt something cold, and his fingers explored the edge of a small stainless-steel door until they reached an inset latch. He pulled up on the latch, restraining his impulse to rip the door off. He pulled out the phone and cried, "Hello, hello."

"Herbert, listen to me! This is Anne Simpson."

Inside the black elevator, the sound of Simpson's voice provided tremendous relief. "Thank God! What do we do now?"

"Listen carefully. This is important. I want you to pull out the IV. The needle is in Sheri's left arm. Feel for the needle and pull it out. Then come back to the phone." The IV containing pitocin was working too well.

"Don't, Herbert! You'll kill me," Sheri said, but Herbert assured her that he was doing exactly what Dr. Simpson told him to.

"It's out, doctor," he reported into the phone.

"Listen. The baby might come before they can get the doors open. If that happens, you just follow my instructions. Now, have Sheri draw up her legs."

"She has them up already." He stopped talking. When he resumed, it was almost a plea. "You mean they won't get here in time?" he asked.

"Are the contractions lessening?" Anne hoped that with the IV out, labor would slow down, but she heard a loud cry over the phone.

"She's having another one!" Herbert was shouting. "This one is stronger. They're getting stronger, doctor. What can I do?"

"You're doing everything you should. Keep reporting to me." Anne held the phone tight against her ear, hoping for a word from Herbert which would indicate that labor had finally slowed up. Time was what was needed. But only seconds later she heard a terrible scream from the elevator. "Herbert, what's happening?" she asked. There was no response, but Anne could tell from the cries she heard that the phone was not dead. At last Herbert returned.

"Dr. Simpson, she's having a lot of pain," he whispered into the phone. "We don't have any medicine for pain." He waited desperately for some advice that would help Sheri. He had been alternating between the phone and the side of the gurney, and he didn't know where he was needed most. He realized that Sheri might lose the baby, and worse—he didn't want to think about that possibility—Sheri's life itself was in jeopardy. As he considered the implications of what just had occurred to him, he knew with certainty that if he was going to be able to help his wife, he would have to control his own fears.

"Have Sheri stop screaming," Anne said. "She's going to have to work with you. Remember the exercises? Have her concentrate on her breathing." Anne experienced her own anxiety. Trapped in the elevator was a primipara close to forty years old without access to any help. If there were to be a complication . . .

Suddenly Sheri screamed, and Herbert went to her. "I have to push!" she yelled. "It's coming now!" Her bag of waters broke, and the amniotic fluid splashed over the gurney and dripped onto the floor of the elevator.

Herbert rushed to the phone and shouted, "The water broke! I can feel the baby's head!"

Anne could hear grunting sounds. "Herbert, you're going to have to deliver your wife yourself," she said. "Stay at the foot of the gurney. Just talk loudly, and I will too. You'll be able to hear me. Drop the phone and listen." She waited. "Can you hear me?"

"Yes. I can feel the head pushing out, and then it seems to slide back a little. Water comes out each time. What should I do?"

"Just go slowly, Herbert. It's normal for the baby to slide back a little after each contraction, and also for fluid to come out. Don't force anything."

She could hear Herbert ordering his wife to pay attention to him: "Sheri, you have to be quiet. I can't hear Dr. Simpson. You have to help me." Now he yelled at the phone: "The head is halfway out!"

"Is the baby faceup or facedown?"

There was a brief pause. "Facedown. I can feel hair on top."

"Good. Have Sheri bear down, and tell me when the head has crowned—I mean, when the head is farther out."

"What is Dr. Simpson saying?" Sheri groaned.

"It's farther out now!" Herbert said to Anne. "She says to bear down," he told Sheri.

"There's nothing else I can do. I have to bear down," Sheri answered. "Can you put your hands on either side of the head yet?" Anne asked. "Can you feel the baby's neck?"

"Yes. I have the head in my hands now. Everything's slippery."

"Herbert. This is important! Be very gentle! Don't do any forcing."

"I won't."

"All right. Pull down very slowly and very gently on the baby's head. Gently! Try it and see if you can feel a shoulder."

"I can feel a shoulder. I pulled gently. The baby's head is facing sideways now. Is that all right?"

"That's normal. You're doing fine. Now, take the head between your hands again and pull up. Very gently!"

"I'm doing it!"

"Soon you should feel the other shoulder."

"I can feel it! I can feel both shoulders now!" Herbert sounded less frightened.

"Good! The tough part is over. Now the baby will almost slide out after a contraction. Just pull very gently."

Anne heard a loud grunt followed by a long pause. Then she heard the cries of a newborn mixed with excited cries from both Herbert and Sheri. "The baby is out," Herbert shouted. "What do I do now?"

"Put the baby on Sheri's stomach. Have her hold it."

A few seconds later Anne heard the new mother exclaim: "Herbert, you're wonderful. I love you. You're wonderful," and she heard Herbert reply: "You're the wonderful one, Sheri. You gave us our baby."

Anne's telephone voice came into the joyous elevator. "Herbert. The baby's cord attaches to the afterbirth. Has the afterbirth come out yet?"

There was a pause until Herbert finally said, "It's all out! What next?"

"Just stay close and help Sheri hold the baby. Don't worry about cutting the cord. We'll do that later. Check Sheri and the baby and tell me how they are."

"They seem fine." Herbert's voice was relaxed for the first time. "Sheri and our baby girl are just great. . . . I felt to make sure." He sounded embarrassed.

"That's fine. How are *you* doing?" Anne finally was able to relax.

The feeble protests of a newborn continued to echo through the elevator. Herbert reported again. "I think Sheri is bleeding a little. Is that okay?"

"That's normal. Remember, we never got a chance to do the episiotomy, and Sherri probably has a slight tear. You don't have to do anything else. Just be a proud father."

In the dark CCU, Leo Vanni was the only physician present. He had been in the unit for the past hour, during which time the medical resident had been called away. The intern, Arnie Jacobs, was tied up in ICU with Susan Royal.

Vanni had just completed a brief examination of his patient Tom Neely. With severe heart attacks, things had to get worse before they got better, and things *were* getting worse. Neely's blood pressure had dropped further and this, combined with newly developed chest pain, had put a sheen of cold perspiration on Neely's face. Part of his heart was infarcting, dying now, and would continue to do so for over a week if he survived. Then the healing process could begin and the dead heart muscle would begin to contract, until only a thin linear scar remained as evidence of the damage suffered. But there was an additional complication. From time to time, Neely's heart would "skip" a beat; actually this represented an extra beat, but the exact nature of these extra beats could not be determined, sinc the EKG machines were not working.

Vanni, standing outside of Neely's cubicle, shone his light at a wooden box mounted on wheels. Attached to it were two large circular metal electrodes. The machine, a defibrillator, was as useless now as the darkened oscilloscopes of the EKG attachments. The newer defibrillators had capacitors, stored charges not dependent on outside electricity, but none of the hospitals of Thornton had a new machine. It had seemed impossible that both outside power and emergency hospital power could fail at the same time, but this had happened, and Vanni unxiously awaited the return of either source; if Neely's occasional arrhythmic heartbeats should come more frequently and become suddenly the killer arrhythmia, ventricular fibrillation . . . But no use dwelling on that. Neely was getting lidocaine in an IV drip, and hopefully this local anesthetic medication would reduce the heart's irritability, would prevent Neely from developing anything more serious than the occasional premature contractions, the extra beats he now was having.

Looking around the CCU, illuminated only by the flashlights of Cathy, the charge nurse, and her assistant, Vanni was reminded of his internship days. Then, nobody knew about monitoring systems, and defibrillators were primitive, just coming into use. But even during those early years, Vanni had never been without an EKG machine to feed him information. He glanced at the desk and watched the nurses at work. They were filling the last of four large syringes with bicarbonate solution. Smaller syringes with small amounts of pharmacological TNT, adrenaline, lay side by side on the desk, and several tourniquets cut from strips of condomlike rubber tubing rested in a row alongside the syringes. These were preparations for cardiac arrest, specifically for Neely. The other two CCU patients were in no immediate danger, and an RN was checking them.

Vanni moved back into the room, and Neely turned his head. "That you, Leo?" he asked weakly.

Vanni propped his flashlight on a bedside table so that it shone on the patient's chest. "Yes, Tom. Until this blackout is over, I'm going to bother you a lot. I'm just going to be a human monitoring machine, and I don't depend on electrical power." Vanni checked Neely's blood pressure and found it lower. "How's the chest pain, Tom?" Vanni asked.

"It's better now. Seems to be letting up. That shot must be working."

Vanni palpated Neely's wrist, the radial reflection of the center of life itself, the heart. There were still extra beats. Vanni knew that the low blood pressure was the result of heart-muscle damage. Neely's heart was acting less like a pump and more like a flappy bag. Vanni placed his stethoscope on Neely's chest and listened carefully. *TIC-TAC. TIC-TAC.* The weak but healthier *LUB-DUP* had been replaced by more fragile sounds. *TIC-TAC. TIC-TAC. TIC-TAC.* Another extra beat, probably from the ventricle, *TICTACTIC-TACTICTACTICTACTICTAC*, but Vanni had no way of knowing. *TIC-TAC. TIC-TAC.* "Ventricular tachycardia!" Vanni called out to Cathy. Neely's pulse had jumped to 180.

Cathy was now inside the cubicle with a syringe filled with lidocaine. "I thought the drip would hold him," she said, handing the syringe to Vanni.

"Your heart is beating faster than I want it to, Tom," Vanni said. "I'm going to play it safe and give you some more medicine." Vanni continued to work as he talked. He injected the bolus of lidocaine directly into the IV tubing and then took Neely's pulse again. He counted fifteen beats in five seconds. The rate was still 180.

Suddenly Neely stopped breathing. There was no pulse. *"Arrest!"* Vanni shouted, and the assistant nurse phoned the switchboard. Within seconds the words "Code Blue: CCU" echoed throughout the hospital, summoning house-staff help. Vanni ripped off the monitoring chest electrode and the tubes in Neely's nose. He placed the heel of one hand on Neely's chest and pushed rhythmically on it with the other hand. His hands were doing the work that Neely's own heart was unable to do, propelling blood around the body. After each fifteen compressions, Cathy placed her mouth against Neely's and blew into his lungs twice in rapid succession. This action inflated them, and hopefully oxygen would pass from Neely's lungs into his circulation.

House staff using flashlights began to arrive, and everyone was working at once. Tourniquets were applied to Neely's arms and legs, and adrenaline and bicarbonate were injected. Occasionally, resuscitation efforts would stop for brief seconds to see if Neely's own heart was responding. Even as he kept pressing against Neely's chest, Vanni knew that the federal mediator had no chance. Everybody kept trying, but it was all over.

March had the eight men lined up. There had never been a platoon quite like this. Two security guards, four orderlies, one janitor, and one patient wearing a pair of pants under his hospital gown. Each of the men held tightly to a mattress. Eight men, eight mattresses. Not bad, March thought as he played his flashlight across the line.

"Here's the problem," he announced. "Water is coming in from over there." He shone his light on the visquine covering the space where the wall had been jackhammered out. "The fire department is on the way to do some pumping, but we have to slow down the water entry with these mattresses," March explained.

He led the group toward the wall. Water was coming into the basement rapidly, and the storm was not letting up. A purple flash of lightning showed through the plastic sheeting.

"Lay them this way," March shouted. He took one mattress and placed it flat on the ground, cursing Swanson, the missing wall, and the excavation site all the while. When the eight mattresses were in place, the water flow stopped almost completely, although March could see trickles between the mattresses. He wondered how long it would be until the water soaked through, but hoped that the pumping unit would arrive in time. He decided to let well enough alone. "All right. Go to the lobby and wait. If I need you for anything else, I'll call."

As the men headed out the door, March started to return to the generator room. He stopped in front of the boiler. The steam drums, the tubes, the headers, the refractory itself—a crack anywhere, and the ball game was over. Evacuation of a hospital in daylight with the sun shining was risky, but under these circumstances, March knew it would be disastrous. He turned from the boiler and continued his trek to the generator room.

Once there, March moved to the wall phone. "Mabel. Get me Dusty Rhodes at Rhodes Tractor Company. Call their night number and tell them it's an emergency and I have to speak to him. Get him fast and call me back." He paced back and forth. A minute later the phone rang. "Dusty, Sam March. We have real trouble at the hospital. Power is out. We need a new governor. You know our unit. Are you at home?"

"No." The voice at the other end sounded troubled. "I'm working late at the plant. But we don't have any governor units packaged, Sam."

"You have a new diesel with the governor attached, don't you?"

"Yes. But that's a brand-new unit."

"Dusty. Break it down and hold the governor in your lap. I'm sending an ambulance to come down and get you. I want you to install it."

"It's a new unit. It's going to be expensive."

"Don't worry about the expense. We'll take care of it. Now, for Christ's sake, Dusty, get on it!"

As March completed a call to the ER, dispatching an ambulance, he heard noises. He shone his flashlight ahead and saw two firemen. They were carrying a portable pumping unit. He called to them to follow him, and they moved back toward the boiler area. "How soon can you start?" March asked. He shone his light on the basement floor. The mattresses had helped, but the water level was still rising. He sloshed around to the other side of the boiler and looked. About two inches to go. Two more inches until the cold water reached the steam-drum level. Two more inches until metal fracture, and then . . .

"We're practically set." The fireman continued to work. He and his partner had already connected the hose which would pump the water to the outside sewers. The first fireman started the gas-driven pumping unit. At last water was being pumped out of the basement.

"That's a good sound," March commented. He returned to the other side of the boiler, to the side where water from the excavation site continued to pour in. The mattresses, March noticed now, were saturated and no longer stemmed the flow from the outside. He was glad the portable water pump was working. At least something was going right. Maybe now the water level would begin to fall. He heard the side door open and pointed his light at the door. O'Brien and Armstrong, soaked, came in carrying auto batteries.

"I've got a twelve and a six," Armstrong announced, "And Frank's got a twelve."

March grabbed one of the batteries from Armstrong, and the three men made their way back to the generator room. March gathered the connecting wires together and told the two labor leaders to begin hooking up the batteries in series.

"Three people are sure going to be pissed off," O'Brien said as he worked. "When they turn their car keys, they're going to hear big fat nothings."

March remained silent. He was busy on the chair unbolting the four hold-down bolts of the damaged governor. When he had completed that, he disconnected a wire and lifted the damaged governor, placing it off to one side. Then he moved over and began to help O'Brien and Armstrong.

A few minutes later, George Rhodes, president of Rhodes Tractor Company, climbed the stairs to the generator room. He was carrying a governor in his arms, and he cradled it like a baby.

"Dusty." March sounded insistent. "Over there." He beamed his light at the empty space. "Need anything?"

"No," said Rhodes, who had moved in and started to work.

"Are we in your way, Dusty?" March, Armstrong, and O'Brien continued their hook-up, close to Rhodes.

"No problem, Sam," said Rhodes as he continued his installation. Light from the battery lamp March had placed nearby illuminated the area.

"This wire to this pole," March said to O'Brien. "Good. You all set to connect over there?" He beamed his light to the side of the diesel motor, to the negative grounded pole.

"I'm set," said Armstrong as he began to make the next-to-last connection. The three batteries were now hooked together, negative to positive, negative to positive. Armstrong attached his lead from the negative pole of battery number three to the connection at the side of the diesel engine. Then he stepped back. March took the long wire connected to the positive pole of battery number one. He fastened its free end to the insulated connection of the diesel motor. The circuit was complete.

Rhodes, who had been watching the three men for the past thirty seconds, spoke up quietly. "I hope you fellows aren't waiting for me. I'm all set."

March had been anticipating this moment, and now that it was here, he dreaded it as much as he relished it. He walked quickly to the diesel-engine starter and let out an audible sigh. He shone his light on the switch as the other men in the room watched. "Ah, what the hell," he said as he turned it RRR RRR RRR and then the music of humming machinery. The diesel engine had started, and the men in the room cheered. Now for the big test, thought March. He moved over to the control panel. He pulled the first circuit breaker, and the diesel was offered its first load. Gradually he added to the load, until he had engaged the final circuit breaker. Now, at 7:55 P.M., lights came on, pumps began to work, and the diesel engine responded, powering the big generator into bringing the hospital to life again. For the first time, March, Armstrong, and O'Brien could afford to be jubilant. They hugged, and March shouted to nobody in particular, "Goddamn son of a bitch, goddamn son of a bitch, we did it!" Only George Rhodes stood by watching the men with amusement. After a few minutes Armstrong turned to March. "Sam, I'm glad for you and I'm glad for the hospital." He was smiling. "Look," he continued, "it's been a rough day and you've probably got a lot to do. So do we. See you in the morning."

March waved to O'Brien and Armstrong as they left. Nothing like an honest emergency, he thought, to get good men together.

Music from the car radio soothed Asa Porter with reassurance of power. The cost of the four custom-ordered stereo speakers was commensurate with the price of the sports car, and expensive things were ingredients of the gallimaufry of Porter's sense of superiority. As he drove toward Thornton, his mind turned, as it invariably did, to the contemplation of his achievements. Porter had developed, from childhood on, an ability to self-delude. As a physician, he was successful by almost all standards, but his arrogance did not permit him, at least on a conscious level, to admit that he had received help along the way. He dreaded impotence at any level, and so he eschewed realistic acceptance of himself for the fantasy that he was an island of accomplishment, created pristinely from the bowels of the earth, that he was a human island created without original sin. He was not bothered by the contradiction inherent in his concept of himself as a self-made aristocrat. So as he drove carefully along the wet highway, he mentally arranged the events of the day to correspond to his wishes. Beulah, a bit huffy this morning because of an understandable insecurity. She had begun to realize that her progressive involvement with the affairs of Pacific Hospital was not because she once had been Beulah Thornton but because she was now Mrs. Asa Porter. Eventually she would learn to accept this gracefully, as she would learn to bow out of hospital politics when he deemed the time appropriate. His performance at the CPC . . . well, there really was nothing to quibble about. His presentation had been lucid, interesting, and entirely correct. The consult—he was looking forward to its fallout. Karen—he was certain now that she would make overtures within a week, and because she was a tasty dish, he would accept her back as his mistress; of course, he first would receive assurances that the type of unpleasantness he had experienced on the boat never would recur. Yes, all in all, the day had gone well and he was entirely content.

Now, as he reached the outskirts of Thornton, the 7:30 news segment interrupted the music. *The blackout that began at six-forty this evening in the Pacific Hospital area of the city continues. The rainstorm is thought to have caused a short circuit in a feeder line.* Porter had noticed that the traffic was heavy, even for a rainy night, and now he understood why.

The newscaster continued: *PG and E crews are working on the scene, but the power failure at Pacific Hospital itself remains unexplained. Approximately one-half hour ago, the emergency generator at that institution ceased functioning. In developments abroad, the strained situation in . . .* Porter flipped off the radio. He was damn lucky, he thought, that he had no desperately ill patients in the hospital. As he reached the perimeter of the blackout area, traffic had slowed practically to a halt. Porter proceeded carefully. Under different circumstances he would have gone home, avoiding the snarled blackout area. But it was important that he set Vanni straight. And he was certain that Vanni would be at the hospital.

At each intersection now, red flares sputtered at the four corners, and policemen as well as PG and E crewmen in yellow slickers were directing traffic, allowing the north-south lanes to proceed alternately with east-west-direction cars. After a long delay, he finally was waved across the intersection, and he moved slowly to the next, and then the next. At last, Pacific Hospital came into view. Porter felt a chill run through him. Despite the fact that he had been forewarned by the radio announcement, he was not prepared for what he saw. By straining, he could make out the darkened bulk of the hospital with great difficulty. The darkness itself was chilling, but its punctuation by jets of moving flashlight beams denoted a frantic sense of desperation that signified the thing that Porter dreaded the most in himself and others—loss of control. He deserved a well-ordered world. Then, while he was stopped before an intersection two blocks from the hospital, lights suddenly appeared in the windows of Pacific. It was as if the hospital itself had responded to the malaise he had experienced from the darkness and the flashlights. Even though the building was not a mass of lighted rectangles the way it usually appeared at night, it was clear that emergency power had been restored. Among other responsibilities, Porter realized with satisfaction, Buildings and Grounds belonged to Sam March, and since emergency power had failed, it certainly was possible that the assistant administrator had fouled up somewhere. Not that Porter had any animosity toward March himself. He didn't. But it was satisfying that Karen might see another instance of the difference between the man to whom she was married and the man whose complete effectiveness was one of the reasons she rushed to the *See-Sick* each week.

Porter began to chafe over a new delay. A fire truck was leaving the hospital, and all other traffic was at a complete standstill. Finally the stream of cars began to move again, and Porter carefully made a right turn into the doctors' parking lot. It was eight P.M. The drive, normally a twenty-minute one, had taken him almost an hour and a half. He entered the hospital and noted the hubbub resulting from the return of emergency power. The corridors were partially lighted, and visitors were coming out of the stairwell doors. Some of them, concerned about traveling along wet and unlighted streets to get home, had worried looks. Security guards, nurses, and other evening personnel walked quickly down the main hallway, apparently en route to speed completion of various postponed tasks. Porter had intended to see Karl Morley before his encounter with Vanni, but as he passed the doctors' lounge, he saw the latter sitting on a couch. Vanni looked disconsolate. Porter decided to delay seeing Morley. Accolades from the patient would have to wait. After all, Vanni might take off, and now was the time for reckoning. Tomorrow, everything would be diluted as the details of the consult blurred.

"Hello, Leo." Porter was disappointed that Vanni was sitting alone in the lounge.

Vanni looked up and nodded a greeting. He did not smile. He looked defeated.

"What's doing?" Porter asked, fencing.

"I just lost my patient," Vanni said softly.

Porter blanched. It couldn't be! There was no way it could have happened, and yet . . . "Karl Morley?" he asked, holding his breath for the response.

"Tom Neely, the federal mediator. Massive coronary, ventricular fibrillation, a dead defibrillator and a dead patient. We shocked him when emergency power came on again, but it was too late."

"What happened to the power?" Porter asked. "I was away."

"Who knows?" Vanni answered. "We lost it at the wrong time for poor Tom. I don't think he could have made it even if we could have shocked him back to sinus rhythm, but that's something I'll never find out." Vanni sighed and became silent.

Porter did a mental tally. Two of Vanni's patients, Neely and Chernock, dead, and a gross miscalculation on a third all in the same day. How fortunate it was, Porter reasoned, that he had intervened to prevent a needless surgical procedure on Karl Morley. Vanni seemed to have gotten his comeuppance. But no matter how dejected Vanni might be at the moment, he was and would continue to be a major irritant to Porter; he definitely would have to go. Of course, the actualization of his plan would have to wait until June, when he would become chief, but at least now he could begin to lubricate the skids. "Bad day, Leo?" he asked without any inflection of his voice.

"Very bad," Vanni answered. He knew that Porter, although seemingly without rancor, was enjoying his, Vanni's, misfortunes. "I just saw my diabetic patient, Susan Royal. She's still in coma after the amputation. In addition to everything else that has gone sour, I compounded my troubles by bad judgment," he added.

"You can't blame yourself because a defibrillator won't work during a power failure." Porter knew Vanni's reference about bad judgment referred to the Karl Morley case, not to the Neely mishap, but he decided to have some fun and stretch it out a bit. The only trouble, he thought with some regret, was that Vanni was ready to apologize right now.

"I'm not talking about Tom Neely," Vanni said.

"You're not?"

"No. My fuckup was Karl Morley."

There it was. Porter savored the moment for what it was about to lead to. Still he refrained from making things easier for Vanni. His instinct to seek Vanni out had not been wrong. His "clinical hunch"—Vanni's words again—had been entirely correct. "Meaning what?" he asked, again controlling the modulation of his voice. There was no need to appear eager.

"Meaning the surgical consult, of course." Vanni looked at Porter with some curiosity now. The man was not present during the blackout. Was it possible that he didn't know about Morley?

"I thought you would get around to that in time," Porter said. Malice infiltrated his tone. "You were so certain, so goddamned sure of yourself."

"You don't even know about Karl Morley, do you?" Vanni asked. His eyes narrowed in anger. "You didn't bother to follow up."

"What about Morley?" Porter felt a queasiness at the pit of his stomach. He fought for the control he must not lose.

"Morley damn near died. At surgery. During the blackout. That was my mistake in judgment."

"What happened?"

"He was bleeding to death from a ruptured spleen," Vanni answered. "Oh, not to worry. He's fine now. But no thanks to you, and certainly no thanks to me. I risked a man's life by allowing an idiot to delay surgery. Mea culpa, not yours."

"Watch your tone, Vanni." Porter had recovered. "If you waited till the last minute, you're the idiot, not me."

"I made two mistakes," Vanni continued, ignoring Porter's comment. "I caved in to Morley. He had rights as a patient, but I had rights also. If I had refused to equivocate, Karl would have taken my advice. Mistake number two, Asa Porter. I underestimated your stupidity or your vanity or both. It seemed impossible that you would do what you did."

"Wait a minute." There was no mistaking the anger in Porter's voice.

"No, Asa. You wait a minute," Vanni said. "I don't pretend to understand you. Most people I know come in shades of gray, light to dark. But I don't see any gray in you. You're a total hypocrite. You're one hundred percent self-indulgence and zero percent feeling for anybody else." Vanni was silent for an instant as he watched Porter's face redden. "Asa," he concluded. *"Va fangulo!* I don't like you."

Porter clenched and unclenched his fists. He was at a loss for words. "Vanni," he muttered finally, "this is a promise. Your days at Pacific Hospital are numbered, beginning right now. If I ever accomplish anything here, and I assure you that I will, the very least of it will be to drive you from this place. You are not needed here."

It was time to see Susan Royal again. Vanni stood up and put his face close to Porter's. "Just you try!" he said.

For the third time of the evening, Arnie Jacobs began the testing procedure on Susan Royal's blood. Emergency power had been restored, and while the house-staff lab was dark, at least the corridors were partially lighted. Filtration—sodium hydroxide—boiling. Fifteen seconds, thirty seconds, forty-five seconds. Only fifteen more seconds would spell out a message of life or death. Sixty seconds. He lifted the boiling tube and removed it from the flame of the Bunsen burner. At the same instant, the lights in the lab came on. The area blackout was over. He looked at the tube. *YELLOW!* He stood there smiling. He couldn't believe it. *YELLOW!* He felt so great, he almost forgot to test for acetone. That too was improved. He could hear cheering noises in the hall, and for a brief instant he thought that the whole hospital was cheering the beginning of Susan Royal's recovery. Then he understood that the patients, visitors, and staff were celebrating the return of full power to the hospital. All elevators were working again, and the lights were on brightly everywhere—in corridors, in rooms, at stations. He noted the time—8:15 P.M.—finally an end to the physical and emotional darkness. He hurried back toward the ICU, anxious to tell the nurses that the lab work confirmed what he had barely dared to believe: Susan Royal was going to make it.

Outside of ICU, Alex, the man Susan wanted to marry, stood quietly. As Alex saw Jacobs approaching, he went up to him.

"How is she, doctor?" he asked.

"She's going to be okay." Jacobs was jubilant. "It was a son of a bitch of a fight, but she won it. By the way, you can help speed her recovery."

"I can help?" the man asked. "How?"

"Susan has this idea that because of the amputation, you're not going to marry her. I'm telling you this in confidence. I know it's silly, but I suppose it's a natural fear. Reassure her, will you? She can use a lift when she really comes to."

The man stood for a second, saying nothing. Then he

cleared his throat. "It was never that heavy, doctor," he replied. "I know Susan understands that. Marriage was never an issue. But I'm grateful to you for the care you've all given her, and I'm very thankful that she's going to recover."

Jacobs listened without surprise. "You had her fooled for a while," he said, "but you're no great loss. She's going to end up with a lot better man than you!" Jacobs turned and entered the ICU.

"I don't know how you did it, Sam," Lester Whitesides said. "You're a miracle man."

The two men were sitting in March's office. Beulah Porter was downstairs trying to console Mrs. Neely. "I had some help, Lester," March answered.

"You don't have to be modest," the older man said. "You put everything together. Some union bastard tried to ruin us, and thanks to you, he didn't get away with it. What a day!" The administrator sighed.

"Where were you when the lights went out, Lester? We were still in the boardroom, and it scared me shitless. Were you in CCU?"

"Yes. I'm sorry I got so hot under the collar during the negotiations. I had to cool down. I stopped off at CCU to check on Tom Neely. Poor fellow. When the lights went out, I wasn't sure of what the best thing to do was. I tried to call the boardroom, but I couldn't get a line. Later I did get through, and Beulah told me that you and the others were in the basement. So I decided to go back to the boardroom. I'm glad I did, because after you told me about the sabotage, I knew you were having your hands full in the basement. You didn't need a fat old man in your way."

"When the area blackout was over," March said, "I checked around the hospital. I'm trying to piece together a report of exactly what happened and when. I asked Cathy in CCU who was there when the hospital went dark. She said that besides the patients, only she, another nurse, and Leo Vanni were present. She remembers that you asked about Neely's condition a few minutes after the lights went out. Are you sure you were there earlier? Maybe she just didn't notice you. You're easy to miss."

"Well, I'm probably a little confused. Maybe I was in the

hall outside of CCU. I'm not sure. Say, what the hell is this? A cross-examination?"

"Yes," March replied.

"You've got a nerve, Sam." The administrator began to perspire. He reached in his pocket for a handkerchief but came up empty.

"Is this what you're looking for?" March held out a blood-stained handkerchief with Whitesides' maroon monogram embroidered on it. "Souvenir from the generator room. You almost killed Phil Wray."

Whitesides paled and reached for the handkerchief, but March put it back in his own pocket. "You have to be the stupidest son of a bitch I've ever met," he said to the administrator. "Why, for Christ's sake? What were you trying to do?"

Whitesides slumped back in his chair. He seemed to have aged ten years. "Don't you see, they were trying to kill the hospital," he said finally. "I thought that we would lose a battle and win the war. I figured that PG and E would restore outside power, and public opinion would force the union to its knees." His face brightened with hope. "Even now, Sam, everybody thinks that the union did the damage. Can't we just leave it that way?"

"*Everybody* doesn't think the union did the damage. *I* know who did the damage."

"You want me in jail?" the administrator asked.

"It's not up to me," March answered. "I'll be taking it up with the hospital's legal staff and the police."

Fifteen minutes after Whitesides had left, there was a knock at the door. "Come in," March called out, and Beulah Porter entered the office.

"Mrs. Neely has a lot of courage, Sam. There would have been more tragedy tonight if it hadn't been for you. We are all grateful. Lester and I were just talking about it. I guess everyone thought you would be a good man in a crisis, but we didn't want you to have to prove it to us in quite the way you did."

"Everybody pitched in, Beulah. That's not bullshit. Armstrong and O'Brien were great."

"The point I'm leading up to," Beulah said, "is that I've

watched you for a long time and I know you very well. Lester just told me he is retiring immediately. He can't handle administrative duties any longer and he has recommended you as his successor. It's sad that Lester is leaving, because he has given a good part of his life to this hospital. He's been devoted to it, but I concur with his decision to quit. It's time. And I also completely approve of his recommendation of you as his successor. I will propose your name at the next board meeting, and I can foresee no difficulty."

Beulah Porter smiled, and so did March. When Beulah wanted something to happen in Thornton, she *never* encountered difficulty.

"Thank you, Beulah," March said. "But Lester had no choice. I'll explain it to you tomorrow." He became almost morose for an instant. "Someday," he added, "you and I are going to have to have a long talk. There are some things I have to fill you in on. But now's not a good time. It'll hold."

"You're talking about Asa," Beulah said.

March, astounded, was speechless for a few seconds. "You've got to be a mind reader. Do you know what I planned to say about your husband?"

"Yes, Sam, and I know you're hurt. I told you I knew you well. What I didn't say was that I've known about Asa's extramarital activities. I know about Karen, and I'm sorry. But I can tell you two things. His affairs are trivial and never last more than a few months, so he'll leave Karen."

"I've got news for you, Beulah. I beat him to it. But what was the second thing?"

"Asa will never become chief of medicine. He thinks he will, but he won't."

Sam March stood up and laughed. "Christ, Beulah. You're something else again. Just tell me one more thing. Why do you stay with him?"

Beulah looked directly at March and spoke without hesitation. "You know something, Sam. If I planned to stay with him, he *would* be the next chief of medicine."

PART IV

The Next Day

March was always an early riser, but this morning, rays of sunshine pouring through the windows of his office substituted for his internal alarm clock. He opened his eyes and remembered all that had happened the previous day. The blackout had not been a bad dream, the negotiations had not been a bad dream, and the lovely girl lying naked beside him certainly was not a bad dream. March reached for his watch—6:15 A.M.

"Where are you going?" Liz's voice was filled with love and contentment as she forced herself awake. A fair amount had happened to her, and her mind could not encompass it all. But, she thought, from yesterday's lunch meeting to right now, she had been kissed, made love to, proposed to—she accepted—and made love to again. This—she remembered her mother's singing—is a fine romance.

March leaned over and took her in his arms. He kissed her with a tenderness he never had been able to feel for Karen, and then other feelings, less tender, took command. He pulled her tight against him, his hand stroking her buttocks.

"Sam . . ." Liz implored. Her voice was husky. "I want you so bad it hurts, really hurts, but let's wait until tonight. You're exhausted and you have a lot to do today." She kissed him again, a lingering kiss, and then pushed him away.

"You don't have a headache, do you?" March asked.

"I have an aching, all right," she answered, "but it's not in my head. I still can't believe it," she continued. "Say it again."

"Say what again?"

" 'Mrs. Sam March.' You whispered that to me, among other things, all night long. Say it again."

"Mrs. Sam March." He said it as if he were reading the Constitution, and she shook him as she laughed.

"Say it right, damn you."

He pulled her close to him again and put his mouth to her ear. "Mrs. Elizabeth S. March," he whispered slowly. Then he slid down farther and kissed her breast. "Are you sure you really want to wait?" he asked.

"No, darling, I'm not sure, but I'm going to. Get dressed, Sam, before you make me do something lecherous."

March moved off the side of the hide-a-bed and grabbed his underwear shorts from the chair. He walked to the small office bathroom and brushed his teeth and shaved. He returned to the office, looked at Liz, who was watching him, tore his gaze away, and finished dressing. "What about you?" he asked. "Are you planning to spend the rest of this gorgeous day flaked out on some administrator's bed?"

"It's early, Sam." She saw his look and quickly said, "Not *that* early." She stopped talking, trying to remember what it was that she had been about to say. "Let me concentrate, blue-eyes. Oh, yes, I know. I want fifteen minutes by myself. Just let me lie here for a while and appreciate the fact that my dreams came true. Okay, Sam?"

"Okay. Relax and contemplate our good fortune. But I'll be back in twenty minutes, and you better be dressed, or else . . ."

"Or else what, Sam?" she asked.

He left quietly, shutting the door gently and making certain it was locked. He walked to the elevator and waited. When it arrived, he appreciated more than ever before what he had taken for granted. He wanted to see how the hospital looked in daylight, especially in daylight filled with sunshine instead of rain. In a sense, he would be observing everything in the capacity of administrator of Pacific Hospital. He stepped out of the elevator at the main floor and walked through the deserted lobby, wondering what time Armstrong and O'Brien would come today to complete the negotiations. If they didn't call him, he would call them. He had never felt quite this expansive.

The glass doors opened as he stepped outside to sample the crisp air of this December morning. Pickets carrying strike signs were slowly walking in a circle in front of the hospital.

March surveyed the scene and saw Armstrong talking to one of the picket captains, while O'Brien was leaning against a telephone pole drinking coffee. March had trouble believing what was happening. He walked over to Armstrong. "What gives? You know damn well that the blackout interrupted our session. I thought you would have the decency to extend the deadline."

"Obviously you thought wrong," Armstrong replied.

"But last night, for Christ's sake, you and Frank and I were all working together. I never would have believed that—"

"Believe it, Sam. Look around again. These signs don't read 'We love Pacific Hospital.' You're all mixed up. We helped out in the emergency, sure. But our grievances have been ignored for the last time. We helped you out with your problem, now it's your turn to help us with ours."

"You didn't have to strike." March shook his head in disgust before continuing. "You could have had the decency to extend the deadline."

"You're repeating yourself, Sam. Look, we didn't cause last night's blackouts, although Whitesides will probably try to lay that trip on us, too. We promised a marathon session, and we fulfilled our obligations. What's the use of discussing this anymore? The deadline passed without the hospital giving us our rights, and that's that."

"Now that you have your pickets out," March said, "what neutral place do you want to meet?"

"Thornton Hotel. Incidentally, I'm sorry about Tom Neely. We'll need a new federal mediator. You have access to phones. Will you set everything up?" Armstrong asked.

"I'll reserve one of the hotel conference rooms for ten-thirty this morning. Agreed?"

Armstrong nodded. Then he called over O'Brien, "We're meeting at the Thornton Hotel later."

O'Brien looked at the two men and nodded.

"Whitesides won't make the meeting, but Mrs. Porter and I will see you there," March said. Then he turned and walked back into the hospital. There was a lot to do. He had to return to Liz and have her initiate the contingency plan at once. The census had to be further reduced, the other Thornton hospitals had to be alerted, and several more emergency measures had to be invoked. He was glad that advance alternate arrangements had been made for dietary, laundry, and janitorial services. We're like an old sailing ship in the doldrums, he thought as he walked through the lobby. We're stocked up on every kind of supplies, and now we have to see who can hold out longer, the wind or ourselves.

Nothing could take away the good feelings Arnie Jacobs felt this morning as he looked around ICU. All of the patients on the unit were doing well, and even the equipment, humming normally again, sounded better to him than it ever had before. Jacobs was exhausted from his all-night vigil at Susan's bedside, but not too tired to fully experience the elation of seeing her awake, alert, and sitting up. The coma and the horror of dealing alone with its complications during the blackout were part of the recent past. From where he stood, he could see the girl who had taken an overdose of sleeping pills; she was now breathing on her own. He could see Phil Wray, the engineer who had undergone surgery for a cardiac laceration; Wray looked good and was talking to one of the nurses. But as Jacobs walked toward Susan Royal, he felt a proprietary pride in his role in her recovery from the diabetic coma that almost had claimed her life.

"He's gone, isn't he?" Susan asked when Jacobs reached her bedside. "Alex isn't here, is he?"

"No, he took off last night," the intern replied. "You had him pegged right. He won't be back. He doesn't go for commitments, apparently."

Susan leaned forward and patted the bedsheets where her leg used to be. "It would take more than an ordinary commitment," she said wryly. "*I'm* having trouble accepting what's happened."

"I know you are," Jacobs said. "You're going to have to make yourself experience it all, every lousy thing that's happened to you. You have to grieve for yourself before you can accept yourself. You have the courage to do it."

"I'm not sure of that. I knew I had diabetes, although I tried to forget it as much of the time as I could. But now I'm a cripple. How do I forget that? How do I live with it? My God, what am I going to do?"

"You're going to get some help, to begin with," Jacobs

said. "Dr. Andruss from the Department of Psychiatry is coming to see you this afternoon. He's a good man."

"I need something, that's for sure."

"Dr. Vanni thinks that you need to sort out your feelings, and Andruss will help you do that. In the last analysis, it will be up to you. And you'll make it."

"What makes you so sure, Arnie?"

"You have guts. That's it, plain and simple. You have guts."

"I hope so," Susan said.

It was 7:45 A.M. when Asa Porter returned home from spending the night on the boat. He was surprised to find his wife dressed and drinking a cup of coffee.

"Why so early, dear?" Porter asked. "Another meeting?" As he leaned over to kiss his wife, Buelah turned her head away and stood up. She walked to the buffet, poured her husband a cup of coffee, and returned to her chair.

Porter sat down opposite her. "I can't stay long," he announced. "I caught up on my reading last night, and the boat was relaxing, but it's time to go to work again."

"You obviously don't know that the hospital is on strike. Sam March just called, and I'm meeting him in his office in a little while. We'll continue negotiations later this morning at the Thornton Hotel. Now that the union has walked out, we have to meet at a neutral place."

"A strike!" Porter was upset. "What does this mean for the hospital? Are you going to be able to settle it soon? I don't relish the idea of crossing a jeering picket line."

"You wouldn't have enjoyed the blackout last night either," Beulah said, unaware that her husband had returned briefly to the hospital. "It was an area blackout, and then there was a power failure of the emergency system itself." Porter started to talk, but his wife silenced him. "You can read about it in the paper after I leave. I don't have much time, but before I go, I have something to say to you."

Porter, startled by her abruptness, stared at his wife. He felt uneasy.

"I'm going to divorce you, and I want you out of the house today," Beulah said. "I don't want you to sleep in this house tonight. Pack what you need now and you can get the rest of your things when you get settled at your club or wherever you end up."

"My God!" Porter was stunned. "What are you saying? We've been married thirty years. We're a perfect couple. We've raised a family and we get along. What is it? You're not making any sense at all." Porter now felt desperate.

Beulah spoke with studied precision. "It's true that we've been married for thirty years and it's true that we've raised a family. But we've never been a happy couple."

Porter thought for a moment before responding. "You're angry about the boat, aren't you? You think I never should have spent nights on the boat. Then why didn't you say anything?" Porter had another thought. "You don't think I was with another woman on the boat last night, do you? I was alone. I've always been alone."

Beulah looked directly at him. "No, *I've* always been alone. I've known that for years, but I never accepted it until recently. I can thank you for that. I always thought that I had to tolerate your affairs, but I don't. You've caused me so much pain and humiliation, but you can't hurt me anymore. I always thought that I needed you, but now I know I don't. I don't need you, I don't love you, I don't even like you."

"I imagine that you've heard about my few indiscretions, but I can assure you that there has never been anyone but you in my life since our marriage."

"That's most reassuring, Asa. But that really doesn't make any difference. I simply do not want you. There's nothing more to talk about. I have to leave for the meeting."

As Beulah went to get her coat, Porter followed her to the closet. "Look, regardless of our problems now, at least you will work for my appointment for chief of medicine, won't you?"

"So far as that is concerned," Beulah replied before opening the door leading to the garage, "I would strongly suggest that you learn to get along with Leo Vanni."

Porter stood in the hall after Beulah closed the door. He returned to the breakfast room and poured himself another cup of coffee. He found that his hands were shaking so badly that he was forced to put the cup down. He had taken for granted the financial and social position his marriage had given him. So far as his affairs were concerned, he thought that he had been entirely discreet and had covered his tracks well. Maybe he had slipped up somewhere, he allowed, but still, his extracurricular love life had been trivial. Beulah should understand that, he thought. When he lived at the club, she would miss him, as, to his surprise, he was already beginning to miss her. Eventually she would plead for him to return home. But even with this assessment, his hands continued to tremble, and although he had no way of knowing it at the time, his shaky optimism was ungrounded. Beulah would never have him back.

"I don't mind telling you, Dr. Vanni, that this tube is causing me almost as much discomfort as the pain here." Karl Morley pointed to the incision site of last night's surgery. "When can I get rid of this thing?" Now he pointed to the nasogastric tube.

"Maybe today," Vanni answered. "That's up to Dr. Chase."

"I hear that there was a blackout when they operated on me. I know I can manage very well without my leaky spleen, but would you tell me how many sponges they left inside me?"

"Don't you think you owe a few kind words to 'knife-happy' Madden Chase?"

"I know I owe some unkind words to Asa Porter." Then Morley's voice softened uncharacteristically. "I'm not used to saying thank you, but I know that the surgery saved my life. I appreciate what you both did."

"I didn't mean for you to get maudlin, Karl," Vanni said. "I can't take that this morning."

"Very well, then," Morley said. "When do you plan to spring me from this hospital? I don't like it today any more than I did yesterday. In fact, my affection for this place grows less with each passing hour."

Vanni looked pleased. "That's more like it, Karl," he said. "Between the blackout and the strike, something or someone around here has to remain normal. Now, so far as your question is concerned, you'll go home when I damn well tell you that you can!"

Paul Diamond was driving Marian Zabriskie to the funeral

parlor to make arrangements for Sim's burial. His eyes were red from crying, and at intersections he wiped them with a handkerchief. "I'm some consolation for you, Marian," he commented. "It's just that Simeon was such a great guy—I'm saying 'was' already—and if anyone, it should have been me. I feel so sorry for you and Sara and for me too."

Marian touched his shoulder lightly. Curiously, she was dry-eyed. Sara was with her grandmother for the day, and Marian was relieved that she could talk openly to her husband's best friend. "It was coming, Paul," she said. "I knew it was coming, and I was helpless to stop it."

"But why?" Diamond asked as he braked at a stoplight.

"You and Simeon were different from the start," Marian said. "You couldn't see it, Paul, because my husband kept his defenses high and he put on a good act. But I knew that he was reacting to dialysis differently from you." She paused before continuing. "I don't know what makes one person respond to a situation differently from another. All I know, Paul, is that life on the machine was intolerable for Simeon. Thank God he's at rest now."

Diamond leaned over and kissed Marian tenderly on the cheek. "Thank God, thank God," he repeated. "You're right. Sim's last words show that you're right." His voice broke, and he sobbed for a few seconds until he was able to control himself. "Sim said, 'I'm very tired and I want to sleep.' Thank God he's at rest now."

The light changed to green, and Diamond forced himself to step on the accelerator.

The scrawny man sat on a bench in the dingy Thornton bus terminal. His worn suitcase rested on the floor next to his legs. He was struggling to complete a letter, and the poor lighting of the waiting room added to his difficulties. He carefully read what he had already written, his lips moving in concentration as he did so. "Dear Phil, Im at the bus depot because Im leaving town. Im going to Denver in one hour from now. I think I got a nefew living there but if not it dont matter. I seen the pickets this morning. Like I told you I got no futur now with the lousy hospital. They can all go to hell the hospital and the union. Not you, Phil! Ha! Ha! When I get setteled someplace Ill send you my address. Then do me a favor. Tell the lousy payrol office to send me what they owe me. Thanks pal and so long." That's enough, the man thought. He pressed his pencil against the paper and wrote the closing line: "Your good friend, Victor Bates." Then he folded the paper and placed it in the stamped envelope he had prepared earlier. As he went to mail the letter at the mailbox inside the waiting room, not even one of the four people slumped over half-asleep on the benches followed his progress.

The door opened and David Raymer involuntarily held his breath for a second. He guessed that it was Dr. Oliver Lusk who had just entered the room. All of his resolutions to be cynical, to be stoical, to expect nothing, dissolved in an instant. He realized that he had never really lost hope, but he also knew that he could not tolerate any more procedures. He knew about the blackout and wondered if it had affected his surgery. His heart began to beat rapidly as the footsteps approached the bed. He was glad that Patton, his roommate, was out of the room.

"Good morning, Mr. Raymer," the surgeon said. "Let's have a look at the eye."

"I suppose you know that I'm praying right now," Raymer said softly. As Lusk began to remove the aluminum guard and bandage from his left eye, the agonies of the last years intruded themselves into Raymer's thoughts. All the pain, and all the defeated hopes, and all the darkness. And here he was again on the threshold, and what ended up emblazoned in his brain was a trite but potent "Now or never." He held his breath for what seemed like minutes while Lusk removed the dressing and carefully examined the new cornea.

"We have a good graft," Oliver Lusk finally announced.

Raymer tried to control the myriad emotions flowing through him. This has happened before, he told himself, and things did not work out in the long run. But those five words and the sight of Dr. Lusk, clear and in focus, the beauty of the form and color of the flowers on the shelf opposite his bed, the splendor of the rays of sunshine slanting into the room, were too much for him. He began to cry softly. "I'm sorry, doctor," he murmured. "I can't help it. I'm not blind anymore." He was silent for a moment and then summoned his courage. "I know you can't give me any guarantees, but do you think that this operation will be a success?"

"I'm very optimistic," Lusk replied. "Frankly, I was most worried about the technical aspects of your surgery, and that all worked out well." Lusk put in prednisone drops, applied a fresh dressing, and then replaced the aluminum guard and taped it. "In a few weeks you can begin brushing up on your chemistry. You'll be teaching again in the fall."

Although his tear ducts had been pitifully scarred by the accident, Raymer sobbed unabashedly after Oliver Lusk had left the room. The tears were meager, but the sentiment could not have been greater.

The word had been spread that agreement had been reached on a contract and a ratification meeting had been called. Now, at 3:30 P.M., there was murmuring and excitement in the union hall. Rumors of all sorts about the terms had been circulated during the past fifteen minutes. On the small raised platform in the front of the room, O'Brien and Armstrong sat impassively looking at the crowd of rank and file. Almost ninety-five percent of the members of the union local were present waiting for the meeting to begin. Finally Armstrong stood up, and the room immediately quieted down. "Members of Local 175" Armstrong began. "Frank and I want to report to you what happened today at our negotiation session. We won the strike."

Armstrong was interrupted by cheers. "The laundry will be phased out over a six-month period, but every single one of the laundry workers will remain employed at the hospital. Let me tell you about the laundry issue. We knew from the beginning that there was no way the hospital could keep the laundry going, but we never let on. We used the laundry issue as a basis for the strike, and as a result, we got everything we wanted."

Armstrong paused for breath. He wanted to sell the package to the membership. It would be good for his people and it would be good for him personally. "We got a wage increase, better dental benefits for your health plan, and a seniority clause. Also, the hospital will not subcontract out dietary or janitorial during the length of the agreement. But the biggest thing we forced the hospital to do was to stop the system of dead-end jobs. We've got the career ladders we've wanted. Pacific has guaranteed that if you want more training or education, the hospital will not only permit it so you can upgrade your job, but they have agreed to pay all the costs. They'll pay half the tuition right away and the other half when you get a passing grade. You may not know now just how good this is, but it's not only a big breakthrough for every one of you, it's the best thing that has ever happened to our union. Some of you will end up in the business office, some of you in upgraded service jobs." Jax knew that this would ultimately enlarge the jurisdiction of the union and give it more power than it had ever had. "This is a summary of the things we won. Now I'm going into the details of each item, and then Frank and I will answer any and every question you have about this contract. After the question period, we'll take a vote from the membership as to whether to accept or reject this agreement. I strongly recommend that you accept it."

Sam March sat quietly in his office. He had just received the phone call from Armstrong notifying him that the union had voted to accept the new contract and that the strike was over. March's sigh echoed his relief. He had not relished the idea of a long strike. He had been certain that although the Teamsters had not joined the strike, they would in time, and he knew that everything would have become more acrimonious. Nonstriking personnel would have been insulted and humiliated more and more with each passing day. So far as the contract itself, he recognized that wage increases were almost automatic during inflationary times, and this was only fair. The hospital would, on the other hand, save a million dollars over the next three years by closing the laundry. The self-improvement program for the union workers that Pacific Hospital would finance was, he felt, a good thing for both sides, even though he and Beulah had made it appear that a concession was being granted. He also realized that had Lester Whitesides participated in the negotiating session instead of Beulah Porter, the approval of these benefits never would have been given. All in all, Sam March was pleased with the contract.

Despite the blackout and the brief strike, Pacific Hospital

had functioned well. All problems had not been solved—they never were—but he would be a more flexible administrator and he would make certain that morale at Pacific Hospital was high. Like Armstrong, he sincerely believed that a hospital—administrators, employees, doctors, and patients all—was indeed a family. He put his feet up on the desk and leaned back in his chair, waiting for the pickets to be pulled off the line.

The ringing of the phone on his desk jarred him. He picked up the receiver. "Yes, Pru," he said to his secretary.

"Dr. Fraser just called up from his office in Pathology. He said he didn't want to discuss it over the phone, but it's important that you come down there right away. Something's happened."

March stood up quickly and left his office. As he headed for the stairs, he wondered what else could have gone wrong. Yesterday, and the pickets this morning, were enough. And Fraser never had called him with urgency before. He took the stairs two at a time. When he reached the fourth floor, he walked with long strides down the corridor. He opened the door to Fraser's office and saw the pathologist and Leo Vanni sitting in chairs. Between them was an old galvanized bucket filled with ice and containing a bottle of champagne.

"What the hell happened?" March asked, disoriented by the entire scene. "Pru said—"

"Pru is an alarmist, Sam," Fraser said calmly. "You'll have to train her better. I would have thought that after so many years working for you . . . But never mind. We have to proceed with our celebration."

March turned to Vanni. "Leo, do you mind telling me what's going on? Pru said that there was urgent business here, that something had happened and—"

"Something *has* happened, Sam," Fraser interrupted, "and that's why we've called you. There's a rumor that you're going to become administrator of our hospital, but before we open the bubbly, we want to hear it from you. Is it true that you are going to lead us?" Fraser put on his most worshipful look.

"There's nothing official, so I can't . . ." March stopped talking as he watched Fraser wag his finger in mock warning.

"Don't equivocate, Sam," Fraser said. "That means, no deception please," he added in explanation.

"What the hell," March said after a brief pause. "It's true. I'm your new boss, so don't waste any more of my time. Open the bottle."

"Not so fast, my good man," Fraser said. "It's no big deal. This hospital cannot run on the abilities of one man alone," he intoned, "a lousy little administrator at that. Now, *you* know that beginning in June I will become the chief of pathology. What you have not learned is that my very dear friend, Leo here, will become chief of medicine at that time."

"How do you know?" March asked.

"Because my very dear friend Beulah Porter told me this morning. We aristocrats talk to each other, you know," Fraser said haughtily. "I just told Leo here, and I implored him not to accept the position. I told him that his modest abilities were not sufficient, and besides, all of that power would spoil the sweet, modest, unassuming Leo that we've all come to love and admire, and may I add that—"

"He's been like this all afternoon," Vanni said. "He gets withdrawal symptoms when he doesn't have at least two autopsics to look forward to." Vanni's face clouded for a minute. "You better buy some new defibrillators, Sam. I told Lester six months ago."

"I know," March answered. "Too bad about Tom Neely. The hospital may get some fallout from that." He paused for a brief time as his quizzical expression changed to one of belief. "I guess it's true about you, Leo. Congratulations. Beulah told me, too. Until yesterday I thought that the prick she's married to would get the job."

"I can see that you're going to be a diplomatic administrator," Fraser said to March. "I like your reasoned tone, your smoothness in disguising overt dislike by—"

"Open the champagne," March commanded. "I don't have all day to listen to your bullshit. I'm the fucking administrator of Pacific Hospital."

Fraser opened the bottle, watching the parabolic path of the extruded cork. "No cheap stuff, you notice," he said as he filled the three glasses. "A toast," he ordered. "To the three of us, the new troika of power at Pacific Hospital. May we exercise our limitless authority wisely, bearing in mind that the less fortunate in the Pacific Hospital flock look to us for direction, for compassionate guidance to allow them to pursue their miserable little lives with . . . You're not listening." He pouted.

"This is good champagne," Vanni said. "Ed, you're weird but you're very generous. Thank you, my old and very dear friend."

"Fill 'em up again, doctor," March said to Fraser, extending his empty glass.

"Listen," Fraser said conspiratorially as he filled the glasses. "There is no limit to the changes we three can initiate here, working together. Nobody can stop us. We can start by having a giant sauna built on the roof for our relaxation, because—now, don't say it isn't so—I can feel the tensions building already. It will be for the private use of the three of us, and we'll stock it with naked nubile dancing girls and crazy tropical drinks and a midget bartender in a little white uniform. Next we build . . . No. I won't tell you what we'll build next. That's a surprise. But I can tell you that within six months—"

"I won't be here in six months," March said. "Thanks for the drinks. I have to go."

"What do you mean you won't be here in six months?" Vanni asked. "Where the hell will you be?"

"On my honeymoon," March said. Then he turned and left the office, noting with satisfaction the expression of complete confusion on the faces of his two friends.

About the Author

Robert H. Curtis lives in San Francisco, California, where he practiced internal medicine for many years before becoming a full-time writer. He is a graduate of the United States Naval Academy and Cornell University Medical College. His published works include mystery stories and several non-fiction juvenile books.

SIGNET Books You'll Enjoy

- [ ] **THE DOCTORS ON EDEN PLACE** by Elizabeth Seifert.
  (#E8852—$1.75)*
- [ ] **THE DOCTOR'S DESPERATE HOURS** by Elizabeth Seifert.
  (#W7787—$1.50)
- [ ] **THE STORY OF ANDREA FIELDS** by Elizabeth Seifert.
  (#Y6535—$1.25)
- [ ] **TWO DOCTORS AND A GIRL** by Elizabeth Seifert.
  (#W8118—$1.50)
- [ ] **EYE OF THE NEEDLE** by Ken Follett.   (#E8746—$2.95)
- [ ] **DEATH TOUR** by David J. Michael.   (#E8842—$2.25)*
- [ ] **WINGS** by Robert J. Serling.   (#E8811—$2.75)*
- [ ] **THE YEAR OF THE INTERN** by Robin Cook. (#E7674—$1.75)
- [ ] **COMA** by Robin Cook.   (#E8202—$2.50)
- [ ] **TWINS** by Bari Wood and Jack Geasland.   (#E9094—$2.75)
- [ ] **THE KILLING GIFT** by Bari Wood.   (#J7350—$1.95)
- [ ] **THE CRAZY LOVERS** by Joyce Elbert.   (#E8917—$2.75)*
- [ ] **THE CRAZY LADIES** by Joyce Elbert.   (#E8923—$2.75)
- [ ] **BELOVED CAPTIVE** by Catherine Dillon.   (#E8921—$2.25)*
- [ ] **THIS IS THE HOUSE** by Deborah Hill.   (#E8877—$2.50)

* Price slightly higher in Canada